PESTILENCE

A break-in at the hospital morgue, explained disappearance of certain bodies, intrigue among the senior staff, and a chance encounter with a grieving widower, prompt Dr James Saracen to question irregularities surrounding the death of a woman at Skelmore General Hospital. Narrowly avoiding personal disaster, he unearths a conspiracy to conceal the fact that she died of a disease believed to have faded out in England hundreds of years ago.

The legend of the Curse of Skelmore, the lost site of a monastery, a young boy's delirious rantings—all add to the mystery. Saracen, putting both his job and his life on the line, must enter the realms of a medieval nightmare before the sinister and near-fatal answer is found.

Please note: *This book may have some material which may not suit all our readers.*

PESTILENCE

PESTILENCE

by
Ken McClure

MAGNA PRINT BOOKS
Long Preston, North Yorkshire,
England.

British Library Cataloguing in Publication Data.

McClure, Ken
 Pestilence.

 A catalogue record for this book is
 available from the British Library

 ISBN 0-7505-0180-4
 ISBN 0-7505-0184-7 pbk

First Published in Great Britain by Simon & Schuster Ltd., 1991

Copyright © 1991 by Ken Begg

Published in Large Print 1992 by arrangement with Simon & Schuster Ltd., London.

Printed and bound in Great Britain by
T.J. Press (Padstow) Ltd., Cornwall, PL28 8RW.

Have you built your ship of death, O have you?
O build your ship of death, for you will need it.

The Ship of Death
D.H Lawrence

ONE

James Saracen carried a loaf of bread in one hand and a carton of milk in the other as he climbed the stairs to his flat. When he got to the third floor he put the loaf under his left arm, leaving his right hand free to search in his trouser pocket for the key. The pocket was empty. 'God, was it ever different,' he muttered, changing over the groceries to his other arm. He found the key and opened the door; it swung back like a snowplough, clearing mail behind it. He closed it again with his heel and put down his things before clicking on the hall light and picking up the assorted pile of post. This consisted of a card to say that a man from the electricity board had called, a circular from Safeways promising ten pence off washing powder, a brown envelope marked 'Inland Revenue', and a white one with a Northampton post mark which said it was a Visacard bill. Good, there was nothing to make him change his plans. It was Saturday, it was eight o'clock in the evening, and he had promised himself something special: he was going to take off his clothes, get into bed, and sleep until he woke up.

Saracen woke up two hours later, but not of his own accord. The bleeper in his jacket pocket had just gone off.

'I don't believe it...I just do not believe it,' he complained, as he struggled to free an arm from the bedclothes. He lifted the telephone from the bedside table and balanced it on the edge of the bed while he dialled the hospital number.

'Skelmore General,' said the voice.

'Dr Saracen, you were paging me.'

'One moment.'

Saracen scratched his head sleepily as the operator put him through to Accident and Emergency.

He recognised the duty houseman's voice.

'James? I know this is your first night off in God knows how long, and I know you have just worked an eighteen-hour shift...'

'But?'

'The fact is, we need you. A & E is going crazy and now there has been an accident up on the bypass. Someone will have to go up there. It's a fire brigade affair.'

'So why don't you go?'

'I'm the only one on.'

'What?' exclaimed Saracen. 'Where's Garten? He's supposed to be on tonight.'

'You know how it goes. Something social cropped up at the last moment and our leader wriggled out of it. Said he "felt sure I would

10

cope'', had "absolute confidence" in me, the usual shit, before it was Hi-Ho Silver, away.'

'I'll come, I'll go out with Medic Alpha.'

As Saracen turned into Skelmore General he saw Medic Alpha standing outside Accident and Emergency. The vehicle, a white Bedford van with appropriate markings, was Skelmore's latest acquisition, and the nearest thing to a hospital on wheels. It was designed for attendance in situations where on-the-spot medical treatment might make the difference between life and death, and had been donated to the hospital by a wealthy local man whose son had died after a road accident.

Saracen saw that the windscreen wipers on Medic Alpha were operating and that the driver was already aboard and waiting. He parked his own car alongside and shouted to the gate porter to park it before climbing into the back of the ambulance.

'Have a good sleep?' asked Jill Rawlings, the staff nurse who was checking the vehicle's inventory.

The question had been tongue-in-cheek. Saracen didn't reply. He struggled into the jacket that Jill Rawlings handed to him as the vehicle gathered speed and cleared the way ahead with a siren that proclaimed its origins from the streets of San Franciso rather than the English Midlands. He had both hands in the armholes behind him when the ambulance lurched to the right to avoid a car emerging from a side street. Saracen crashed against the side of the van, his head narrowly missing an oxygen cylinder. The driver gave a quick glance back.

'Sorry,' he said sheepishly.

Saracen grunted and did up the rest of his jacket.

'Now we all know who we are,' said Jill Rawlings, referring to the white plastic jackets they had to wear. Each carried a fluorescent strip with the designation, Doctor, Nurse or Ambulance, according to its wearer.

'I always feel as if I'm part of one of those costume sets you get when you're a child,' said Jill.

'Could be a money-making idea,' said Saracen. 'Any details on the accident?'

'An articulated lorry and two cars.'

Saracen screwed up his face. 'Direction?'

'Head on, then a rear shunt.'

Saracen gave a low whistle, then asked, 'Morphine shots?'

'All ready.'

'Cutting gear?'

'All ready.'

The rain lashed against the windscreen as Medic Alpha lost the protection of town buildings and sped out on to an exposed section of the ring road. From where Saracen sat

12

in the back, the lights outside merged into blobs of yellow and red in the rivers of water flowing down the pane. Somewhere up ahead blue blobs appeared, and Medic Alpha slowed down as they reached the scene of the accident. Two fire appliances were present, their arc lights already in position, while three police cars sat angled across the carriageway.

Blue lights flashed asynchronously in the night sky as Saracen got out and bowed his head against the rain, which was whipped into his face by a malevolent wind. The firemaster led him into the lee of one of the police cars to brief him, but still had to shout above the sound of the generators.

'First car nose-dived under the artic, decapitated the two in the front. There's a kid in the back; we think it's dead but we don't know for sure.'

'And the other car?'

'Driver's dead, steering wheel crushed his chest. His passenger, wife I think, is trapped by her feet. My lads are trying to free her right now.'

'Is she conscious?'

'No.'

'Staff Nurse Rawlings will see to the woman. I want to see if I can reach the child,' shouted Saracen through cupped hands.

The firemaster gave an exaggerated nod to signify that he had understood and indicated that Saracen should follow him. They picked

13

their way through cables and hoses to reach the towering front of the truck, now deformed into a giant mouth that had half-swallowed a Ford saloon.

'Your best bet is to go in from the left,' yelled the firemaster against the noise.

Saracen got down on the cold wet tarmac and wriggled under the front bumper of the truck. He paused to reach out behind him and accept the powerful torch that a fireman handed him, before crawling in deeper to search for some breach in the car's side where he could gain access. The wetness of the road changed to stickiness where blood had poured out from the floorpan to form a puddle. Somewhere behind him rainwater had found a path through the twisted metal and was now flowing steadily on to the back of his legs.

Saracen finally managed to get his arm between the rear door of the Escort and its pillar, which had bowed on impact. He levered himself against the inside of the truck's front wheel to reach in deeper and felt his way along the rear seat until he touched something. It was a hand and it was cold and limp. He tried for a pulse but could feel nothing.

Saracen pulled the child's wrist until its body flopped over on to his forearm, then he drew back a little and felt for the head. He touched curly hair and moved his hand down to search for a carotid pulse. Still nothing. As he tried

14

to remove his arm from the crack, he brought the child tumbling forward to lie against the back of the gap. He brought up his torch and shone it through the opening. He could now see that it was a little girl. Her eyes were open but she was quite dead.

Saracen started to wriggle out backwards, for there was no room to turn round, when a woman started to scream. He looked out from under the truck and saw the yellow leggings of a fireman running towards him. A face squatted down to look under the truck.

'Doctor! The trapped woman has come round. She's in a lot of pain.'

Almost before he had had a chance to reply, the screaming subsided and Saracen knew that Jill Rawlings had taken care of the situation. The strict, who-does-what régime of hospital life did not always apply in the searching reality of Medic Alpha's world.

Saracen was aware of a fireman recoiling from him as he got to his feet, and looked down to see that the front of his jacket was covered in blood where he had been lying in the puddle. A policeman handed him some rags and he wet them at the trickling end of a hose that had been used to flush away spilt fuel, before sponging away the sticky mess.

'How is she?' he asked Jill Rawlings.

'They can't free her. Take a look.'

Jill moved back and Saracen knelt down to peer into the crushed footwell of the car that

15

had ploughed into the back of the Escort. He could see the problem, for the woman's foot had been snapped at the ankle and crushed between an engine support member and the bulkhead of the car. Her foot was a bloody, broken pulp sticking out at right angles from her ankle. There was no room for the firemen to use hydraulic jacks in such a confined area.

Saracen withdrew from the front of the car and said, 'I'll have to amputate.'

'I thought you'd say that,' said Jill. 'I've prepared the instruments.'

'What did you give her?'

Jill told him and he nodded. 'Ask the firemen if they can rig up some kind of shelter to keep this bloody rain off, will you?'

Saracen returned to examining the trapped woman's foot with the aid of a better torch while Jill went to speak to the firemaster. Now satisfied that he knew exactly what he was going to do, he began to assess his patient in more general terms. She was a woman in her early thirties, well-dressed, slim, attractive and apparently in good health before this accident, which had just shattered her life. Probably the wife of a successful professional man, thought Saracen, considering the make and year of the car and the quality of her clothes. She was a woman with everything going for her, who, would wake up a widow with no left foot.

Saracen stood up and moved out of the way while two firemen rigged up a makeshift shelter

16

out of a tarpaulin. While he waited he asked one of the senior policemen about the contents of the woman's handbag. 'Anything I should know about? Any discs or medallions?'

The policeman shook his head. 'She did have a kidney donor card, though.'

'Did her husband carry one, too?'

'I put it in the ambulance with the body and alerted the hospital.'

Saracen nodded. That might be something else to tell the woman when she came round. 'All right?' he asked Jill Rawlings.

'All ready,' she nodded.

The firemen and policemen knew what was going on behind the screen but had only their imaginations to fill in the details, until the sound of Saracen using a saw painted too vivid a picture for one of them. A constable retched up the contents of his stomach on the wet road, supporting his head on his forearm as he leaned against one of the fire appliances.

'Clips!' said Saracen.

Jill Rawlings pressed them into his hand and knew that Saracen was now working on stemming the blood-flow from the stump. She anticipated each request before it came. Swabs, pressure pads, tape. The seconds ticked past, then Saracen sighed and said, 'All right, she'll do.' He got to his feet stiffly and rubbed at his legs to restore the circulation, then he moved out of the way to allow the ambulancemen to lift the woman gently from the wreckage and carry her to Medic Alpha.

'What happened to the truck driver?' Saracen turned to the senior policeman as he cleaned his hands and watched Jill Rawlings gather together their equipment.

'Minor cuts and bruises. He went to hospital for a check-up in the first ambulance.'

Saracen nodded and said, 'That's it, then. I'll leave the rest to you.' He started to walk towards the ambulance with Jill.

'Be seeing you,' said the policeman.

'All too soon,' replied Saracen.

As Saracen climbed into the back of Medic Alpha he paused to look across at the houses that bordered the ring road. Most of the people who had been at their windows earlier to see the excitement had returned to their television sets. Real life drama had begun to pall. Saracen had picked up some road grit in his mouth; he spat it out on to the tarmac.

The rain still had not relented by the time Medic Alpha arrived back at Skelmore General and one of the ambulancemen stepped in a puddle up to his ankles as he wheeled the trolley up to the doors. Saracen accompanied the trolley with the intention of handing over his patient to the surgical registrar on duty and then going home. He could hardly believe the sight that met his eyes. Accident and Emergency resembled the Beggar's Court of eighteenth-century Paris.

'What's going on?' he asked Tremaine, who had telephoned him earlier.

'Three things,' answered the flustered houseman. 'It's Saturday night, the weather is bringing in the drop-outs, and City were playing United at home. There was trouble.'

Saracen looked around him and swore under his breath. The treatment room was full, the waiting room was full. Half a dozen policemen were talking to people and writing things in notebooks. The sound of gagging and retching came from one of the side rooms. Saracen looked in and found Sister Lindeman cajoling a teenage girl into swallowing a gastric aspiration tube.

'OD?' Saracen asked.

'A hundred aspirin. Her boyfriend left her.'

In a corner of the main treatment room Saracen caught sight of a nurse sitting down. It was so unusual that he knew something must be wrong. He went over and saw that the girl was holding the side of her face.

'What happened?'

'One of the drunks,' replied the nurse.

Saracen lifted her hand away to assess the damage and saw the early signs of bruising. 'Did you tell the police?' he asked.

'Jack Lane dealt with him,' replied the girl.

'Do your teeth feel all right?' asked Saracen.

The nurse smiled and said, 'I'm all right, really I am. Just give me a moment.'

Saracen squeezed her shoulder and continued

19

on a quick inspection tour. He looked in on the waiting room but the smell that hit him there made him wish that he had not. It was a mixture of vomit, urine and wet clothing. All the chairs were full and people were squatting on the floor. A woman was wandering up and down with tears flowing down her face and Saracen recognized her as one of the regulars in Accident and Emergency when it rained. She was known to the unit as Mary.

Mary was one of the people that the Sunday supplements liked to call the 'twilight people' in their intermittent features on life's unfortunates between advertisements for Porsche cars and Swedish furniture. She was alone in the world and had the IQ of a child, although she was now in her early thirties. She had spent her entire adult life either sleeping rough or in a succession of hostels and assessment centres, having fallen through one of the many gaps in the Welfare State. She could not be admitted to a regular hospital because there was nothing physically wrong with her; neither could she be admitted to a mental establishment because, although retarded, she was not mentally ill. This left her alone in a world which had little sympathy for a thirty-year-old bed-wetter with the mind of a ten-year-old child.

On the occasions when being turned out of a hostel coincided with bad weather, Mary would turn up in Accident and Emergeny in floods of tears and stinking of urine, in the

20

hope of a bed and a little kindness. She was rarely successful, for the simple truth was that Mary was not alone. There were a lot of 'Marys' on the streets, out of sight and out of mind.

'Come on now, Mary, you know the rules,' said Saracen gently.

'But, Doctor, I'm ill,' whined the woman.

A porter came up to Saracen and whispered in his ear, 'We've been on the blower and the church hostel in Freer Street will take her for tonight.'

Saracen nodded, grateful that he was not going to have to turn Mary out on the street. 'C'mon Mary,' he said, 'We've found a nice warm bed for you.'

The sobbing subsided and Mary came towards Saracen with open arms. Saracen steeled himself for the embrace and held his breath. He patted her back and hoped that she would release him before the stench of ammonia overpowered him.

'I'm sure one of these nice policemen will run you round to the hostel.'

The nearest constable raised his eyes to the ceiling before saying, 'Of course,' with less than marked enthusiasm. He whispered to Saracen as the porter led Mary out, 'It took us three days to fumigate the Panda last time.'

Saracen returned to find Tremaine and said to him, 'You'll need some help, I'll stay.'

'I wasn't going to ask...honest,' said Tremaine.

Saracen smiled and put on his white coat.

Sister Lindeman had finished pumping out the teenage girl's stomach. She left her in the care of another nurse while she returned to the main treatment room to see how things were going. She saw Saracen and grinned. 'Couldn't stay away, huh?'

'That's about it, Sister. Who's next?'

Saracen started working his way through the aftermath of a violent Saturday. Tiredness prevented any kind of small talk and limited him to asking only relevant questions before working in silence. He accepted the answers with no sign of emotion, for exhaustion had brought on a detachment that shielded him from the boring, mindless monotony of the reasons given for the injuries he was treating, from bottle and beer glasses to steel combs and bread knives.

Saracen was working on his fourth patient when reception alerted the unit to the arrival of an ambulance carrying victims of another road accident. A few minutes later a trolley was wheeled quickly into Accident and Emergency with an entourage of police and ambulancemen. A distraught woman with blood running down her face from a cut on her forehead ran alongside the trolley, unwilling to let go. Saracen guessed correctly that it was her husband lying on it.

'It was the rain, it was the rain—David has always been such a careful driver, but it was the rain. The car just spun, there was nothing he could do. It was the rain...'

In the background Saracen saw one of the ambulancemen shake his head. He said to one of the nurses, 'Nurse, would you find a seat for Mrs...?'

'Lorrimer,' replied the woman. 'With two rs,' she added nervously.

Saracen smiled reassuringly at her as she was led away to the waiting room, then he turned to her husband.

'I think he's had it,' said the ambulanceman who had previously shaken his head. He filled Saracen in on the details of the accident while he examined the man. Saracen stood up from the table and said, 'You're right, he's dead. Ribs probably punctured his heart. The PM will say for sure.'

'Will you tell his wife?' asked one of the policemen.

Saracen said that he would and went to find the woman. She had been taken to one of the side rooms by a nurse. She got up as Saracen entered and smiled nervously before starting to speak quickly, as though she believed that she could make something true by repeating it often enough.

'He is all right, isn't he? Just a bit of a bump. I thought so. This weather really is the limit. I was just saying to David before the accident...'

Her voice trailed off as Saracen took both her hands in his. 'I'm sorry,' he said. 'Your husband is dead, Mrs Lorrimer. There was nothing we could do.'

The woman's eyes widened, then filled with tears as the bottom fell out of her world. She began to sob uncontrollably and Saracen held her against his shoulder, raising his hand to stop the nurse who made to move forward and take her away. He let the woman cry herself out before lifting her gently away from him and asking if there was anyone they could contact to be with her. A relative? A friend? 'Nurse will clean you up and get you some tea,' he said, ushering her into the waiting arms of the nurse. Saracen returned to the main treatment room just as a heavily-built man lurched in from the waiting room.

'I wanna see a doctor,' he demanded, his voice slurred with drink. He transferred his weight unsteadily from one foot to the other as he tried to focus on the scene in front of him.

'You'll have to wait your turn,' said Saracen. 'Go back to the waiting room, please.'

'I wanna see a fuckin' doctor now!' demanded the drunk. He brought his fist down on the edge of an instrument tray, sending a shower of steel up into the air. He staggered back as if amazed at the consequence of his action.

'You'll have to wait your turn like everyone else. Go back to the waiting room,' said Saracen.

'Who fuckin' says so?'

'I do,' said Saracen evenly.

The drunk sniggered. 'Are you gonna make me, like?' he whispered hoarsely.

'No, he is,' said Saracen matter-of-factly. He nodded to the porter, Jack Lane, who had just returned from taking a patient to X-Ray. He looked down at the drunk from a height of six and a half feet and said quietly, 'This way, my son...there's a clever boy.' He led the drunk out by the scruff of the neck.

Tremaine shrugged and said to Saracen. 'Twenty minutes ago this place was full of policemen. Now, when you want one...'

Saracen stitched up another head wound then walked over to the sink to wash his hands. He levered on the taps with his elbows and took in the sights around him as he washed. The clock on the wall said twenty past two, and exhaustion was inducing a cynical numbness. How different it all was from his pre-medical school view of medicine, when family and friends had encouraged him in the notion that he was about to become one of God's chosen people or, at least, society's. He smiled faintly as he recalled the image he had nurtured throughout his student years; the one where, dressed in a neat grey suit, he was standing on the steps of a bright, modern hospital waving

25

goodbye to a grateful family who looked as if they had stepped out of the pages of a glossy magazine. 'How can we ever repay you, Doctor?' they were saying.

'Oh, it's nothing really...'

Saracen saw the symbolism in washing his hands as he looked at the last of that Saturday night's clientele at Skelmore General.

'Barabas it is, then,' he said softly, but not so softly that a passing nurse did not hear.

'Did you say something, Saracen?' she asked.

'No, nothing,' he replied.

The stream of patients dwindled to a trickle and the last one finally limped out through the swing doors at twenty minutes past three. Saracen sat down slowly on one of the tubular frame chairs and tilted it back to rest his head against the wall. Alan Tremaine joined him and read aloud from the clipboard in his hand.

'Forty-three patients, fourteen admitted to the wards, four palmed off on to the County Hospital, one dead on arrival, the rest discharged.'

'Tea?' asked Sister Lindeman.

'Please.'

Tremaine put down the clipboard and stretched before putting his hands behind his head. 'Only two more months of A&E to go,' he sighed. 'How long have you been doing it, James?'

'Six years.'

26

Tremaine expelled breath loudly and said, 'You know, I can't begin to tell you how grateful I am to you for helping out tonight.'

'Forget it,' said Saracen.

'Something should be done about Garten,' said Tremaine, 'How does he keep getting away with it? I've got a damned good mind to complain to the authorities about him.'

'You will do no such thing,' said Saracen, with an air of finality that took Tremaine aback. 'You will keep your mouth shut, finish your residency and leave with a good reference. Understood?'

'If you say so, but it's so unjust.'

'Don't waste your time looking for justice. Keep your nose clean and get on with your career.' With that, Saracen got up and left through the swing doors.

Sister Lindeman returned with the tea, and looking around her asked, 'Has Doctor Saracen gone?'

Tremaine replied that he had. He accepted the mug that she held out and asked almost absent-mindedly, 'How come James is still only a registrar? He must be, what, thirty-five? Thirty-six? Come to that, why is he still working in A&E?'

'I'm sure I don't know what you mean, Doctor,' said Sister Lindeman. Her voice was cold enough to ensure that Tremaine knew not to pursue that line of conversation.

Tremaine sipped his tea, still deep in thought.

'And as for Garten...'

'Drink your tea, Doctor.'

Saracen raised his collar against the wind and walked up the hill to find the duty porter. The man emerged from his turreted gate-house when he saw Saracen approaching.

'Where did you leave my car?' Saracen asked.

'It's round the back, parked behind the bins.' The man dropped the keys into Saracen's hand and said good-night. Saracen turned and walked back down the hill, taking care not to slip on the wet cobblestones. It had stopped raining but only recently, for water still trickled down the hill through the joints and crevices of a surface that had been laid before the turn of the century.

Unlike the front of the building, which had an array of neon signs and direction indicators, the lighting was poor at the back for the rear of the hospital boasted no public buildings except for a small chapel attached to the mortuary. The lighting was therefore minimal, and solely consisted of electric conversions to the original gas mantle-holder on the walls.

Saracen saw that a notice had been pinned to one of the two tall mortuary doors. He stopped to read it, but had to manoeuvre himself until he achieved an angle where there was enough light to make this possible.

MORTUARY CLOSED
DUE TO
REFRIGERATION FAILURE
For transfer arrangements call ext 2711.

His curiosity satisfied, Saracen walked on past the row of large bins that held the hospital's refuse. Each was mounted on a wheeled trolley and fitted with a grab-ring to match the hydraulic hoists of the collection vehicles that called every other day. He took a sharp intake of breath as a cat leapt from the top of one of the bins in front of him and disappeared off into the shadows.

Saracen found his car squeezed into a small space behind the row of bins, for parking was always a problem within the precincts of the hospital. He had to sidle between it and a wet stone wall to reach the driver's door. As he fumbled for the lock in the gloom he dropped the keys and cursed softly as he found difficulty in bending down in the narrow space.

As he groped for his keys, Saracen became aware of a faint hissing sound. At first he thought it must be coming from one of the tyres but as it grew louder he realized that it was coming from the other side of the bins. Intrigued, he stood up and squeezed out from behind the car to peer through a gap between two of the bins where he could see out into the courtyard.

The sound grew louder and Saracen recognized it as the noise car tyres make on wet cobblestones. A vehicle was freewheeling slowly down the hill from the gate. He waited for its headlights to illuminate the courtyard but nothing happened. Instead he saw the dim outline of a dark van come slowly round the corner, without lights, and stop outside the mortuary.

The light coming from the single bulb above the mortuary doors enabled Saracen to see that three men had got out of the van. He watched spellbound as they donned some kind of protective clothing which they took from the back of the van. The unlikely possibility that they were refrigeration engineers was totally dispelled when Saracen saw them put on hoods and full face visors, and then pull on gauntlets.

Looking like astronauts about to enter their space craft, the men approached one of the mortuary doors in single file. There was a brief pause while the lock was undone, then they disappeared inside.

Saracen began to wonder if he was hallucinating. Perhaps it was all a vision brought on by tiredness. He even screwed up his eyes before looking again and finding that the van was still there.

A few minutes later two of the men re-emerged carrying a long box that appeared to be wrapped in plastic sheeting. They loaded the box into the back of the van, then turned to wait for the third man who was still inside. Through the open door Saracen saw the darkness of the mortuary become eerily bright, as if candles had been lit inside. The third man came out and closed the door.

Saracen walked out into the open and approached the van. 'What's going on?' he demanded.

Three dark visors turned to look at him, but no one spoke.

'I asked you what you were doing,' said Saracen as he got closer. Still no reply. Saracen suddenly felt apprehensive. The lack of response and the fact that he could not see the men's faces made him feel that it might be unwise to get any closer. 'Just stay where you are!' he ordered, and turned on his heel to make for the gate-house. He made it only to the foot of the hill before something hit him on the back of the head, and unconsciousness swept over him like a black fog.

TWO

It was daylight when Saracen came round and opened his eyes. The pain inside his head brought on a sudden wave of nausea when he tried to move, so he lay quite still for a moment, trying to put his thoughts into some kind of order. He remembered the incident outside the mortuary and assumed, correctly as it happened, that he had been attacked from behind. But where was he now?

The silence and the cold grey light suggested that it could be dawn, but if the dull rainy weather had persisted from the previous day it could be any time, he reasoned. It was particularly hard to tell, for he was not lying outside on the road. There was a ceiling above him and the air, although unheated, was perfectly still.

'Nurse!' Saracen croaked, in the hope that he might be in a hospital bed, but somehow he knew that he was not. It felt all wrong.

Still unwilling to move his head for fear of awakening the pain dragon, he felt about him with his hands and discovered that he was lying on something hard. It was metallic—cold smooth metal—stainless steel, perhaps?

At intervals his fingers sank into narrow slots that ran longitudinally. Was that the word? Saracen found it hard to concentrate. Try as he might, he just could not think clearly. Was it the head wound or was it something else, he wondered, for there was a smell in the room, a heavy, sickly sweet smell, a smell that was now more of a sensation really, as if his senses had been overloaded with it after a long period of inhalation.

Had he been chloroformed? No, he decided,

it wasn't chloroform, neither was it ether. It was something else, another chemical that he felt sure he should recognize but could not because it was impossible to think clearly.

Unable to make any progress through deductive reasoning, Saracen tried moving his head again. He tried shifting it slowly to the right but found it difficult, not because of the pain, but because the back of his skull seemed to be resting in some kind of mould. The mould was not metal, for it felt warm through his hair and softer, though not much. He had it, it was wood!

All at once, Saracen realized where he was and the shock made him sit bolt upright. An agonizing pain reminded him that this was a mistake and momentary blindness followed a wave of nausea. Fear and pain vied inside his skull until he opened his eyes and peered out through the fingers that cradled his head. A long row of bone-handled knives on the wall confirmed his worst fears. He was lying on a post-mortem examination table.

It was another full minute before Saracen could bring himself to try moving his legs off the table. He slid the left one slowly over the edge of the steel surface and let it dangle down while he brought the right one round to join it. Then, holding his breath, he attempted to stand up. It was a disaster. His legs buckled beneath him and, as he fell, his fingers caught in one of the channels that were etched into the table for the drainage of blood and body fluids. His wrist was wrenched painfully as he slid to the floor.

Saracen cursed in frustration as he dragged himself up on to his hands and knees. He had to stop and hang his head for a moment as the pain increased in successive waves like an incoming tide. He knew that he was going to be sick but there was little he could do about it. He just had to let it happen and threw up on the floor. The involuntary convulsing of his stomach brought on an exhaustion that made him feel faint. He felt that consciousness was slipping away from him fast, and his last act before passing out was to push himself to one side so that he would not fall into his own vomit.

When Saracen came round for the second time he felt icy cold and was shivering uncontrollably, but this time he could think more lucidly. He had to get to the telephone. There was one in the room and he knew where it was, it was just a matter of reaching it. He did not attempt to stand up this time. Instead, he dragged himself across the floor, keeping as horizontal as possible to maintain the blood supply to his head, and having cause to be grateful for the smooth, sluicable surface that minimized the friction factor in his progress. He reached the far wall and risked pulling himself up into a sitting position by reaching up and gripping a metal hose-reel that was mounted low down on the tiled wall. He could see the pathologist's telephone sitting invitingly on the desk above him. It encouraged him to make the final effort and he stretched up to take the receiver from the hook.

'It's Saracen—I'm in the PM room—send someone.'

The voices in the tunnel suddenly lost their echo and began to make sense.

'So you are back with us!'

Saracen understood the words but could not reply at first.

'Care to tell us what happened, old man?'

Saracen opened his eyes and recognized Martin Saithe, the Physician Superintendent at Skelmore General, a man he did not much care for; contact between them had been minimal, however, so this had not been a problem. Standing beside Saithe was Alan Tremaine and beside Tremaine a policeman in uniform. The face of Sister Vera Ellis swam into view and told Saracen that he was in ward four, the ward immediately above Accident and Emergency.

When his power of speech returned, Saracen told the assembled group of the incident outside the mortuary and how he had been hit from behind. He was puzzled to find that no one seemed particularly surprised. Saithe nodded and said, 'Yes, we had concluded as much. You had the misfortune to disturb our intruders last night.'

'Intruders?' asked Saracen.

'Thieves,' said Saithe, with an air of distaste. 'Dr Garten informs me that a new compressor due to be fitted to the refrigeration system in the mortuary was stolen last night. A grubby little crime.' Saithe assumed the expression that Saracen associated with him most, a narrowing of the eyes and the adoption of a pained expression that was meant to convey an extreme sensitivity to all things vulgar and distasteful. He now betrayed a restlessness and obvious desire to be off. 'Well,' he said, eyeing his watch, 'I think it's quite clear what happened. You got a nasty crack on the head, but nothing too serious. Dr Garten will have to soldier on without you for a few days but then you'll be back, right as rain.'

The idea of Garten 'soldiering on' made Tremaine look at Saracen and raise his eyebrows. He was grateful that Saracen, in his present state, did not feel much like smiling.

Saithe said to Saracen, 'Perhaps you might tell the constable here anything that you think might be useful or helpful in the investigation.' With that he gave a dutiful smile, said thank you to the ward sister, and left.

'If there is anything you can tell me, sir,' said the constable, 'anything at all.'

'Yes, I'm going to be sick,' said Saracen.

'Nurse!' Sister Ellis conjured up a student nurse with a suitable receptacle before Saracen could even contemplate defiling her smooth

36

blanketry or mirror-shine floors.

The stomach convulsions ceased and Saracen lay back on the pillow and closed his eyes until the throbbing in his head had subsided. When he felt better he turned to the young policeman and said, 'There were three of them.'

The policeman looked pleased and started to write in his notebook. 'Did you get a good look at any of them?' he asked.

Saracen told him about the overalls and visors.

The policeman nodded thoughtfully and said, 'That could be very helpful. From what you say it sounds like the sort of gear they wear to strip out asbestos from old buildings and the like. That could be a valuable lead.'

'Good,' said Saracen, without much enthusiasm, for he still felt sick.

'I'll let you get some sleep, sir,' said the constable, rising to his feet and pocketing his notebook. He placed his helmet on his head using both hands, coronation style, and adjusted it well before nodding to Saracen and Tremaine and saying goodbye for the moment.

'You look awful,' said Tremaine, when he and Saracen were alone.

'I feel awful,' conceded Saracen.

'You know,' Tremaine began cautiously, 'the bump on your head isn't that bad and the X-rays were perfectly okay. I'm surprised you're having so much discomfort.'

Saracen's first thought was to hit Tremaine,

but physical effort was beyond him for the moment. 'There was more to it than the bump on the head,' he said.

'What do you mean?'

Saracen screwed up his face at the question that he himself had invited, but could not answer. 'I don't know exactly, but I think I may have been poisoned. There was something in my lungs when I came round, something that stopped me thinking clearly.'

'You're serious?' exclaimed Tremaine.

'When I came to, my chest felt as though I had been breathing in some sickly sweet gas. It was heavy, unpleasant, but by the time I woke up I had been inhaling it for so long that I couldn't recognize it. Were you one of the people who came down to the PM room when I called?'

'Yes, I was.'

'You didn't notice any strong smell?'

'Formaldehyde, but you'd expect that in the PM room.'

'Formaldehyde,' repeated Saracen slowly. 'It could have been that, but there would have had to have been an awful lot of it. You didn't come across a broken bottle, did you?'

'No, but then I really didn't look. We were all too concerned with getting you out of there. If you like I'll go down and check.'

'I'd be obliged. Tell me, did you go into the mortuary itself?'

'The connecting door between it and the PM

38

suite was locked.'

'It's not usually kept locked,' said Saracen.

'Probably to keep these fridge engineers out of the autopsy room. Mortuaries are bad enough in themselves for the morbidly curious, but PM paraphernalia tends to lend wings to already vivid imaginations.'

'I suppose you're right.'

Tremaine got to his feet and said, 'Do you know what I'm going to do now?'

'What?'

'I'm going to call Garten and tell him that you will be out of action for a few days. That should obviate our leader's need for a morning laxative. He is going to *have* to come in.'

'Who are the housemen on A&E today?'

'Doctors Prahash Singh and Chenhui Tang,' Tremaine announced.

Saracen closed his eyes and pursed his lips silently.

'Exactly,' said Tremaine. 'Neither outstanding in their command of English.'

'How is your Urdu and Chinese?' asked Saracen.

'Not good enough to practise in Pakistan or China,' replied Tremaine.

'Point taken,' conceded Saracen. 'But push off now, will you, I feel like death.'

Tremaine smiled and shrugged his shoulders. He turned as he got to the door and said, 'If there's anything you want, just yell out.'

Saracen nodded.

By late afternoon, Saracen felt a whole lot better. So much so in fact that he signed himself out of the ward at four thirty, assuring Sister Ellis that he was now perfectly all right. The speed of his recovery had surprised even him, but reinforced his view that he had been subject to some mild form of poisoning. When the substance had cleared from his system he had immediately begun to feel better, just as if he had been suffering from an alcoholic hangover. Now all that was wrong with him was a sore head not out of keeping with the minor knock that Tremaine had originally diagnosed him to have taken.

Saracen had to walk round to the back of the hospital to collect his car, which was still where the gate porter had left it the previous night. He was trying to remember what he had done with the keys when he came to the mortuary doors and paused for a moment to take comfort in the fact that everything looked normal again. There were no strange vans, no men in hoods and black visors, and the door was securely locked. He examined the padlock and wondered for a moment about the doorlock, when a sudden whiff of ammonia filled his nostrils and made him reel back from the doors. 'What on earth?' he exclaimed, but the smell had already gone.

It was over so quickly that Saracen began to wonder if the smell had ever really been there, for now there was no trace of it. On the other hand, a breeze had sprung up after the rain had stopped and that could just as easily have borne away the gas fumes. He approached the doors again and sniffed. Nothing. It must have been his imagination, some trick of his olefactory system, still upset after the events of the night before.

Saracen shrugged and turned. He now remembered having dropped his keys beside the car in the darkness and went to look for them. Finding them in daylight presented no great problem and he was back at his flat within fifteen minutes, pouring himself a large whisky.

Saracen took a gulp before placing a Vivaldi album on the stereo and adjusting the volume before sitting down and picking up the local paper. The big news, as it had been for the past three weeks, was concerned with predictions of Skelmore's success in attracting the giant Japanese company, Otsuji Electronics, to the area. True, the final agreement had not yet been signed and there were other towns competing for the factory, notably in Scotland and the industrial north-east, but all the signs indicated that Skelmore was the favourite and it was all settled bar the shouting. There was, in fact, nothing new at all in the newspaper story, but in this case Saracen found the euphoric repetition excusable, for this was more than just an industrial story; it was something that meant life for the whole area.

During the time that Saracen had been in Skelmore he had seen the industrial heart ripped out of the town. The giant steel works of Lever Hanah had closed, the iron foundry had gone and the local colliery had been declared no longer economically viable, and shut down after a bitter strike.

The economic depression had cast a great shadow across the area and it showed in the streets, where boarded-up shops and *For Sale* signs sprouted like weeds reclaiming the earth. It showed in the faces of the people in whom hope had been destroyed. A greyness and a passive submission to the yoke of hard times had replaced the air of cheerful optimism that had once been the hallmark of the town. The crime rate had also risen, particularly cases of violence, where larceny might have been the crime predicted to increase the most. It seemed that people who were at the end of their tether ran on an extremely short fuse. Minor irritations became major bones of contention in a town without a future.

But then came the news of Otsuji and the creation not merely of five hundred jobs from the company alone, but a great many more through the knock-on effect it would have, as smaller firms flocked to the area like pilot fish to satisfy Otsuji's requirements for components and services. Already the building trades in the area were flourishing and new housing was springing up on every available plot of land.

Capital was being ventured on the well-proven assumption that prosperity and home owner-ship went hand in hand.

The new air of optimism was not confined to the private sector alone. New council departments with grand-sounding names seemed to materalize overnight to deal with the floods of trade enquiries, and brightly-coloured brochures were being rushed off the presses to extol the virtues of Skelmore and its surrounding district as the development area of the future.

There was even talk of the hospital modernization programme, which had been on ice for the last five years, being brought down from the shelf and dusted off. There seemed to be a real possibility that essential renovation work at Skelmore General might actually be carried out before the place fell down.

Skelmore General was a disgrace; at least it was a disgrace to anyone who believed in the highest standards of medical care. Of course, if you have lived in Britain for the last five to ten years then Skelmore General was fast becoming the norm in a health service at odds with government policy. Understaffing, low pay, and impotent resentment manifesting itself in trade union bloody-mindedness, had all conspired to bring morale to a dangerously low ebb.

Even the Press seemed to realize this and had stopped flogging an all-but dead horse. Stories of leaking ceilings and cockroaches in hospital kitchens, no longer appeared under crusading headlines. It was a waste of time, for there was no incompetence or laxity left to expose. Britain's health service was simply falling to pieces for lack of money.

Skelmore General felt the effects of economic stringency particularly badly because it had been a rambling Victorian slum of a building to start with. Its plumbing and electrics were antiquated and the style of its design, with its high ceilings and arches, made it prohibitively expensive to heat and very difficult to clean.

Frequent outbreaks of diarrhoeal illness in the wards was the norm and was almost certainly due, though never admitted publicly, to unhygienic food standards. Ironically, this problem tended to work in the General's favour, for any kind of outbreak that looked as though it might be infectious allowed the hospital to unload affected patients on to the Infectious Diseases Unit of Skelmore's County Hospital, a ploy that the County was only too well aware of.

On the last occasion of a transfer Saracen's friend and opposite number, David Moss, at the County Hospital, had good-naturedly claimed that anyone who farted too loudly in the General was in danger of finding themselves in an ambulance on their way to the County. Saracen had countered with the claim that Moss had deliberately pushed two of his geriatric patients downstairs during the previous week in order to have them admitted to the General Orthopaedic Unit.

Saracen was idly wondering what to do with his unscheduled two-day break when the telephone rang; it was Nigel Garten.

'Hello, James. I've just been up to ward four to see you. Found you'd flown the coop. How are you? All right?'

'I feel a lot better, thanks.'

'Excellent. Nasty business all round really; still, can't be too bad if you signed yourself out, eh, what?' Garten gave a forced laugh to augment his one-of-the-chaps act.

Saracen could see what was coming. He was right.

'Soon be back in harness, eh?' continued Garten, still forcing the laugh.

'Shouldn't be too long,' agreed Saracen flatly. There was a pause.

'Any idea exactly...how long?' probed Garten.

Saracen smiled at being proved right. 'A couple of days,' he said.

'Of course you mustn't come back until you feel absolutely well again. I'm sure sick leave can be arranged.'

'I'm not taking sick leave, Nigel; I'm due a couple of days off anyway.' Saracen left out the 'at least'.

'Oh, absolutely, old chap, no question about it. It's just that, well, you know what A&E is like. Having you off will be an added strain on all of us.'

'A couple of days.'

'Right, well then, look after yourself and, of course, if you do happen to feel better in the morning...'

Saracen put the phone down, swore once and went back to his newspaper. He skipped through the advertisements that comprised eighty per cent of it and found the weekly feature that he particularly liked on the history of Skelmore and its surrounding district. This week's offering was entitled, *The Curse of Skelmore*, and recounted the legend of the Skelmoris Chalice, a vessel reputed, like so many others over the course of two thousand years, to have been the Holy Grail, the dish that Christ had eaten from on the occasion of the Last Supper.

According to the story, Skelmoris Abbey, a Dominican foundation, had occupied the site where the town of Skelmore now stood. In the fourteenth century, the chalice had been brought there from London for some unrecorded reason and handed over to the abbot, one Hugo Letant, for safe-keeping.

Unknown to the church authorities, Letant and the brothers of Skelmoris could hardly have been a worse choice as guardians for they were evil men who preyed on travellers unwise enough to seek food and shelter at the abbey. The story went that God, in his anger at having seen the chalice fall into the hands of such villains, had struck them all dead and, in the years that followed, a similar fate had befallen any other mortal who had approached the abbey in search of the chalice. In the end, the place had been destroyed by fire. The chalice had disappeared with the abbey, and only the legend had survived the mists of time.

The Chronicle reported that interest in the abbey had been awakened recently with the arrival in Skelmore of an archaeological team from the University of Oxford to begin exploratory excavations. Saracen smiled and had to put down the paper as the telephone rang again; this time it was Alan Tremaine.

'I checked out the PM room. I didn't find any broken formaldehyde bottles, I'm afraid.'

'Just a thought,' said Saracen.

'It's funny. I thought the place actually smelled of ammonia, not formaldehyde.'

Saracen felt his pulse rate rise a little. He had been right. It had not been his imagination after all. 'Really?' he said noncommittally.

'God knows what they'd want with ammonia in the PM room,' said Tremaine.

Saracen agreed, but somewhere in the back of his mind a vague memory had begun to stir. There was something he could not quite recall, some kind of a connection between formaldehyde and ammonia, if only he could remember.

'Garten was up looking for you,' said Tremaine.

'Yes, he called me.'

'Asking if you would be back tomorrow?' asked Tremaine.

'Something like that,' agreed Saracen.

'I hope you told him what to do.'

'I said I would be taking a couple of days off.'

'That man is incredible. Do you think he has ever worked himself?'

'I'm on leave. I don't want to think about him,' replied Saracen.

'Enjoy the break. You deserve it,' said Tremaine.

Saracen put down the phone and stared thoughtfully out of the window. There was something decidedly odd about the whole affair at the mortuary, something that tales of thieves in the night did not answer satisfactorily. Apart from the unexplained chemical smells, there was another detail that had begun to bother him. The man who had opened the door at the mortuary could not have picked the lock with such speed as he had; he must have had a key, which implied that it was an inside job, someone on the maintenance staff maybe, or perhaps someone connected with the refrigeration firm.

Saracen permitted himself the luxury of a second drink and lingered over the pleasing thought that he did not have to go out tonight. There were no patients to consider, and he could get as drunk as a lord if he had a mind to. He did not intend to, but it was nice to know that he had the choice. He added a little water to the whisky and sat down with the glass between his palms. Good whisky was one of the few luxuries that he allowed himself, not a single malt, but a deluxe blended whisky, The Antiquary. He sipped it from a crystal glass, one of a set of six that he had won a long time ago as a prize in an essay competition at medical school.

Saracen followed the engraving in the crystal with his thumbnail and remembered how different his world had been then. It seemed like a hundred years ago. He had been bright eyed, bushy tailed and ready to take on the whole world, but instead he had taken on the medical establishment and come a poor second.

Saracen had been a very new doctor in his first residency, having obtained a position in a world-famous professorial unit, as befitted the top student of his year. He had set out to impress his chief, Sir John MacBryde, with his capacity for study and hard work, but it was this zeal that had led him to probe a little too deeply into the case histories of a group of MacBryde's patients who were being used to illustrate a point being made by the great man.

MacBryde had submitted a paper to *The Lancet* and Saracen had discovered that he had falsified certain aspects of the data in order to make his proposed 'MacBryde Effect' even more pronounced. No one had been at risk over the misrepresentation and no one would have come to any harm, but Saracen, with all the holier-than-thou rectitude of the young, had exposed the misdeed publicly. MacBryde's reputation had been destroyed and he had retired a broken man.

While outwardly praising his vigilance in the matter, the medical establishment had never forgiven Saracen for putting feet of clay under John MacBryde. Although nothing had ever been said to that effect, he had been left to figure it out for himself as one career avenue after another had closed in front of him, and all his applications for research grants and fellowships had been politely declined. He no longer appeared to have the Midas touch.

When he had finally realized what was going on, Saracen had been filled with impotent anger; impotent, for there was nothing to be done about it. No one would ever tell him to his face why he had not been appointed to a particular position. That was not the way things were done. He had been blackballed by a club that would not even admit its own existence. The incident had also destroyed his marriage; being married to a loser had not figured in Marion's plans.

Saracen had been captivated by Marion from the day he had met her. She was beautiful, she was charming and she was vivacious to the point of being larger than life. Other women paled into insignificance in her presence. She had all the self-assurance and confidence that stemmed from being the daughter of a career diplomat, and for some strange but wonderful reason she had always made Saracen feel that he belonged; without her, his much more humble origins as the only son of an insurance clerk would have made him feel that he did not.

Saracen had been beside himself with joy when Marion had agreed to marry him in the face of all the odds, for she captured the hearts of all the men who met her—and was loathed by just about as many women for the same reason. They had been married in the university chapel on the day after Saracen had graduated first in his year, and he had felt that there was nothing he could not do, that no goal was beyond reach. With Marion at his side he could ride the wind, catch the stars, talk to the angels.

True, money had been a consideration, especially when he had discovered that Marion's dress allowance from her father was actually more than twice what he would be earning as a houseman, but Marion's father, although never in favour of the marriage, had been prepared to indulge his daughter until such time—and it must be sooner rather than later —as Saracen became a successful consultant. When Saracen suddenly found himself having to take any job that he could get, invariably junior posts in unpopular specialities in third-rate hospitals, things began to change.

There had never been a big scene between Marion and himself. Instead, Marion had started seeing more her old friends, taking advantage of the legion of admirers ever willing to wine and dine her while her husband worked all the hours that God sent. Being Marion, she had always been quite open about it, as if it were the most natural thing in the world to do and, for her, it was. Saracen had been sad but, strangely, never angry. He had tried to keep a beautiful butterfly in a net and that had been against the laws of nature.

What bitterness and anger there was in the situation came between Saracen and his father-in-law, and it was to prove final. Saracen stubbornly refused all offers of financial help to set himself up in private practice, having resolved to rehabilitate himself in 'real' medicine rather than pander to the often imagined, ills of the rich. It was an attitude that Marion's father could not accept and Saracen could never fully explain. What relationship they did have, and it was never very good, foundered over it; Marion's father set out to break up the marriage and recover his daughter from the 'failure' she had wed.

Apart from being an inveterate snob, Saracen's father-in-law was a clever and devious man, as befitting his profession, and he had succeeded in distancing Marion from Saracen in a number of seemingly innocent but effective ways. Marion's mother had died some two years before and her father's need for a woman to play diplomatic hostess was exploited to the full. He managed to persuade Marion to accompany him on trips abroad more and more, until finally she just wasn't there at all.

In the interim, Saracen had moved three times, changing from one dingy little flat to another, the fate that his father-in-law had prophesied for him, as he took the only jobs in medicine that were left open to him. Accident and Emergency Units were rapidly becoming 'his thing', largely because working in them was so unpopular with his contemporaries. The hours were appalling, the work more often social than medical, and the prospect of advancement practically nil. Consultancies in A&E were rarer than hen's teeth.

In his own mind Saracen bitterly regretted having exposed the short-comings of John Mac-Bryde, not because of what had happened to himself over it, but because the consequences for MacBryde had far outweighed the crime. All the good that the man had done had been wiped out and forgotten. He would be remembered only as a cheat. The man had been destroyed and he, James Saracen, would have it on his conscience for the rest of his life.

It had been two years since Saracen had last

seen Marion and he had come to terms with the fact that his marriage was over. The hurt and pain had even cleared enough for him to be able to see in his ex-wife the faults that love had made him blind to for so long. Like many beautiful things she lacked substance, she was weak, fragile, ephemeral, and now she was gone.

The loss of Marion and deep self-criticism over the MacBryde affair had led to Saracen becoming something of an expert in human nature, and his own personality had changed accordingly. He had become a loner, a spectator at the game rather than a participant. No longer fettered or driven by professional or social ambition, he had discovered the practice of medicine for its own sake and, in that, he found a satisfaction beyond all expectation.

This fact seemed to communicate itself to colleagues and patients alike, and he was universally regarded and respected for his genuineness. He either said what he thought, or nothing at all. He had no acquired bedside manner, no instant smile etched with insincerity, no eye to the future in whatever he said or did. Being a loner did confer on him a certain remoteness but it was not a hostile remoteness and the shutters went up only when someone tried to get too close to him. But even that was done with elegance. He simply sidestepped anything he saw as an intrusion into his privacy with a practised ease and charm.

He had a quiet intelligence that inspired confidence, and an air of gentleness that the nurses in particular regarded more highly than any of his other qualities.

The staff in Accident and Emergency at Skelmore General knew that Saracen was a far better doctor than Nigel Garten, the unit chief, and had even been known on occasion to voice that opinion within Saracen's earshot. But he would have none of it. He had never been known to say a word against Garten in public, something that only made the staff respect him more.

Nurses tended to feel something more than respect for Saracen, for women found him attractive. Not that he was overly handsome in the classical sense, but his gentleness, his dark eyes, and the enigma of his being a loner ensured that female company was always available should he desire it. And desire it he did, but only ever on a casual basis: that was always made clear from the start. Friendship and fun was as far as the relationship was likely to go. It was for this reason that Saracen tended to avoid involvement with young, impressionable student nurses who might conceivably see sex as a bargaining measure. Relationships with older women were always more relaxed and satisfactory.

Saracen looked out of the window and wondered what he should do with his time off. He thought about going up to the hospital in the morning and poking around the mortuary in search of some answers to the things that were troubling him, and then he considered just forgetting the whole matter. The whisky helped him to see the attraction of the latter option. It seemed a shame to spend a precious day off at the hospital. Why not do something entirely different? Why not? Saracen thought for a moment and then he had it. Sea air! That's what he needed. A good brisk walk by the sea would clear away the remaining traces of poison from his lungs. He would drive down to Gerham-on-Sea and walk along the beach. It was only a ten-mile drive, and he could have lunch at the Ship Inn. That's what he would do.

THREE

The fact that Gerham-on-Sea was close to Skelmore was one of the few points that the job at Skelmore General had in its favour as far as Saracen was concerned. He had a soft spot for the English seaside resort, not knowing whether this was a legacy from the happy holidays he had spent as a child with his bucket and spade on British sand, or whether it was something he had acquired after the obligatory period of outgrowing it. Whatever the reason Saracen liked Gerham; for him it was the perfect example of its kind.

According to Saracen's rules, Gerham-on-Sea had everything a resort should have: a long pier with a theatre at the end, a lifeboat station, and rows of boarding houses with absolutely predictable names. Indeed one of the joys of his first visit had been looking for 'Seaview' and finding it. He had followed up with 'Bella Vista' and had completed a successful hat trick by coming across 'Dunromin' at the end of Beach Road.

Many of the other houses were obvious amalgams of their owner's names and it always brought a smile to Saracen's face when he thought of people inventing them in the first place.

'I've got it, Margaret! We'll call it "Jimar"!'

'That's a wonderful idea, Jim.'

There was no sneer involved. Saracen's affection for the place was quite genuine.

On an April day, Gerham-on-Sea was almost completely deserted, but then, as Saracen reasoned, it was really still in hibernation. It would be another couple of months before hustle and bustle returned to the streets, blinds were raised, shutters flung back and baskets of coloured beach toys tumbled out on to the pavements. The Punch and Judy tent would be erected on the promenade at 3pm precisely every day, and ice-cream vendors would parade slowly up and down. Menus of the day would be chalked up on blackboards outside cafés and deckchairs would be stacked at the top of the beach steps. Then the whole town would hold its breath as it waited to see if the value of sterling against the Spanish peseta and the fickle English weather would let them survive one more season.

Several of the beach cafés and shops had already conceded the battle to Majorca and the Costas, but Saracen, in spite of everything, was still optimistic that places like Gerham might win the war and 'Jimar' might once again proudly display its 'No vacancies' sign in its front bay window.

Saracen pulled up the collar of his jerkin as he left the shelter of the narrow cobbled streets and crossed the promenade to negotiate the steps down to the beach. A cold wind, full of salt and the tang of sea weed, was whipping along the shore, but the sky was bright and a watery sunshine caught the tops of the waves as they dashed themselves against the beach. He crossed the soft sand and began to walk along the firm wet plateau that the receding tide had created.

Saracen was glad that the tide was out, for he liked the feeling of space and freedom that the wide beach gave him. To his right he could see half a mile of unbroken water line, to the left, the entire sea front of Gerham.

At intervals Saracen would pick up a pebble and throw it into the water. Distance was the only relevant criterion, direction was unimportant. He had to keep reminding himself that forty-five degrees was the correct angle for achieving maximum distance but, like a Wittgenstein example, it seemed wrong. He doggedly went for the satisfaction of a steeper trajectory.

Saracen left the sands when he drew level with Jacob's Ladder, a meandering path that traversed to and fro across the face of the cliffs which, at this point, rose some two hundred feet above the shore. He paused half way up to lean on the guard-rail and look out to sea while he recovered his breath. The water turned a cold, grey colour as a cloud drifted across the sun.

The wind was much stronger at the top of the cliffs, but Saracen did not mind for it would be behind him as he walked back to the town and lunch at the Ship Inn. Gulls screamed overhead as they caught the up-draught from the cliff face and wheeled to keep their motionless wings at the correct angle to the wind. They looked fat and well fed, the bully boys of the air, scavengers and thieves. Saracen wondered if they would be so kindly regarded if evolution had decreed them to be black instead of pristine white.

He suddenly became aware that he was no longer alone on the landscape, there was a man sitting in the Victorian gazebo at the inter-section of the three paths. As he passed, Saracen looked towards him and said, 'Good morning.'

The man, who sat with his arms resting on his knees, looked up and moved his lips slightly without saying anything.

In his brief glimpse of the man Saracen noted that he looked prosperous, with neatly clipped hair, an immaculate suit and a deep tan that said he had recently been abroad. But some-thing had made a bigger impression than any-thing else: it was the look in his eyes. Saracen recognized it as despair. He slowed his pace as he wrestled with his conscience over whether or not he should interfere. The fact that the man was sitting near to the edge of the cliff decided the issue. He turned and started to walk back to the gazebo. As he walked, he un-fastened his wristwatch and slipped it into his pocket.

'Excuse me, I wonder if you could tell me the time?' said Saracen.

The man turned his wrist and replied, 'It's twelve thirty.'

'Thank you,' said Saracen, desperately try-ing to think of a way to continue the conversa-tion. 'You didn't get that tan in this country, I'll bet,' he smiled.

The man looked up and seemed to pause for a long time before saying, 'I've lived in Africa for twenty years.'

60

'Really? That is interesting,' said Saracen, taking the man's reply as a cue to sit down. 'So you are back here on holiday, then?'

'My wife and I came back here to retire.'

'It's a nice place,' said Saracen.

The man did not reply.

Saracen took the plunge. He said softly, 'Something is troubling you. I know it's none of my business but, for what it's worth, I'm a doctor. Can I help?'

The man looked up sharply at the word doctor and snorted, 'Doctor! I need doctors like I need smallpox!'

Despite the sentiment, Saracen was glad to see that he had kindled some spark in the man. 'I'm sorry,' he said. 'You've had some kind of bad experience?'

'Bad experience? Myra is dead, for Christ's sake!' The man broke down and started sobbing silently as he covered his face with his hands.

Saracen put his hand on the man's shoulder but did not say anything and, in a few moments, the man had recovered his composure. He blew his nose and said, 'I'm sorry, that was unforgiveable. Please accept my apologies.' He dabbed hurriedly at his eyes with a large handkerchief.

'There's nothing to apologize for,' replied Saracen. 'I'm going to have lunch down at the Ship Inn. Join me?'

The man hesitated, then agreed. He stood up

and held out his hand. 'I'm Timothy Archer.'

'James Saracen.'

The two men walked down the winding cliff path making small talk about the weather until they reached the inn that nestled at the foot of the cliff at the east end of the town. A model of a three-masted schooner was fixed to the wall above a doorway that was so low that they both had to duck their heads to enter. They stepped into the warm, calm air of the bar and immediately became aware of the wind-burn on their faces.

'What'll it be, gentlemen?' asked the landlord.

Saracen ordered whisky and turned to his companion. 'And...'

Archer looked along the bar and asked, 'Do you have Jack Daniels?'

'Should do.' The landlord ran his finger through the air from left to right. 'Yes, there we go.' He kicked a small footstool along the floor and stood on it to reach up to a very dusty bottle, bringing it down with a grunt.

They picked up their drinks and Saracen retrieved a menu from the bar counter and took it with them to a table where they could look out at the sea view. After a few minutes a girl, summoned by the landlord, came across to the table to take their order and wrote it down on her pad with a very blunt pencil.

Saracen waited until Archer had finished

most of his drink before suggesting that he might like to talk about what was troubling him.

'Frankly, I wouldn't know where to begin.'

'I'm in no hurry,' said Saracen. 'How about you?'

Archer threw back what was left of his drink and looked to the landlord. He stabbed two fingers at the empty glasses on the table without saying anything. Saracen noted the gesture. Archer had been in Africa a long time and it showed. The landlord brought over the drinks and Archer began to speak.

'Twenty years ago Myra, my wife, and I sold up here and went to live in Rhodesia—Zimbabwe—as it now is.'

Saracen noticed the edge in Archer's voice.

'It was a big step for us. We had known each other since we were kids and neither of us had ever been abroad before, not even on holiday. We had both grown up here in Skelmore but we wanted more out of life than forty years in the mill and a two-up two-down in Station Road.

'Africa was a big adventure but it worked out for us. We became successful and had everything we wanted, except children, but that didn't matter too much. We had each other and that was enough. Then, one night last year, I confessed to Myra that I still missed the old country. Would you believe it? I actually missed Skelmore. And do you know? Myra said that she felt exactly the same!' Archer smiled as he recalled the moment and took a sip of his drink before continuing. 'Well, we laughed and we laughed, then Myra suggested that we go back. We were both getting on a bit. We could sell the farm and retire, buy a little place back in Skelmore or down here in Gerham. We could visit all our old haunts and pretend that we were kids again.

'At first I baulked at the idea, for selling the farm was not going to be easy and, with things being the way they were, there was no way that we were going to get what it was really worth. But Myra pointed out that it didn't matter, as long as we got enough to buy our place back here and had some left over to live on. So that's what we did. We wrote to an estate agent in Skelmore and asked him about houses in the area and to our amazement, he wrote back saying that new houses and flats were springing up all over the place; something about a Japanese company opening up a factory here.'

Saracen nodded.

'He sent us some brochures and we decided on one of the new flats on Palmer's Green. Myra came over two weeks ahead of me to get things ready, and I stayed on to tidy up the loose ends.' Archer paused, as if composing himself for what he had to say next. 'When I got here last Tuesday, a neighbour told me that Myra had been taken to hospital.'

'Which one?' asked Saracen.

'The neighbour said Skelmore General, but when I got there they told me that she wasn't there, she must have been taken to the County Hospital. I went immediately to the County, but they said that Myra wasn't there either. I was at my wits' end, I didn't know what to do.'

'I can imagine. What did you do?'

'I went back to the General and told them what the people at the County Hospital had said. Eventually they apologized for the mix-up, as they called it, and admitted that Myra had been brought to the General. She had died shortly after admission.' Archer wrung his hands as he stared at the table in front of him.

'What did your wife die of, Mr Archer?' asked Saracen softly.

'They said that she had had a heart attack. I can't understand it, Myra was always as strong as a horse. She'd never had a day's illness in her life.'

'It can happen like that,' said Saracen.

'But it was all so cold and callous, as if Myra was some vagrant they had found dead on a parking lot. They wouldn't even let me see her.'

Saracen was puzzled but very much aware that Archer was on the verge of breaking down again. 'Did they give you a reason why not?' he asked gently.

'They said that an autopsy had been carried

out on Myra and it would not be "appropriate" for me to view the body. They said that they hadn't realized that she had had a husband or indeed any relations and had arranged for her body to be cremated.' Archer's voice fell to a whisper as he said, 'But I managed to stop them doing that. Part of our reason for coming back to Skelmore was that we both wanted to be buried in St Clement's church-yard when the time came. We went to Sunday school there when we were kids, and we were married there. I managed to fix that yesterday for Myra.'

Saracen nodded but was still puzzled. If the woman had died of a heart attack the post mortem would have been confined to the thorax. The site of incision could have been concealed easily and the body displayed in the viewing area of the mortuary chapel. Why had Archer been treated so shabbily? Had it really been too much trouble for someone to arrange for him to see his wife?

'Who did you speak to at the General?' he asked Archer.

'Dr Garden, I think he said his name was.'

'Garten,' corrected Saracen.

'Yes, that was it. You know him, then?'

'I work in Dr Garten's unit at the General,' replied Saracen.

'I see,' said Archer quietly. Saracen remain-ed silent, letting Archer come to terms with the information.

It suddenly occurred to Archer that Saracen might actually have seen his wife at the hospital. He was anxious to find out.

'I'm afraid not,' said Saracen, conscious of the disappointment he was causing. 'It must have been my night off.'

'She was admitted on Monday the twelfth.'

Saracen confirmed that he had not been on duty on the Monday night.

Archer's face fell and he said, 'I know it probably sounds silly, but I just want to speak to someone who might have seen her since she got here, someone who might have met her. Twenty-three years married and I end up standing in an office being handed a plastic bag with some of her things in it. They even asked me to sign a chit...' Archer put his hand over his face and held his fingers lightly against his eyelids for a moment.

Saracen was aware of the landlord's curiosity; the man was wondering what was going on. Saracen spread his fingers silently in a gesture that said that everything was all right. He could not help but appraise the situation professionally. Archer, he concluded, was not the type to respond to platitudes about time being a great healer and the like, so he came straight to the point and said, 'Mr Archer, you need some help.'

'Pills, you mean,' answered Archer, with scorn in his voice.

'Yes, pills,' said Saracen flatly. 'There is

nothing noble in going through agony unnecessarily. Your wife is dead and feeling the
way you do is not going to bring her back.
What you need is a breathing space before you
start getting your life in order. Medication can
help.' Saracen had made his gamble with a
firm, almost bullying approach. He waited for
Archer's response, not at all confident of the
outcome.

Archer capitulated. 'I suppose you are right,'
he conceded.

'Good. Have you registered with a doctor
since your arrival?' asked Saracen.

Archer replied that he had not and Saracen
told him how to go about it. Then he wrote
down the telephone numbers of his flat and the
Accident and Emergency Unit at the hospital
before saying, 'If you have any trouble or
even if you just want someone to talk to, call
me.'

Archer accepted the beer mat on which
Saracen had written the information and slipped it into his pocket. 'Doctor, I don't know
how to begin to thank you. Up there on the
cliff I was seriously thinking of...'

'I think I know what you were considering,'
said Saracen.

'At least let me pay for lunch,' said Archer.

Saracen protested, but finally agreed.

Saracen tried to rescue what was left of the
day with a slow walk round the harbour, but

thoughts of Archer remained uppermost in his mind as he located a smooth stone to sit on near the mooring wall. He found it hard to believe that Nigel Garten would have treated a dead patient's relative in such an off-hand way, for being charming to strangers was one of his fortes, as it was with many shallow people. Perhaps Archer's account of what had happened had been distorted by grief or, even more likely perhaps, the truth of the matter might lie somewhere in between.

It was sometimes difficult for a doctor, however well-meaning, to adopt the proper degree of sensitivity or concern over the death of someone he or she had scarcely known, or in the case of a 'dead on arrival' someone they had not known at all. People expected too much. He didn't blame them; he accepted it.

When he got home Saracen decided to return to duty the following morning and telephoned Nigel Garten to tell him so. The news was greeted enthusiastically by Garten, who wondered if Saracen 'could possibly' take over his period of duty with Chenhui Tang as he had been called to an all-day meeting of the Skelmore Development Committee at the Council Chambers. Saracen bit his lip and agreed. Involvement with the Development Committee was rapidly becoming the jewel in Garten's crown of excuses for avoiding work. This would be the third all-day meeting he had attended in the past month.

Saracen sensed political ambition awakening in Garten and thought the man well-qualified: all front and no substance. He was of the right age and status in the community to present himself in the political arena. The more usual qualification of business success was provided, in Garten's case, by his father-in-law Matthew Glendale, a wealthy and prominent local builder. It was a connection that had cost Garten dear, for Mildred Glendale, Garten's wife, had achieved uniqueness in Saracen's mind as the most unpleasant woman he had ever met. Tremaine, on meeting her, had summed her up succinctly with the comment, 'Sensitivity of a dead pig, manners of a live one.' Saracen might have argued with the ethics of such a remark but not the accuracy. From time to time Saracen had wondered if Garten might have been different had he not married the malicious Mildred, but he concluded not. To be so lazy and parasitic demanded congenital shortcomings, not just acquired ones.

Chenhui Tang smiled when she saw Saracen come through the swing doors of Accident and Emergency. She touched her head with her hand and said with a strong accent, 'Your head, it is all right now?'

'Fine,' smiled Saracen. Conversation with Chenhui invariably involved a lot of smiles. They filled in the gaps where words should have been. 'Are we busy this morning?'

'Yes, yes, busy,' said Chenhui, with an exaggerated series of nods and smiles.

Saracen liked Chenhui and thought that she would make a good doctor. He respected her for that and would have liked to have known her better, but the communication barrier between them was just too great. He had visited her once in her room at the doctors' residency and had found it full of tutorial books on the English language. They had occupied an entire shelf along one wall, a monument to complete failure, he had thought at the time.

Alan Tremaine, who had been on duty during the night, signed off officially and handed over responsibility to Saracen with a report on the night's 'business'. There had been an accident in the local brewery resulting in several cases of severe scalding; a motorcyle accident resulting in the death of the pillion passenger. The police were still trying to contact relatives; they would probably turn up during the morning.

Saracen nodded and noted the location of the burns cases in anticipation of telephone inquiries. 'Anything else I should know?'

'The police brought in a man at three this morning. He had "collapsed" in the cells, hit his head on something.'

'Did it wash?'

'No other bruises on him.'

Saracen nodded.

71

'The X-rays were okay, he just knocked himself out.'

'Good. Off you go, then.'

As the doors closed behind Tremaine, Chenhui came up to Saracen looking harassed. 'You come, please!' she said.

'I come,' smiled Saracen, and followed her to the treatment room to begin another day.

The mid-morning admission of a housewife who had overdosed on Valium made Saracen wonder how Timothy Archer was getting on. He had decided not to ask Nigel Garten about the Myra Archer case lest his interest be misconstrued, or more correctly, construed as unwarranted interference or even implied criticism. However, he did resolve to check up on the case details recorded in the admission book when he got the chance.

His chance came in the early afternoon when a lull developed. Nurses were chatting as they polished and tidied instrument trays and re-stocked cupboards and shelves. Chenhui sat with one of her English language books, her mouth moving silently. Saracen flicked through the pages of the admissions book and scanned down the entries for the evening of the twelfth. His index finger stopped on the entry for Myra Archer. Medic Alpha alert: Myra Archer, Flat 2, Palmer's Green Court. Dead on arrival. No known relatives. Medical Officer, Dr Chenhui Tang. There was no mention of a post-mortem report.

Saracen closed the book and replaced it on the shelf. He went and sat down beside Chenhui, who looked up from her book and smiled. He glanced at the page she had been studying. It was headed, 'At the seaside: How is the weather? The weather is fine. What colour is the sky? The sky is blue.'

'Chenhui, do you remember a Mrs Myra Archer?' asked Saracen. He fully expected her to smile, repeat the name slowly and then look thoughtful. Instead her smile disappeared instantly, her eyes filled with something that looked like fear and she became so nervous and agitated that she dropped the book she had been looking at. Saracen picked it up and handed it to her.

'No, no Myra Archer,' said Chenhui, looking more and more like a frightened mouse.

'But...' Saracen stopped himself. 'No matter,' he smiled. 'It must have been a mistake. Forget it, it wasn't important.'

Chenhui got up and excused herself, leaving Saracen to look thoughtfully after her as she left the room.

'Now what was that all about?' he said quietly. It suddenly appeared as though Archer had been right. There had been something odd about the way his wife's case had been handled. The question was, what? He considered everything he knew about the affair. According to Timothy Archer there had been some kind of mix-up over which hospital his wife had been admitted to and, with Chenhui involved, a misunderstanding was certainly on the cards. Had that been it? Had some failure in communication been responsible for a delay in admitting Myra Archer to hospital and, if so, had it been a serious delay? Could it have been responsible for her death?

If it had been, then there had obviously been a cover-up and Nigel Garten must have been involved for he was the one who had spoken to Archer. Saracen felt a hollowness creeping into the pit of his stomach. This was exactly the kind of situation he did not need in his life, not a second time.

His inclination was to do nothing and he tried to rationalize this course of inaction by telling himself that whatever he did it was not going to bring Myra Archer back to life. Any kind of inquiry would be sure to cause embarrassment, anguish and a great deal of unpleasantness. Chenhui might end up being dismissed, maybe Nigel Garten too, after a sacrificial inquiry by the health board for the benefit of the Press. He himself would establish his credentials beyond doubt as a viper who would never find another nest in medicine. Was that the real reason for doing nothing, he wondered. If someone really had died because of Chenhui it could happen again and, if it did, would it not be as much his fault as hers for having said nothing?

As business began to pick up in Accident and Emergency, Saracen did his best to pretend to Chenhui that nothing was amiss. He still had not decided what to do for the best, for both options seemed equally unattractive, but by tea time he had produced a third alternative. He would carry out an investigation himself and reach his own conclusions about the death of Myra Archer. If he discovered that a foul-up had contributed to her death then he would speak out. If, on the other hand, he felt that she would have died anyway, he would be content to let the matter rest.

The question now for Saracen was how to go about making inquiries discreetly, how to find out what he wanted to know without having to make any direct approaches. That, he concluded, meant paperwork, always assuming that it existed, for there was nothing more to be gleaned from the Accident and Emergency records. Myra Archer had been admitted as dead on arrival, no file would have been opened on her. That left the post-mortem report, which would record the exact cause of death, something that may or may not prove useful for Saracen's purpose; and, as an afterthought, Medic Alpha's log book. If there had been any untoward delay or mix-up it would be recorded in the log.

Nigel Garten appeared in the department at six thirty pretending that he had just had an exhausting and demanding day. He had 'popped in' to ensure that everything was running smoothly. Saracen assured him drily that it was, and smiled thinly when Garten announced that he would have to rush off again. 'Dinner with the in-laws, old man. You know the form.'

Garten checked quickly through the mail lying on his desk before leaving and Saracen kept watch out of the corner of his eye to see whether Chenhui made any kind of approach towards him. To his relief she did not, although he could not be sure whether this was because Garten appeared to be in such a rush or whether he had managed to convince her that his question about Myra Archer had been quite innocent. With a bit of luck, thought Saracen, her lack of English might have pushed her towards the latter view.

Soon after Garten had left Tremaine and Prahesh Singh arrived to take over the night-shift in Accident and Emergency. Saracen went through the report with Tremaine and made a conscious effort to appear humorous and relaxed for Chenhui's benefit, for he could sense that she was watching him in what he feared might be a textbook case of guilty conscience. When it was time to leave he said good-night to her with an extra big smile, then waited round the corner in the car park until Chenhui herself left. Then he walked down the hill to the ambulance depot to look for a member of the Medic Alpha crew.

He found the rest room empty, the only signs of life being a thermos flask sitting on the middle of the table with its lid screwed on the wrong thread and a piece of greaseproof paper that had recently held sandwiches. He looked out of the window and saw an attendant cleaning the windscreen of one of the vehicles.

'Where is everyone?' asked Saracen.

'Try the duty room.'

Saracen walked slowly through the corridor to the back of the building. He passed a room which was emitting bursts of static noise, and looked round the door to see the sole radio operator engaged in conversation. He continued along to the door marked 'duty room' and heard voices coming from inside. They were arguing about football. Saracen knocked and went in. The talking stopped.

'Can I help you?' asked a short, bald man in shirtsleeves.

Saracen looked around for a familiar face and picked out Leonard Wright, a driver he knew to be on the Medic Alpha rota. 'Could I have a word?' he asked.

Wright followed Saracen out into the ambulance yard and asked, 'What can I do for you?'

'I'd like to examine Medic Alpha's log book if that's possible,' said Saracen. Saracen thought he saw the smile on Wright's face waver but it was only for a second and it could have been his imagination.

'What's the problem?'

'No problem, really. I just need some information about the time of the smash-up on the ring road the other night. I forgot to make notes at the time.'

Wright appeared to hold his gaze for a moment before saying, 'I'll get it.'

Saracen was aware that his pulse was racing. Lying was hard work when you weren't used to it and the guilt of knowing that you were lying changed your perspective on everything.

Wright returned with the log book and Saracen smiled in what he hoped was a relaxed fashion, but he felt the strain at the corners of his mouth. Wright had opened the book at the correct page for the ring road accident. That made it more difficult for there was no excuse for thumbing through the pages. Saracen's pulse grew even faster.

'I'll just make a note of these,' he said stalling for time. He fumbled in his pocket for a pen and found an excuse instead. He left his pen where it was and said, 'What a twit! I don't seem to have a pen with me. I wonder...'

Wright held his gaze again and Saracen read accusation in it, or imagined that he did, before Wright said that he would fetch one and turned to go back inside.

Saracen flicked through the pages with what he felt were five thumbs and found the entry he was looking for: *'Call to Flat 2, Palmer's Green Court. Patient Myra Archer, severely cyanosed, suspect cardiac arrest, medical officer on board, Dr Tang. Alarm raised by neighbour, Mrs M Le Grice. Time of call, 21.34 hours. Arrival at Palmer's Green, 21.47 hours. Arrival at Skelmore General, 22.04 hours.'*

Saracen felt a strange mixture of deflation and relief. There appeared to be nothing wrong at all with the response of Medic Alpha, no suggestion of delay or mix-up. So why had Chenhui Tang behaved the way she had when the name Myra Archer had been mentioned?

Saracen noted that the driver on the night of the twelfth had been Leonard Wright, whom he now saw returning with a pen. He let the pages fall back but as he did so he felt the one he had been looking at come loose. There had been no reason for it to have done so apart from the one that flew into Saracen's head. It was not the original page! It was a substitute that had been lightly glued in!

Saracen accepted the pen from Wright and wrote down some details of the road accident before returning it to him. 'Good, all done,' he said, closing the book and handing that back too. 'Much obliged.'

'No problem,' replied Wright.

Saracen walked out of the ambulance station with contrived casualness, conscious of every movement of his limbs and convinced that Wright was staring at him all the way up the hill to the gate, but he steeled himself not to turn round and check.

Saracen made directly for the whisky bottle when he got in to the flat and took a big gulp. Just what the hell was he getting himself into, he wondered. The thing seemed to be snow-balling out of all proportion, first with the suggestion of a cover-up and now the deliberate falsification of records. The question of what he should do next bothered him. Commonsense and a desire for self-preservation said that he should drop the whole affair like a hot potato, but he recognized that this was no longer an option. If he were to do that then the unanswer-ed questions would gnaw at him until he final-ly did seek the answers and put the matter to rest.

It occurred to Saracen that there would have been a nurse from Accident and Emergency on board Medic Alpha when it had answered the call to Myra Archer. Perhaps he could persuade Staff Nurse Rawlings to make a few discreet inquiries and find out what she could. He pick-ed up the phone and dialled the Nurse's Home. It was engaged; come to think of it, thought Saracen, it always was. He tried twice more before he eventually got through and asked for Jill. There was a long pause while distant voices echoed along corridors.

'Hello,' said Jill Rawlings' voice.

'Hello, Jill. It's James Saracen. Are you free this evening?'

Jill Rawlings agreed to meet Saracen for a drink at the Blue Angel at eight o'clock.

The pub was busy when they arrived. They were served by a teenage girl who sniffed intermittently, as though she had a heavy cold, and spoke very slowly and deliberately. Asking Jill if she wanted ice and lemon in her drink amounted to an in-depth interview.

'Well, no one is going to get drunk around here,' smiled Jill, as her interrogator shuffled off.

'I have a favour to ask,' said Saracen.

'Never on a first date, Doctor.'

When Saracen finally did manage to explain to Jill what he wanted her to find out for him she became more serious. 'Did something go wrong?' she asked.

'That's what I want to find out,' replied Saracen. 'Discreetly.'

'I'll see what I can do.'

'And I will now buy you dinner.'

They went to an Italian restaurant, one of two in Skelmore, and afterwards Saracen drove Jill back to the Nurses' Home where she thanked him for dinner and said that she would be in touch.

FOUR

It was four days before Saracen saw Jill again, when their duty stints coincided on Friday morning. He raised his eyes in question when she came into the crowded treatment room and she nodded briefly and self-consciously in reply. Saracen mouthed the word 'Lunch' to her, and she nodded again.

They ate in the hospital staff canteen, a huge rambling barn of a place which reminded Saracen of a school assembly hall, where the accoustics were such that the air was constantly filled with the clatter of crockery and cutlery from the kitchens. The tiled walls were clean to shoulder height, where the agreement with the unions expired, and then grew progressively filthier as they climbed to meet the vaulted ceiling some twenty feet above the lino-clad floor. Proper cleaning would have required the erection of scaffolding and so was out of the question but, for the most part, poor lighting hid the dirt.

'You spoke to the nurse?' asked Saracen.

Jill said that she had. 'It was Mary Travers, she's a friend of mine. She said that the patient was severely cyanosed when they got to her, almost navy-blue in fact. They gave her oxygen

82

on the way back to the General but then there was some discussion as to whether or not she should be taken on to the County Hospital.'

'Why?'

'Mary didn't know. Dr Tang just told them all to stay on board while she spoke to Dr Garten. When she came back, Dr Tang told Mary that the patient would be going to the County and, as she would be going with her, there was no need for Mary to stay on board. Mary was well over her duty period so she was quite glad. She returned to A&E and signed off.'

'So as far as Nurse Travers was concerned, the patient was being taken to the County Hospital?'

'Yes.'

'And she was alive when Nurse Travers left her?'

'Yes.'

'Did you ask about times?'

'Mary couldn't remember. She suggests you check the ambulance log book.'

'I already did.'

'And?'

Saracen hesitated before replying. It had been his intention to involve Jill as little as possible in the affair, for her own good, but it was becoming increasingly difficult and he did want to discuss it with someone, so he decided to confide in her.

'The records says that Myra Archer was dead

on arrival at Skelmore General. There was no mention of a transfer to the County Hospital.'

'But why?' exclaimed Jill in astonishment.

'Why indeed,' said Saracen.

Jill asked what had made Saracen suspicious in the first place and he told her of his meeting with Timothy Archer.

'Poor man,' said Jill, when he had finished.

Saracen confessed that, at first, he had been sceptical about Archer's story and had put it down to the man being over-wrought. But now there seemed to be grounds for believing that there had indeed been some kind of foul-up over his wife's treatment and a subsequent cover-up.

'But why would Garten involve himself in the cover-up?' asked Jill. 'Surely the blame was down to Dr Tang?'

'That puzzles me, too,' Saracen agreed. 'I can't honestly see Garten putting his career on the line to save a junior doctor.'

'Or anyone else, for that matter,' added Jill.

'Then he must be involved in some way.'

'Tricky,' said Jill.

Saracen nodded in agreement.

'What are you going to do now?' asked Jill.

Saracen shook his head.

'Have you tackled Dr Tang?'

'I tried, but when I mentioned Myra Archer's name she took fright and scurried off.'

'She might tell Garten,' said Jill.

'That thought has not escaped me,' replied

Saracen ruefully, 'but I broached the subject casually; there was no suggestion of an accusation so I think I might get away with it.'

'What happened when the ambulance reached the County Hospital?' asked Jill.

'As far as I can tell it never did. Timothy Archer told me that he had been sent to the County when he first tried to locate his wife but the staff there had no knowledge of her and sent him back to Skelmore General. That's when Garten acknowledged that she had been admitted to A&E and told him that she had died of a heart attack.'

'But we know the ambulance did leave for the County. It must have been recalled en route.'

'Or maybe Myra Archer died on the way?' said Saracen, thinking out loud.

'If that's the case, I can't see what all the fuss is about. Can you?' asked Jill. 'Presumably the decision to send the patient to the County was taken in good faith. If she was so ill that she died on the way it seems likely that she would have died anyway.'

Saracen tapped his forehead and said, 'Then why the big cover-up over an extra five minutes or so in the ambulance?'

'It does seem a bit odd,' agreed Jill.

Saracen stopped racking his brains for answers and smiled at Jill. 'I'm grateful to you for asking around,' he said.

'Don't mention it.'

'There is one more thing.'

'Yes?'

'Alan Tremaine has asked me to have dinner with him and his sister tomorrow evening; apparently she's coming to stay for a bit. He suggested I bring a friend. Would you come?'

'I'd be delighted,' said Jill.

Shared social occasions were rare for Accident and Emergency staff; however, it was sometimes possible, with a bit of duty swapping, for two doctors to be off at the same time. Alan Tremaine had engineered his off duty to coincide with Saracen's, so he could give a small dinner party for his sister Claire who would be arriving on the following day.

In actual fact, the limitations imposed on social life by working in Casualty suited Saracen very well. He disliked parties, a legacy of his time with Marion when their life had revolved around a seemingly endless circuit of social gatherings, outstanding only for their superficiality. Why so many people who so patently disliked each other should have continued to seek each other's company had been beyond his comprehension. But Marion had seen it all as an exciting game, a competition for which she would plan like a military strategist, deciding in advance who to speak to, whom to avoid, what to wear, what to say. The end result had always been a flawless performance. Marion would arrive like a film star, shine brightly, stay long enough to capture the hearts of all the men, then leave before the proceedings had begun to flag.

'Time we were getting back,' said Jill.

Saracen snapped out of his musings and gathered their used crockery to return it to the kitchen hatch as was the regulation. 'Pick you up at seven thirty tomorrow evening?'

'Fine.'

It was raining when Saracen turned into the narrow lane that led down to the Nurses' Home at the General, and the raindrops on the back window made it awkward for him to reverse the car in the small space available, which was made even smaller by illegally parked cars. When he finally did complete the manoeuvre he saw Jill sheltering under the long canopy that fronted the building. He leaned over and opened the passenger door.

'I saw you arrive from the window,' said Jill, as she swung her stockinged legs into the car.

Saracen made an appreciative sound.

Jill smiled and said, 'I thought I'd better make the effort, don't know what the opposition is going to be like.'

'I've never met her before,' confessed Saracen. 'She might be a twenty-stone dumpling.'

'With my luck she'll be a Dior model,' said Jill. 'And there's me with St Michael stuck all over me.'

'You look great,' said Saracen, and meant it.

Jill's prediction proved to be a good deal more accurate than Saracen's, for Claire Tremaine was no dumpling. She turned out to be a slim, confident, elegant woman in her mid-twenties, who proved to be as witty and entertaining as she was attractive. She was not, however, slow to point out the failings of Skelmore as a place to live, a view that Saracen happened to agree with, although he did feel a little irritated that an outsider should be so forthright so quickly.

But such considerations had long since ceased to be important enough for him to take issue with. Throughout the course of the evening he smiled and laughed in all the right places. Jill might have been goaded into some kind of defence of her home town but she was kept fully occupied by Alan Tremaine, who was having difficulty keeping his eyes off her cleavage and kept repeating—due to over-indulgence in Côtes du Rhône—that he hadn't realized what delights had been lurking beneath the drab blue cotton of a Skelmore nurse's uniform. Jill was well able to handle the situation for, at twenty-seven, she had seen a lot of randy housemen come and go.

'So why have you come to Skelmore, Claire?' asked Saracen.

'My first job,' replied Claire. 'I've been doing a PhD at Oxford in archaeology and my supervisor is leading the search for the site of Skelmoris Abbey. He took me on despite the fact that I haven't written up my thesis yet.'

'Why the sudden interest in Skelmoris Abbey?' asked Saracen. 'No one has ever bothered to look for it before, have they?'

'Not in recent times,' agreed Claire, 'but that was because no one really had any idea where the site was.'

'And now?'

'A few months ago a librarian in Oxford was leafing through the pages of some old books that had been bequeathed to the university and he found a map. It was very old and very yellow.'

'How exciting,' said Jill.

'Just like *Treasure Island,*' added Tremaine.

'It included a plan of Skelmoris Abbey and it contained information about the surrounding area. A lot has changed in six hundred years, of course, but we now think we have a reasonable chance of finding the actual site.'

'There was something about this in the local paper,' said Saracen. 'The abbey was supposed to have been destroyed by fire, wasn't it?'

'The fire is fairly well documented,' said Claire.

'And the legend?' smiled Saracen.

Claire smiled and said, 'Legends are legends.'

'So the curse doesn't bother you?'

'What curse?' asked Jill.

Claire explained. 'According to the story, the abbey was entrusted with the safe-keeping of a sacred chalice. Anyone attempting to remove the Skelmoris Chalice would incur the wrath of God and pay with his life. Legend has it that a lot of people did.'

'Creepy,' said Jill.

'What the story in the paper didn't say was that the fire was deliberate,' continued Claire. 'After the deaths of the original abbot and brothers, the Church tried several times to re-open the abbey. Although the new monks were God-fearing and had no intention of removing the chalice, they met with the same fate as the others. In the end the Church gave up and burned the place to the ground.'

'What an awful story,' said Jill, with a shiver. 'I think if it was up to me I would let well alone.'

Claire smiled and said, 'The plan is that I dig during the day and write up my thesis in the evenings.'

'Sounds like a full life,' said Saracen.

'I think the idea is that there won't be too many distractions here in the sticks, so here I am as an uninvited guest of little brother.'

'Consider yourself invited,' said Tremaine, leaning across and kissing his sister on the cheek.

'I wish I had a brother like you,' said Jill. 'Keith and I fight like cat and dog whenever we are together.'

90

Tremaine made a rather unsteady attempt to kiss Jill on the cheek too. 'I'll be your brother,' he grinned.

Jill laughed it off and expertly avoided Tremaine's advance. In anyone else his behaviour might have been considered offensive, but from Alan Tremaine it was accepted with good humour. If anyone was upset by it, it was his sister. Saracen noticed her occasionally betray her impatience with an unguarded look.

The party broke up around midnight, for both Saracen and Jill were on duty in the morning, but before she left, Jill invited Claire to call her whenever she got too bored with writing. They could arrange an evening out for a chat.

Saracen passed his own apartment on the way back to the Nurses' Home. 'Nightcap?' he asked. Jill agreed.

'Brrr. The place is like a morgue,' said Saracen, as he fumbled in the darkness for the light switch. He lit the gas fire, drew the curtains and put some music on before pouring the drinks. 'Did you enjoy yourself tonight?' he asked Jill.

'It was a nice evening,' Jill replied.

'What did you think of Claire?'

'I hated her,' said Jill, with a disarming honesty that made Saracen splutter.

'Why?'

'She's good-looking, bright, self-assured, confident, and totally at ease. Is that enough to be going on with?'

Saracen laughed and said, 'You had nothing to worry about. You held your own beside her.'

'You're too kind, sir,' said Jill. 'But I felt like a country bumpkin beside Claire Tremaine. I could feel the straw falling out of my ears.'

'Nonsense,' insisted Saracen. 'Besides, you were a big hit with Alan.'

'Boys will be boys,' smiled Jill, and returned to thoughts of Claire.

'God, I wish I had that kind of confidence,' she said.

'Maybe it's an act.'

'Do you think so?'

'It often is. Even the most outrageous extroverts insist on being basically shy.'

'They're usually mistaken,' argued Jill. 'They misconstrue selfishness as sensitivity, believing they're "basically shy" because they once managed to have a thought without telling the whole world.'

'That's astute of you,' said Saracen quietly. 'I came to the same conclusion many years ago.'

'Then maybe we both understand people.'

'Maybe,' agreed Saracen.

They finished their drinks.

'I'd better get back,' said Jill looking at her watch.

'Of course. I'll drive you.'

As they got to the door Jill turned and said, 'Thank you, James.'

'For what?'

'Not sticking your hand up my skirt.'

Saracen smiled and said, 'I won't say the thought didn't occur to me.'

'Good. I would have felt insulted if it hadn't. Incidentally, why didn't you?'

'We don't know each other well enough.'

Jill smiled and seemed pleased at Saracen's reply.

Saracen looked at the green digits on the alarm clock and saw that it was thirteen minutes past four in the morning. It was the third time he had looked at the clock in the past hour. Three hours of sleep was not much of a basis on which to begin a long period of duty, but that thought just made matters worse. There was no way that he was going back to sleep and it was all due to Myra Archer and the pricking of his own conscience.

The explanation that the only wrong-doing in the Myra Archer case was a short delay in deciding which hospital she should go to was attractive and convenient, because it trivialized the incident and absolved him from further involvement. In fact, there was only one problem, thought Saracen, as he lay in the dark; it was wrong. Of that he was certain. There had to be more to it to have warranted such a cover-up and falsification of records.

Saracen realized that this was the second time in days that he had lain awake in the early hours feeling troubled about events at the hospital. The first time had been after the affair at the mortuary when the explanation on offer had seemed too convenient, just like now. Thoughts of that incident had been receding but now they surfaced to niggle at him once again. He reached out for the lamp switch and abandoned all hope of sleep. Any remaining reluctance to get up was solely concerned with temperature. The flat did not have central heating and maintained at best a temperature between lukewarm and cold. At four thirty in the morning it was on the freezing side of cold.

Saracen turned on the gas fire and squatted down in front of it for a few moments, trying to cram as large an area of body as possible into the path of the radiant heat before making for the kitchen to switch on the electric kettle. He lifted the kettle first to make sure that it had enough water in it. It hadn't. He breathed a single expletive and padded over the cold lino in his bare feet to the sink. In his haste to get back to the fire he wrenched on the cold tap too hard and overdid it. The mains pressure at that hour in the morning ensured that he received an icy spray all over his bare chest. Single expletives were no longer sufficient, and he launched into an adjectival soliloquy.

As he sat nursing his coffee, Saracen's gaze fell on his textbooks which were arranged in neat rows on the shelves by the fire. The group nearest to him were concerned with pathological technique. Their titles reminded him again of the horror of waking up on the post-mortem examination table. It made him think of how he had come to be there in the first place. He imagined his body being dragged across the courtyard and into the mortuary, his wrists scraping the stone floor, the coldness, the stillness, the sweet sickly smell and the forgotten fact that still eluded him, the connection between formaldehyde and ammonia. He withdrew a large tome on histology and looked up formaldehyde.

Saracen found only what he already knew. Formaldehyde was a gas that could be dissolved up to a concentration of forty per cent in water. A ten per cent solution, known as formalin, was commonly used as a general fixative for the preservation of dead tissue. The book went on to list appropriate occasions for the use of formalin fixation in preference to others. Saracen closed it and put it back on the shelf. He lay back and idly scanned the other titles on the shelves. His eyes stopped at *Cruikshank's Medical Microbiology* and he sat up sharply. That was it! Formaldehyde did have another use. Ninety-nine times out of a hundred it would be used as a tissue fixative, but it could also be used to kill bacteria. It was a powerful disinfectant!

Saracen thumbed quickly to the relevant section on sterilization and methods of disinfection. He found what he was looking for. Paraformaldehyde tablets, when placed in a spirit lamp evaporator, gave off formaldehyde gas capable of disinfecting entire rooms. At the end of the process the toxic formaldehyde gas could be neutralized by throwing in rags soaked in—ammonia! He had found the connection. It made sense. He had been lying unconscious for many hours in a room next door to one that was being disinfected by formaldehyde gas.

One question had been answered, but a much bigger one loomed. Why had it been deemed necessary to disinfect the entire mortuary in the first place, and why all the lies about thieves in the night? Could it be that the affair at the mortuary and the cover-up over Myra Archer's death were in some way connected? The floodgates to Saracen's imagination opened up. Just how did Myra Archer die?

Skelmore General did not have a full-time pathologist of its own. Post-mortems were carried out by a rota pathologist, one of two who covered the County Hospital as well as doing forensic work for the district. They were both based at an office in the County Hospital. Saracen phoned Dave Moss, his friend at the County, to find out which one was on duty. It was an important consideration, for one of the two was approachable while the other was a paranoid alcoholic who attempted to cover up his failing abilities with increasing pomposity. The latter would not take kindly to inquiries coming from someone of Saracen's lowly status. He would almost certainly mention the matter to Garten.

'Dave? It's James Saracen.'

'Saracen! if you are about to tell me that you are sending down a dozen patients knee deep in shit I'm going to put down the phone and pretend you never called.'

'Nothing like that. Actually, it's three nuns with gonorrhoea.'

When the banter had stopped Saracen asked who the duty pathologist was.

'Hang on, I'll look.' After a few moments Moss returned and said, 'It's Peter Clyde. What's the problem?'

'No problem. I just want to check up on something.'

'Uh huh,' said Moss knowingly. 'I see, it's cover-up-your-mistakes time. Say no more.'

Saracen tried to laugh, then asked, 'Is he in the office this morning?'

'I think so. I saw him about half an hour ago, come to think of it. His extension is four-three-one, but I suspect it says that in your directory too.'

Saracen took the point Moss was making and said, 'I'm sorry, I had to make sure it wasn't Wylie today. The inquiry I have to make is rather delicate.'

'I understand,' said Moss. 'I keep hoping that Wylie will retire soon and save us the continued embarrassment of pretending that he's not pissed out of his mind all the time.'

'At least his patients are dead.'

'Just as well,' said Moss. 'A hamster with a hacksaw could have made a better job of the last PM I saw him do.'

They made their usual assertions about having to get together for a drink and Saracen put down the phone. He lifted it again and dialled 431. Peter Clyde answered. After an initial exchange of pleasantries Saracen came to the point and asked about the post-mortem report on Myra Archer.

'The name doesn't mean anything,' said Clyde. 'Hang on a moment.'

Saracen could hear the sound of paper being shuffled at the other end of the telephone while he waited, then Clyde's voice said, 'Not one of mine, I'm afraid. I've only had one from the General in the past four weeks and that was—a man—Robert Nolan, aged sixty-nine, done on the eighth.'

'Damn,' said Saracen softly. 'I suppose that means that Cyril Wylie must have done it.'

'He'll be here tomorrow. You can give him a ring.'

Saracen gave a noncommittal grunt that Clyde picked up on. 'Is there some problem?' he asked quietly.

'It's rather awkward. I'd rather not ask Dr Wylie.'

'I see,' said Clyde thoughtfully, assuming that Saracen's reluctance had something to with Wylie's drink problem. Saracen saw no reason to disillusion him. 'One moment,' said Clyde.

Saracen was left holding the phone again. He hoped that Clyde had gone to check through Wylie's records.

Clyde returned. 'No joy, I'm afraid. I thought that Cyril might have left his filing cabinet unlocked but no such luck. You'll have to approach him yourself tomorrow.'

'Thanks anyway,' said Saracen. He put down the phone and rubbed his forehead with the heel of his hand.

'Problems?' asked one of the nurses.

'You could say that,' said Saracen with a wan smile, but let it go at that.

All thoughts of Myra Archer were dispelled from Saracen's head with the arrival in Accident and Emergency of a badly-injured thirteen-year-old girl who had been involved in a road accident with her bicycle. Both legs had been badly damaged where the car had hit her side on and she had lost a lot of blood.

'Have you alerted the theatre, Sister?' Saracen asked.

'Yes, Doctor.'

'Permission forms?'

'There's a problem.'

99

'Can't contact the parents?'

'No, it's not that. They are here, but they won't give permission for a blood transfusion. Religious reasons. They're Jehovah's Witnesses.'

Saracen's head dropped and he massaged his left temple with the fingertips of his left hand. It was his way of counting to ten.

'Where are they?' he asked.

'The small waiting room.'

'Put them in the office, will you. I'll talk to them.'

Saracen took a deep breath and entered the room to find a middle-aged couple sitting there with their arms around each other. The woman was sobbing quietly into a handkerchief. Saracen explained who he was and came straight to the point. 'Let me be perfectly frank with you,' he said. 'If your daughter does not have a blood transfusion soon, she will die. There is no other possible outcome. Do you understand?'

The man nodded silently. The woman continued to sob.

'Will you please give me your permission?'

The woman sobbed harder. The man squeezed her shoulder and said, 'I'm afraid our beliefs forbid such a thing, Doctor. We cannot give our permission.'

Anger simmered inside Saracen and he remained silent for a moment until he had regained his composure. He was about to say something else when the couple looked up at him and his anger was replaced by frustration. Instead of the smug self-righteousness he expected to find in their faces, he could see only pain and torment. The couple were suffering doubly, first because their daughter had been so badly injured and second because they felt compelled to refuse the one course of action that could save her.

Saracen said, 'I will now apply to have your child made a ward of court for the duration of her treatment. Do you have any questions?'

The couple remained silent but as Saracen reached the door the woman asked, 'How long will that take, Doctor?'

'One hour, maybe two.'

'Will she...' The words died on the woman's lips as she realized that it was a question she should not be asking.

Saracen left the room with the impression that the couple were really quite glad to have had the onus removed from them, although he also suspected that they would never admit as much to anyone, not even themselves. The games people play, thought Saracen, as he returned to the treatment room to check on the girl's condition before entering Nigel Garten's office to find the card that held the numbers and instructions for instigating ward of court proceedings.

The number was engaged and Saracen cursed under his breath. When he still got the engaged tone after the third attempt he slapped down his fist on the desk in frustration and caused some ink to jump out of its silver pot and splash on to the leather desktop. He searched quickly through the desk drawers for blotting paper and found some, but there, just below it was an open letter. Saracen's eye caught the underlined name near the top of the page. It was Myra Archer.

When he had finally reached the authorities and set things in motion Saracen returned to the drawer where the letter was and drew it out. He overcame his feelings of guilt at what he was about to do and read it. The letter came from British Airways and referred to a request made by Nigel Garten that all passengers and crew on the flight that had brought Myra Archer to the United Kingdom be contacted and treated as recommended. The letter confirmed that this had been done.

'What the hell for?' said Saracen softly as he stared at the letter. If the woman had died of a heart attack, what was all this nonsense about treatment for fellow passengers? Did this mean that Myra Archer had not died of cardiac failure? To find the answer Saracen knew that he would have to trace Garten's original letter to British Airways. He started searching through the files.

After a few minutes, which seemed like hours, he found what he was looking for and read the letter while still crouching beside the filing cabinet. It advised the airline that Mrs Myra Archer, a passenger on their flight BA 3114 to London Heathrow, had been shown to be suffering from a Salmonella infection. As a precaution it was deemed advisable for all persons on the flight to undergo a course of preventative antibiotic therapy as there was a possibility that food served on the aircraft might have been responsible.

'Food poisoning?' said Saracen, out loud. Myra Archer had been suffering from food poisoning? He shook his head in puzzlement but did not have time to consider the matter further before Chenhui came through the door and said anxiously,· 'Dr Saracen, I need your help. You come, please.'

Saracen followed Chenhui back to the side room where the teenage girl lay.

'I not happy,' said Chenhui.

Saracen examined the girl and checked the monitors. He agreed with Chenhui. 'We can't wait any longer,' he said. 'We'll have to give her blood right now. Has it come up from the bank?'

Sister Lindeman said that it had.

'Cross-matched?'

'Yes. How about the paperwork?'

'We can't wait.'

'If you say so.' Sister Lindeman enunciated the words very clearly and Saracen recognized that she was inviting him to take responsibility publicly.

'I say so,' he said, with a barely perceptible smile.

Saracen had set up the transfusion and was washing his hands when Chenhui came up beside him and said, 'I puzzled. Why parents say no blood?'

'A religious objection to transfusion,' replied Saracen, pushing off the taps with his elbows.

'I no understand.'

'Frankly Chenhui, neither do I,' said Saracen, baulking at the thought of attempting to explain something he had no heart for. 'It's all part of God's little obstacle course.'

Chenhui looked more puzzled than ever.

'Let's go and have a cup of tea.'

As they walked across the floor towards the duty room a trolley came through the swing doors bearing a tear-stained young boy, gingerly holding his left arm. 'He fell off a swing,' said the attendant.

'I will do,' announced Chenhui, and Saracen nodded. He went to have his tea and found Jill Rawlings had beaten him to it. She was sitting on a corner of the desk holding cup and saucer. 'I hear you gave blood to the JW,' she said.

'No option.'

'The authorities might disagree.'

'Sod 'em.'

'My hero,' grinned Jill.

Saracen ignored the remark and asked, 'Did Mary Travers say anything about Myra Archer having had a Salmonella infection?'

104

'Yes, she did, come to think of it. Some days after the Archer case she and the ambulance crew were given a course of antibiotics as a precaution. It didn't seem to be relevant to what you were asking at the time.'

'I suppose not,' said Saracen deeply in thought.

'You're not dropping the matter?'

Saracen screwed up his face. 'So many things are bothering me. For instance, how did they know the woman had a Salmonella infection if it was a treble nine call to a heart attack?'

'Presumably it was something they discovered afterwards at post-mortem,' said Jill.

'A Salmonella infection is hardly something the pathologist would be looking for in this woman's case,' said Saracen.

'What are you getting at?'

Saracen shrugged his shoulders and sighed. 'To be quite frank,' he said, 'I'm not at all sure myself.'

Jill smiled and touched him on the forearm.

'I have another favour to ask,' said Saracen.

'Go on.'

'Would you ask Mary Travers what day she was given the antibiotic cover on?'

'All right,' sighed Jill, 'if it will make you happy.' Then, as an afterthought she said, 'If they did know that Myra Archer had food poisoning at the time of the call that would explain why they decided to send her on to the County Hospital, wouldn't it?'

'It would,' agreed Saracen. 'But I don't see how Chenhui could have made that diagnosis in the circumstances, and that's what's niggling me.'

Saracen was in the bath when the telephone rang. His first thought, as always when the telephone rang in the early evening, was that it was Nigel Garten trying to unload his duty stint on some pretext or other, so he was relieved to hear Jill's voice.

'I've spoken to Mary Travers. She started her course of treatment on the thirteenth. Is that what you wanted to know?'

'Thanks, you're an angel.'

Saracen felt a weakness creep into his knees. He sat down as the blood began to pound in his temples. Myra Archer had died on the twelfth; the post-mortem would not have been done until the thirteenth at the earliest, more likely the fourteenth or fifteenth. To determine that Myra Archer had been suffering from a Salmonella infection would have required a lab examination of specimens taken from her body. The result could not possibly have been known until the fifteenth or sixteenth. Whatever reason Garten had had for putting Mary Travers and the others on treatment on the thirteenth, it had nothing to do with any discoveries at post-mortem. He must have known beforehand.

The bath water had gone cold. Saracen dried

himself and put on a towelling robe. He sat down to wonder how Chenhui and Garten could possibly have made the diagnosis. From all accounts Myra Archer had been unconscious when the ambulance was called and had not regained consciousness. She had told them nothing and died of cardiac failure, yet they had known that she also had a serious infection. It didn't make sense. Not only had they been able to diagnose Salmonella but they had been able to determine that it was one of the more serious strains, if Garten had deemed it necessary to contact the airline and to disinfect the mortuary. Could it have been typhoid—the 'top' of the Salmonella range? But if so, why the secrecy? There were one or two cases every year. If only he could see a copy of the PM report, thought Saracen, perhaps he could work backwards from the exact cause of death and figure out how they knew. Wylie or no Wylie, he would have to get his hands on that report.

Saracen rested his neck on the back of the chair and looked up at the ceiling for inspiration. He was tracing the path of a thin crack that radiated out from the light fitting when the telephone rang, it was Dave Moss.

'I've just had your Dr Tang on the phone,' said Moss.

'Oh yes.'

'She seemed to be in a bit of a state; trouble is, I don't really know what about. I only managed to pick up every fourth or fifth word. I think she wanted me to take a patient, maybe two, she kept saying "two", then the line went dead.'

'I see,' said Saracen, feeling anger rise within him. 'And you are phoning to find out why a doctor who can barely speak English has been left in charge of A&E at Skelmore General.'

'More or less.'

'Well, I'd like to know the answer to that, too,' said Saracen, getting out of the chair and gathering his clothes. 'Give me fifteen minutes. I'll get back to you.'

Saracen was furious. How could Garten do such a thing? How could he be so irresponsible? His toes got stuck in the heel of a sock in his haste and he cursed out loud as he disentangled himself, then he lost a shoe which led to more cursing. He slammed the door behind him and ran downstairs to the car, making a conscious effort to control his temper and prevent its translation into sheer bad driving. With only partial success in that direction the front tyres screeched as he swung the steering wheel over to enter the hospital gates. In truth, this was due more to the fact that he had wrenched the wheel so sharply than to any excess in speed, but it made the duty porter lift his eyes from his newspaper and half get out of his chair to glance out of the gate house window. When he saw that it was Saracen he slumped back into inertia.

Saracen burst in through the swing doors of Accident and Emergency, ignoring the smile of a junior nurse in his preoccupation with finding Chenhui. Sister Turner, the night sister, came out of the sluice room and looked surprised when she saw Saracen.

'I didn't realize that Dr Garten had called you,' she said.

'He didn't,' replied Saracen.

'Oh, when I saw you there I thought that he must have called you out to cover for Dr Tang...'

Saracen was puzzled. 'Why should he? What's wrong with Dr Tang?' he asked.

'She's had some kind of nervous breakdown. She's been admitted to the wards.'

Seeing that he had read the situation all wrong, Saracen calmed down and felt rather foolish. 'And Dr Garten?' he asked.

'He is with her right now.'

'So she wasn't left on her own in A&E?'

'Good heavens, no, she can hardly speak a word of...'

'Yes, sister,' interrupted Saracen. 'What did you mean, some kind of nervous breakdown?'

Sister Turner, a spinster clinging to late middle-age and fond of tittle-tattle, warmed to her task and said conspiratorially, 'I've never seen anything like it. She was shouting and raving, practically attacked Dr Garten when he tried to calm her down!'

'But why? What happened to upset her?'

109

The night sister looked perplexed. She said, 'The ridiculous thing is, we don't know. She was raving in her own language.'

'But something must have triggered it off?'

'Not really. It's not as if she hadn't seen a dead body before.'

'Go on.'

'We had a dead on arrival at around eight o'clock; Dr Tang was asked to certify the patient dead. When she came back she burst into Dr Garten's office and started shouting and carrying on.'

'In Chinese?'

'Not at first.'

'Could you make out anything that she said?' asked Saracen.

'Not much. She has such a heavy accent but it sounded like, "six days, more than six days", but I couldn't swear to it.'

'Then what happened?'

'She came rushing out of Dr Garten's office and started telephoning. Dr Garten tried to reason with her but in the end he had to get the porters to restrain her while he sedated her.'

'And what did Dr Garten say about all this?'

'He said that Dr Tang had been under great strain recently and was suffering from nervous exhaustion. She would probably be as right as rain in a couple of days, so it would be a kindness if none of us mentioned the incident outside A&E.'

Saracen nodded and said that he was going up to see Chenhui.

Away from Accident and Emergency the corridors of Skelmore General had quietened, as they always did around nine in the evening. The last visitors had gone and custody of the wards had been handed over to the night staff. Saracen had only the echo of his footsteps for company as he made his way along the entire length of the bottom corridor to reach ward eight. He disliked the hospital at night, for it had a Dickensian, dreamlike quality about it which was intensified by the poor lighting in the corridors and the peeling green paint on the walls. To be admitted at night as a patient to Skelmore General, thought Saracen, must be an unnerving experience, being wheeled head-first on a trolley with nothing but the cobwebs and dark shadows of the ceiling vaults to concentrate on while the trolley squeaked and echoed its way along a seemingly endless tunnel to an unknown destination. Poor sods.

Saracen opened one of the two tall glass-fronted doors to ward eight and went in. He winced as the door creaked loudly on its hinges but no one came out to investigate. He looked into the duty room and got a quizzical look from the staff nurse in charge. He told her who he was and why he was there.

'She's in the second side ward. Dr Garten is still with her.'

Saracen went in search of the side ward. He went inside and closed the door quietly behind him. Nigel Garten was sitting beside Chenhui, who seemed fast asleep. He looked up as Saracen came in and seemed startled, but recovered his composure quickly. 'I didn't expect to see you here,' he said, with a smile that seemed less than genuine.

'I received a telephone call,' said Saracen.

'Really? Who from?'

Saracen was slightly taken back at Garten's directness, but he answered anyway. 'Dave Moss at the County.'

'Ah yes, Dr Tang's phone call,' said Garten. He seemed relieved that it had not been one of the Accident and Emergency staff who had phoned Saracen.

'And what did Dr Moss tell you?' probed Garten.

'He thought that Chenhui had been left on her own in charge of A&E,' said Saracen, looking directly at Garten.

'Hardly,' said Garten slowly and quietly, his eyes holding Saracen's gaze as though looking for a challenge. The strained smile on his face was maintained as though carved in rock.

'How is she?' asked Saracen.

'Out for the count. She'll feel better after a good sleep.'

'What happened, exactly?'

'A sudden emotional outburst, complete loss of control. I blame myself, of course, I should

112

have seen it coming. She's just not up to the job. I should have said something to the board months ago but I felt sorry for her, wanted to give her every chance.' Garten looked at the floor in a display of mock self-condemnation.

Saracen was glad that Garten was looking at the floor, otherwise he might have seen the look of distaste on his face. He had never disliked Garten as much as he did at that moment. He looked at Chenhui, sleeping peacefully, and moved over to the bed to feel her pulse; it was slow and regular. He noted the drip feed going into her other arm and asked Garten, 'What are you giving her?'

'Heminevrin.'

'That's a bit drastic, isn't it?'

'I deemed it necessary,' replied Garten with more than a hint of coldness in his voice.

Saracen felt the temperature drop and changed the subject. 'Sister Turner said something about Chenhui dealing with a death in A&E when all this came on?'

'Nothing out of the ordinary. The man was dead on arrival.'

'I see, so it's a complete mystery as to what triggered off Chenhui's outburst?'

'Absolutely.'

'She does seem to have been under some kind of increased strain recently,' ventured Saracen.

'Really? I hadn't noticed,' replied Garten.

Saracen got to his feet and said, 'I'm here

now, so I'll work Chenhui's shift with you, if you like.'

'Wouldn't hear of it, old boy,' said Garten, so quietly that Saracen thought he detected menace in it. 'You go on home.'

Saracen had to work hard to keep the astonishment off his face. 'All right,' he said, and left.

FIVE

Saracen returned to Accident and Emergency and telephoned Dave Moss with an explanation of what had happened.

'That's rough,' said Moss. 'I sometimes feel like screaming myself. Where is she now?'

Saracen told Moss that Chenhui was under heavy sedation.

'Did you get what you wanted from Peter Clyde this morning?' asked Moss.

'No, the autopsy must have been one of Cyril Wylie's.'

'Couldn't Clyde have checked Wylie's files for you?'

'He tried. They were locked.'

Moss snorted and said, 'That sounds like Cyril, all right. Paranoid old bugger. How important is this?'

'Very,' replied Saracen.

'And you really can't go through channels?'

'It's not a case of avoiding channels,' said Saracen, feeling uncomfortable about not confiding in Moss. 'It's just that I don't want Garten to know I've been asking about the case.'

'Oh I see,' said Moss. 'It's one of Garten's cases. I can see the problem.' Moss knew about Saracen's past dealings with authority. 'Look, I can't promise anything, but give me the patient's name and I'll see what I can come up with. Wylie is doing a PM for us tomorrow. If I get a chance to nip into his office while he's occupied, I will.'

'I'd be in your debt,' said Saracen. 'The name is Myra Archer. She died on the night of the twelfth.'

'Anything in particular you want me to look for?' asked Moss.

'The cause of death was given as cardiac arrest and she was also said to be suffering from a Salmonella infection. I'd like to know if the PM confirmed that or if there was more to it.'

'I'll call you tomorrow.'

Saracen put down the phone thoughtfully. Moss's offer was something he had not foreseen; he made a mental note to buy him a drink.

'Will you be working tonight, Dr Saracen?' asked Sister Turner, who had come up behind him. Saracen took pleasure in watching the

115

flicker of surprise appear on her face when he replied that Garten would be covering Accident and Emergency on his own. A comment almost passed her lips but Saracen saw her stifle it and replace it with a professional 'Very good, Doctor.'

'About the death that Dr Tang was asked to certify, Sister?'

'There's not much to say. The patient was one Leonard Cohen, a sixty-four-year-old man, retired, living alone. He had been dead for a good few hours.'

'I take it the body is in the mortuary?'

'Yes, or rather, no. I mean I'm not sure.'

Saracen waited for her to explain.

'Dr Garten said something about the refrigeration system playing up again. He said he was going to contact a firm of undertakers to see if they could help out. I'm not sure if he did, in all the commotion, or whether the body is still here. You could ask the porter.'

Saracen found the duty porter tidying up a clutter of wheel-chairs in the corridor outside X-Ray. He asked him about the dead man.

'The undertakers took him away about thirty minutes ago, Doc. Was it something important?'

'I suppose not. Do you happen to know which firm it was?'

'Maurice Dolman and Sons, Ventnor Lane.'

'Thanks. What's wrong with the refrigeration, anyway?'

'Dr Garten said that the compressor was losing gas and the temperature was rising.'

Saracen nodded and turned away. He walked back along the corridor without seeing anything, for his mind was working full pelt. It was happening again. Garten, Chenhui, a dead patient. What the hell was going on? He turned into Accident and Emergency to say good-night to the nurses, but found it deserted. He could hear voices coming from the duty room where they were having tea.

Saracen was about to walk over when his gaze fell on the small wooden cupboard that held the mortuary key for the night porter. After a moment's hesitation he gave in to the impulse to tiptoe towards it and take it silently from its hook. He sidled out of the room again, holding his breath and grimacing with the concentration of moving soundlessly.

It had started to rain outside, but that did not diminish Saracen's relief at being safely out in the dark. He kept to the shadows and hurried down the hill to the mortuary to unlock the tall wooden doors and step inside.

Everything was still and silent. He felt for the light switch on the wall with his flattened palm and found it at the second attempt. It was loose in its mounting and a slight trickle of plaster fell to the floor when he pressed it. At first glance nothing appeared to be amiss, but Saracen had to admit that he had no real idea what he was looking for. He crossed the floor and examined the temperature gauge; the needle was reading high, just as it would if the compressor had failed. Saracen pulled back the heavy metal clamp on one of the body vaults and swung the door open to reveal the empty interior. He absent-mindedly slid out one of the three trays and pushed it back with the heel of his hand before closing the vault and moving on to the next one. It was empty too, as was the third, but the fourth and last one was not. There were two bodies inside.

Saracen stared at the white, linen-covered heads, unable to think why they should still be there. Why, if the compressor had really failed, had not all the bodies been removed? He pulled out each tray in turn and read the labels. Anne Hartman, Maud Finnegan. The shrouds were still cold but had started to feel damp with the rising temperature. Maybe there had been a number of bodies in the vaults, thought Saracen, and they were being transferred in relays. He found the mortuary register and checked on the idea. It proved wrong. There were only two bodies listed for the vaults, Hartmann and Finnegan, and they were still there, so only one body could have been taken away by the undertakers, that of Leonard Cohen, Chenhui's dead-on-arrival case. It was beginning to look as though the story of the compressor failure had been a subterfuge for the quick removal of Cohen's body from the hospital. On the other hand, the refrigeration unit did seem to be out of action.

Saracen examined the small door in the housing that covered the machinery and saw that it was secured by three screws. He fetched a screwdriver from the tool drawer and undid them. There was no smell of burning or any sign of damaged wiring, so he began a systematic check. He traced the path of the main cable to the motor and then all the lines to subsidiary units and switches, finding nothing amiss until he looked at the mounting panel. There was a hole in it.

Saracen took a closer look and saw that the hole should have held a circuit-breaker fuse. It had been removed. Could that be all that was wrong with the unit, he wondered, excited at the thought of having discovered deliberate sabotage. He searched through the tool drawer again and found a replacement fuse and holder, but fitting it was going to be awkward for the panel was tucked up behind the wiring loom of the motor. He tried first from the right hand side but found that he could not reach, so he changed his position on the floor and reached in with his left hand. He could almost reach the panel, just another few centimetres would be enough. He altered position slightly again and pressed his cheek up against the side of the unit to give himself the extra distance but, as he did so, he caught sight of something black on the floor. It was the toe of a shoe. Someone was standing behind him.

The shock of discovery made Saracen jerk his hand back and in doing so he touched the live wiring on the side of the motor. The mains voltage shot through him like a shower of arrows flinging him backwards across the floor, to land in an ungainly heap.

Fear took precedence over pain in Saracen's head. He looked up and saw Nigel Garten looking down at him as if he were a stain on the ground.

'What on earth do you think you are doing?' demanded Garten.

'I thought I could fix the fridge,' replied Saracen weakly.

'We have engineers for that sort of thing,' said Garten coldly, 'Unless this is a particular hobby of yours?'

Saracen felt foolish and it made him aggressive. 'I think someone removed the circuit breaker,' he said, staring Garten straight in the eye.

'I did,' said Garten calmly. 'The compressor was leaking gas. I didn't want anyone switching the unit back on and ruining it.'

'I see,' said Saracen, feeling more foolish than ever. 'Perhaps you can also tell me why only one body was removed and why two were left behind?'

Garten stared down at Saracen in silence, then he said slowly, 'I beg your pardon?'

'I asked why only one body has been removed and two left behind,' said Saracen, feeling intimidated.

'Could it be that the undertakers' vehicle can only accommodate two bodies at the one time? Three bodies equals—two trips?'

'Could be,' agreed Saracen quietly, now feeling absolutely ridiculous. He got to his feet and started to brush himself down, for his clothes were in a mess. Garten looked at him distastefully and said curtly, 'I'll bid you good-night. Lock up before you go.'

Saracen went back to the locker room in Accident and Emergency to change his clothes, for he kept a spare set there as necessary insurance against periodic dousings of blood, vomit or whatever. Mercifully he met no one and was able to leave again without having to offer an explanation to anyone. As he left the building a posse of policemen were escorting four drunk men through the swing doors. They had been involved in some kind of violent confrontation by the look of them, and two were still trying to get at each other.

'All the best, Nigel,' said Saracen under his breath, as he got into his car and started the engine.

When he had got over the burning embarrassment of having been discovered in the mortuary by Garten, Saracen saw that he could still be right. The removal of the circuit breaker might still have been all that was wrong with the refrigeration unit. Garten's glib explanation might have been nothing more than a lie. It could still have been an excuse for the quick removal of Cohen's body. But why? Unlike Myra Archer, Cohen was definitely dead when he arrived at Skelmore General, so there was no question of any mistake having been made or any delay being involved this time. What was Garten afraid of? Saracen decided that there was now a second post-mortem report he would have to take a look at.

Sudden death demanded an inquest unless the victim's general practitioner felt able to sign the death certificate. A hospital doctor could also sign, but would not in the case of a patient who was dead on arrival. In that instance a post-mortem would be a *sine qua non* for establishing the cause of death and the subsequent issuing of a death certificate. With luck, Dave Moss would get a look at the PM report on Myra Archer in the morning and let him know what it said. Maybe that would shed some light on the matter.

Saracen had an idea. If he got a move on in the morning he could contact the undertakers, Maurice Dolman and Sons, and arrange to examine Leonard Cohen's body himself. That would be better than just waiting for the report on the autopsy. To hell with Garten and to hell with the consequences. He had to know what was going on.

Saracen telephoned Dolman's at nine in the

morning. 'This is Dr Saracen at Skelmore General. I understand you have custody of the body of Leonard Cohen?'

'That is correct,' said the sombre voice. 'We were asked to assist when your refrigeration system broke down.'

'I'd like to see the body,' said Saracen.

There was a pause, then Dolman said, 'Of course, Doctor. When would you like to come?'

Saracen looked at his watch. 'Twenty minutes?'

'I'll expect you.'

Saracen put down the telephone feeling deflated, for the man had shown no surprise at all. It was almost as though he had been expecting the call. Was that a possibility, he wondered. Could Garten have warned them? Saracen picked up the telephone again and contacted the hospital switchboard. He asked for the number of the contract engineer for refrigeration equipment in the hospital and jotted it down on the pad in front of him. He called it.

'I take it you have been informed of the compressor failure in the mortuary at Skelmore General last night?' he asked.

'No,' replied the puzzled voice. 'This is the first we have heard of it.'

'My mistake,' said Saracen, and put the phone down. At least he had been right about one thing.

'Is that you phoning your stockbroker again?' joked Alan Tremaine, who was passing.

'I have to go out for about half an hour,' said Saracen. 'Look after the shop, will you?'

'Sure. Are you going up to see Chenhui?'

Saracen told Tremaine that he was going to Dolman's to have a look at the body Chenhui was asked to certify.

'He was a DOA wasn't he?'

Saracen nodded.

'Do you think that had something to do with her breakdown?'

'I don't know, but I think it's worth checking out.'

'Garten has it down in the book as a straightforward cardiac case,' said Tremaine.

'I know,' said Saracen.

'And if our leader should call?'

'Tell him,' said Saracen.

Parking near Ventnor Lane in mid-morning stretched Saracen's patience to the limit. He could not get into the lane itself because two hearses and a black Bedford van were already parked there and all the surrounding streets were etched with double yellow lines. This in itself had not prevented a caravan of lorries from stopping there with their wheels half up on the pavement as their drivers made their deliveries and obstructed traffic in both directions.

The streets in this area, the oldest part of

124

town, were narrow and overhung with an odd assortment of two- and three-storey buildings which huddled together as if in mutual support, each cemented to the other with the dirt and grime of centuries.

Saracen saw a space among the rubble of a recently demolished warehouse and risked the anger of any traffic behind by stopping suddenly and attempting to reverse into it. A red-faced man driving a Rover blew his horn angrily and made a rude gesture at Saracen. Saracen noted the florid complexion as he smiled an apology and said quietly through his teeth, 'See you soon, old man.'

The premises of Maurice Dolman and Sons were painted black and grey and fronted with double shop windows, each blanked out to just above eye-level, with smoke-grey paint. This had the effect of making the inside of the building artificially dark, even in the mid-morning, and required that the lights—crystal wall lights—be kept on all the time.

There was no one at the counter when Saracen went in, so he took time to take in his surroundings. A tape of solemn organ music was playing and it irked him. Unwilling to accept its celestial origins, he looked for the concealed speakers and found one grille above a photograph of a hearse captioned, '1933'. There was another in a peg board screen on the other side of the room that carried yet more photographs of hearses and the dates when they had served with the company.

Saracen saw the polished brass bell on the counter. It sat beside a leather bound edition of the Bible and a small plate which invited him to 'press for attention.' He slapped it hard with his palm, not that he was annoyed that no one was about. He just wanted to destroy the bogus aura of reverence.

There was a movement from somewhere at the back. A series of slow footsteps seemed to go on for ever before a short man wearing a black jacket and striped trousers appeared at the counter. He had his hands clasped together as if he had been disturbed at prayer.

'May I be of assistance, sir?' the man inquired, in a voice full of practised sympathy and concern.

'I'm Saracen. I telephoned.'

'Oh yes,' said the man, affecting an immediate change of tone. 'This way.'

Saracen followed the man, whom he took to be Maurice Dolman himself, through a narrow corridor flanked by partitioned cubicles. Each was furnished in similar fashion with a desk and three chairs, and was where Saracen deduced the 'loved ones' decided which of Dolman's wares should accompany their departed on the final journey. An elderly typist sat in the last cubicle, her spectacles perched on her nose, hands poised above the keyboard, as she read her notes before committing her fingers to the keys.

They left the front shop and descended some stairs to a basement which joined with that of a neighbouring building. There was a strong chemical smell in the air and the rooms were now lit by fluorescent fittings that filled every corner with cold, hard, shadowless light.

'This is quicker than walking round the outside,' said Dolman. He stopped as they came to a closed door and half turned, saying, 'I am afraid we have to pass through here but you being a doctor and all...' His voice trailed off without further explanation, and he opened the door. Saracen entered to a sight that took him unawares and a smell that brought his hand up to his face.

The naked corpse of an old woman was lying on a marble slab while two men, one with a cigarette dangling from his mouth, worked on it. A series of plastic tubes led out of the cadaver and were draining away the body fluids into a number of stainless steel buckets on the floor. One of the men was preparing to replace the fluids with a chemical mix.

'Embalming,' said Dolman. 'So important that the dead should look their best, don't you think?'

Saracen did not reply. He would cheerfully have blown up the place, but saying so was not going to help.

Dolman spoke to the men. 'Dr Saracen is here to examine the deceased Leonard Cohen. Would one of you take him through and give him every assistance.'

The directive was aimed at the man with the cigarette, who responded sullenly by getting up slowly from his stool and leaning over one of the buckets to release the butt from his lips without using his hands. It fell with a hiss into the stinking slop. Still without speaking, he inclined his head to indicate that Saracen follow him. The man put Saracen's teeth on edge. He found his fingers bunching into fists as he followed him through a narrow stone passage until they came to a room marked 'Morgue'.

Saracen stood back as his reluctant assistant opened up a refrigerator with space for six bodies; four were in residence. Saracen read the name tags over the man's shoulder. Carlisle, Hartley, Finnegan and Cohen. So Garten had transferred the remaining two bodies from Skelmore General after all.

The examination did not take long, and afterwards Saracen washed his hands in the grubby little sink in the corner as he faced up to the fact that he had discovered nothing new. The corpse had been that of a man in his sixties with no unusual features or peculiarities at all. Unless Chenhui had actually known him personally, it was difficult to see anything about the man that could have upset her so badly.

Dolman came into the room, his hands still clasped together. 'Quite finished, Doctor?' he asked with an obsequious smile.

'Quite,' said Saracen.

128

Dolman turned to the man beside him and said, 'Return Mr Cohen to the fridge will you, and get out Miss Carlisle. She is going at noon.'

Saracen was glad to get out into the fresh air, even if it was full of diesel fumes. Anything had to be better than the Hell's kitchen atmosphere of Dolman's. He returned to the hospital, where Alan Tremaine was full of questions.

'So you are no further forward, then?' said Tremaine, when Saracen had finished telling him about Cohen.

Saracen agreed and asked about Chenhui's condition.

'She's not upstairs any more. She's been transferred to the psychiatric unit at Morley Grange.'

'On whose say-so?' asked an astonished Saracen.

'Garten's, I suppose. I don't really know. Why?'

Saracen did not reply immediately. He had to admit to himself that he was in danger of becoming paranoid about almost everything Garten did. Was it really so strange that Chenhui had been taken to Morley Grange? Why should he see something sinister in it? Why should he immediately jump to the conclusion that Garten was getting Chenhui out of the way, putting her some place where people, himself in particular, could not ask her questions? He became aware that Tremaine was still waiting for an answer. 'Oh nothing, I suppose that's the best place for her if she's ill.'

Tremaine looked puzzled but then remembered something. He said, 'Dave Moss phoned while you were out. He wants you to call him back.'

Saracen called the County Hospital, then had to wait while the operator paged Moss.

'You are not going to believe this,' said Moss, sounding slightly embarrassed.

'Try me,' said Saracen.

'That PM on Myra Archer...'

'Yes?'

'There never was one.'

Saracen was struck dumb.

'Are you still there?' asked Moss, as the silence lengthened.

'I don't understand,' said Saracen. 'There had to be one. She was a DOA and she didn't have a general practioner to sign the death certificate.'

'Well, I've been right through Wylie's files. No Myra Archer.'

'Maybe the file has been removed?' suggested Saracen.

'I thought you would say that, so I checked Wylie's schedule from the twelfth to the fifteenth. He had a full list but Myra Archer was not among them. There simply was no PM done on her, James.'

Saracen still found it hard to swallow. 'So

who signed the death certificate?' he asked, thinking out loud.

'If what you say is true I think I would like to know the answer to that one too,' said Moss.

'I'll be in touch,' said Saracen, slowly replacing the receiver. As he stood there, deep in thought, Sister Lindeman came up to him and waited in silence until she had his attention.

'Yes, Sister?'

'If you have a moment, Doctor, I'd like a word.'

Saracen followed her into her office and she closed the door. She looked worried. 'It's about the JW girl you treated,' she began. 'The girl has developed hepatitis. She has been transferred to the County.'

Saracen rolled his eyes up to the ceiling and said, 'God, that's all I need. She must have got it from the blood transfusion.'

'Almost certainly.'

'How is she?'

'She's holding her own and the parents haven't said anything as yet, but in the circumstances, they may read more into the complication than might otherwise be the case. If that happens the ball might well land up in your court.'

Saracen nodded and said, 'No pun intended on the word "court" I hope, Sister.'

Sister Lindeman smiled and said, 'Let's pray it won't come to that. For what it's worth,

I'm with you all the way. You did the right thing in the circumstances.'

Saracen said, 'That's worth a great deal, Sister. Let's go and stitch some heads.'

Saracen was sitting on his own in the hospital canteen, wondering whether or not to eat the mess in front of him or perhaps underseal his car with it, when Jill Rawlings came in and sat down beside him. She joined him in a silent appraisal of what was on the plate before saying quietly, 'Give me a stick and I'll kill it.'

Saracen managed a wan smile and said, 'I think somebody already did, a very long time ago.' He pushed the plate away and rubbed his forehead with the heel of his hand.

'Problems?'

'And how.'

'That bad?'

'Damn near it.'

'My friend Mary is off home for a week; I'm staying in her flat. Why don't you come round this evening? Bring a bottle of wine and I'll make you a decent meal.'

Saracen looked at her and smiled. 'That sounds good,' he said. 'I'd like that.'

'Then it's settled.' Jill gave Saracen the address and they agreed on eight o'clock.

At four in the afternoon Saracen called the County Hospital and asked Dave Moss about the condition of the girl with hepatitis who had been transferred there.

'She's okay for the moment. What's your interest, James?'

Saracen told him.

'Ye gods, Saracen, you certainly have some kind of professional death wish, don't you!'

'What would you have done?'

'The same, I hope.'

'Do you think she's going to be all right?'

'If nothing else happens she'll be fine, and if the parents should ask how she got it I'll tell them that the ways of the Lord are strange.'

'Thanks, I owe you.'

Saracen left Accident and Emergency at seven o'clock. He stopped at an off licence on the way home to pick up some wine and found the experience less than cheering, for he always thought such places depressing at night. After a slow saunter along the wine shelves he decided on a litre of Valpolicella and joined the check-out queue behind a man in dungarees who was carrying a six-pack of beer, and a very small woman, almost lost inside a purple mohair coat. The woman hugged a half-bottle of port to her breast as she counted out the exact amount from the clutches of her purse and paid without comment. Saracen had to work hard to stop himself imagining the woman's life. For the moment he had enough troubles of his own.

He felt better after a bath and a change of clothing and made a conscious effort to free his mind from thoughts of the hospital before setting out to have dinner with Jill. He was pleasantly surprised that the prospect of spending the evening with her made him feel so good, and wondered about it as he drove there. What were his feelings about Jill Rawlings? It was something he hadn't given much thought to until the night they had dined with Alan Tremaine and his sister. After that evening he had found himself thinking about her quite a lot. There was something about her that disturbed him, but not in an unpleasant way. It wasn't just that she was attractive and fun to be with. There was something more, a feeling that he was reluctant to define for the moment, but it made him think of his days with Marion.

Saracen slowed down as he arrived at the street and crawled along the kerb until he came to the right number. Jill answered the door and kissed him on the cheek. Had he come by car, she asked. Saracen said that he had and was scolded. 'You should have left it behind. What you need is to relax and have a few drinks. Still, you can always leave it and get a taxi home if you feel inclined. I can bring it to the hospital in the morning.'

Saracen settled himself on the sofa and said with a smile, 'I offer no argument.'

Jill poured the drinks and joined him on the sofa. 'I take it it's this Myra Archer business that's getting you down?' she said.

Saracen nodded.

'Would you like to talk about it? A trouble shared and all that.'

'Everything?'

'Everything.'

Saracen told her all that was on his mind.

'You're convinced that Myra Archer's death and Leonard Cohen's are linked?'

'Absolutely. I must have disturbed the men who had been sent to move Myra Archer's body on the night I got clobbered.'

Jill sighed and shook her head.

Saracen shrugged and said, 'So there you have it, two dead on arrival, both bodies transferred out of the hospital as quickly as possible on the pretext of the refrigeration having broken down. Chenhui Tang knows what has been going on but she has a nervous breakdown and finishes up in Morley Grange on Heminevrin. Any ideas?'

'Did the patients have anything in common?' asked Jill.

'Not that I can see. A woman in her late fifties who has spent the last twenty years in Africa, and a man in his sixties who has never been out of the country. It's hard to spot the connection.'

Jill nodded and said, 'How about blood and tissue types?'

Saracen smiled as he followed Jill's train of thought. 'Are you going to suggest that Garten has been selling bodies for spare parts,' he asked.

'Just an idea,' said Jill. 'Not on, huh?'

'Not on,' agreed Saracen. 'Cohen had been dead for some hours before he was brought in. Transplant organs have to be fresh and, apart from that, Myra Archer had a Salmonella infection; that would have ruled her out. Besides, removing organs is a job for experts, not those butchers in Dolman's cellars.'

'So who else would want the corpses?'

'No one,' replied Saracen. 'I think Garten was trying to cover up something about their deaths.'

Jill looked sceptical and said, 'Possibly with the Archer woman, because of the ambulance nonsense, but not with Leonard Cohen. You said yourself that he had been dead for several hours before he was brought in? What could Garten possibly have to cover up?'

'I don't know,' Saracen confessed. 'But I want to take a look at the death certificates, particularly Myra Archer's.'

'Do you think Garten signed it without a PM being done?'

'Who else?'

'How will you get your hands on it?'

'Timothy Archer.'

'Her husband? But won't that upset him all over again?'

'Could do,' agreed Saracen. 'I thought I might play it by ear, go and see the man, find out how he is before I start prying.'

'I have another suggestion to make,' said Jill.

'Go on.'

'I suggest that we forget all about it for the rest of the evening and start by having another drink?'

'Agreed.'

'Take your jacket off,' said Jill, as she got up to re-fill their glasses. Saracen did so and loosened his tie before resting his head on the back of the couch and closing his eyes for a moment. He hadn't realised how tired he was. Jill came back and smoothed the hair along his forehead before sitting down.

Saracen looked up at her and smiled.

'Dinner won't be long,' she said. 'I hope you're hungry.'

'Ravenous.'

The evening was interspersed with a lot of laughter; the wine was good and the food delicious. Saracen knew that it had been a very long time since he had felt so much at ease and said so.

'I'm glad,' said Jill, softly.

When they had finished he offered to help with the washing-up, but Jill insisted that they leave it and have more coffee. Once again Saracen didn't argue and let out a sigh of contentment as he sat down on the sofa again. 'That was the best meal I've eaten in ages,' he said.

'Where do you usually eat, James?' Jill asked.

'At the flat.'

'What?'

'Tins of this, packets of that, you know.'

'Fast and easy, I know. There's not much incentive to cook when you live on your own.'

'Have you always lived on your own?'

'I was married once,' replied Jill.

'I didn't know.'

'No reason why you should. We were divorced five years ago.'

'I'm sorry.'

'Don't be. Getting divorced was like being reborn.'

'That bad?'

'Looking back I think our marriage was doomed from the start; in fact I can't think why Jeff ever married me in the first place. He came from what's called a "good family": his father was a solicitor, making a fortune out of other people's misery. My dad worked in the steel mill. His mother always made it plain that she thought I wasn't good enough for her son, but when you're twenty years old and in love things like that don't matter. It's only later that you begin to see things more clearly.'

'Was your husband a lawyer, too?' asked Saracen.

Jill smiled and said, 'No, he didn't have the brains. Jeff was in creative advertising. At first

138

I tried to share his ambitions and help him all I could, but he grew more and more remote and, one day, it suddenly dawned on me that I embarrassed him, my background and my being a nurse embarrassed him in the presence of his smart new friends. My Jeff, my hero, my knight in shining armour, was turning out to be exactly the same as his mother and father, a pathetic little snob.

'Every time he failed to get a promotion he would blame it on my social shortcomings and grow even colder towards me, until I couldn't stand it any more. One night I just snapped and told him exactly what I thought of him and his cronies with their gold medallions and Gucci shoes. I think I may have suggested that the intellectual capacity to design a bean can was just about all that they could rustle up between them.'

Saracen smiled.

'You were married too?'

Saracen nodded and said, 'I think you could say I had much the same experience. My wife's family never felt I was quite worthy of their daughter.'

'Must be something about the medical profession,' said Jill.

'Lowest of the low,' agreed Saracen.

'Would you like another drink?' asked Jill.

'No, I'm fine.'

'Is there anything you would like?'

Saracen turned and looked at Jill sitting

139

there beside him and said, 'I want to kiss you.'

'I'm not complaining, Doctor,' said Jill.

Saracen leaned over and kissed her softly. He ran his fingers light round the line of her cheekbone and felt her shudder slightly. 'Are you all right?' he whispered.

Jill sighed unevenly and nodded. She said, 'I'm sorry, it's been so long.'

'Perhaps I shouldn't have...'

Jill looked into his eyes and smiled. 'Oh yes, James Saracen,' she said. 'Oh yes, you most certainly should.' She put both her hands behind Saracen's head and pulled him towards her.

Saracen felt a passion, stronger than any he had known for many years, grow within him. He felt Jill's tongue enter his mouth as he cupped his hand over her breast and sought her nipple with his thumb. Her back arched to press herself to him. 'God, how I want you,' Saracen murmured.

'I'm still not complaining, Doctor,' she whispered. Saracen lifted her gently from the couch and looked towards the two possible doors. Jill smiled and pointed lazily over her shoulder with her thumb. 'That one,' she said.

With all passion spent, Saracen buried his head in Jill's hair while her fingers soothed the back of his neck in a circular motion. 'There, there my gentle James Saracen,' she whispered. 'I only hope you feel as good as I do.'

Saracen laughed and kissed the side of her neck. 'I'd forgotten it could be that good,' he murmured.

Jill's arm tightened around him a little. 'I'm glad,' she said.

After half an hour or so of nuzzling tenderness Jill said, 'Do you know what I think?'

'What?'

'I think we should shower together.'

'You do?' smiled Saracen.

'Uh huh,' replied Jill, running her forefinger down Saracen's upper arm.

Saracen gave in to Jill's giggled demand that she be allowed to soap him all over. She applied the suds with the palms of her hands with a gentleness that made Saracen's skin tingle. 'You've got hard thighs, my prince,' she murmured, her fingers kneading them as she watched his face. Saracen groaned with pleasure as Jill's hands continued their odyssey over his body.

'And strong arms...'

Saracen tilted his head back to rest it against the wall. Jill's hands moved over his chest. 'I want to know every inch of you. How tall?'

'Six, one,' groaned Saracen.

Jill took his now erect penis into her soapy hands and said, 'I can see that you're not Jewish...'

Saracen drew Jill towards him and brought his mouth down hard on hers, but suddenly he froze and pulled away. 'But Cohen was,' he said slowly.

'I beg your pardon?'

'Would you say that someone with a name like Leonard Cohen was Jewish?'

'Almost certainly,' replied Jill, bemused by what was going on.

'Have you ever known a Jewish male not to be circumcised?'

'Well, I've not examined them all, but no.'

'The body they showed me at Dolman's was that of an uncircumcised male. It was the right age but the wrong religion. They didn't show me Leonard Cohen at all. They must have switched the bodies!'

'Maybe they just took the wrong body out of the fridge?' suggested Jill.

Saracen considered that, but then said, 'There were only four, and three of them were women, the two from Skelmore General and a Miss Carlisle who was being buried at noon. Don't you see? Leonard Cohen's body wasn't even there!'

SIX

The telephone rang. 'I think you'd better get over here,' said Tremaine's voice.

'What's up,' asked Saracen.

'Chenhui Tang. An ambulance has just brought her in.'

'What?' exclaimed Saracen.

'She's in a bad way. She fell from a window at Morley Grange.'

'How the hell...'

'I don't know any of the details. I just thought you should know.'

Saracen was at the hospital within ten minutes.

'She's in Intensive Care,' said Tremaine.

Saracen nodded and backed out through the swing doors to hurry along the bottom corridor to the Intensive Care suite. As usual he was aware of the sudden rise in temperature when he entered. Clothes and covers were a dispensable encumbrance in Intensive Care. Naked patients were easier to deal with, easier to keep electrodes attached to, tubes inserted into, needles in place.

There were three patients in the unit which was equipped to accommodate six. One was being ventilated artificially and the intermittent hiss of air and the click of the change-over relay interrupted the soporific calm of the place, breaking up the regular flow of soft bleeps from the cardiac monitors.

Chenhui, her head swathed in bandages, lay in an apparently deep and peaceful sleep. Saracen thought how like a little girl she looked, her body so frail, her skin so smooth, marred only by a recent graze along her left cheekbone. The sister in charge came up and stood beside Saracen. 'Severe skull fracture,' she said quietly.

Saracen nodded but did not say anything. He watched as pulses chased each other along the screen of the oscilloscope and wondered about their regularity. 'Are the X-rays up here?' he asked.

'In my office.'

Saracen followed the sister and took a large envelope from her. He removed the film from it and clipped it up on the light box to wait for a moment until the fluorescent tubes had stuttered into life. 'God, what a mess,' he said softly, as he followed the crack lines on the image of Chenhui's skull.

'Dr Nelson says it's a wonder she's still alive,' said the sister.

Saracen unclipped the X-ray and returned it to its envelope. He said, 'If by any chance she should come round, Sister, I'd like to know as soon as possible.'

'Yes, of course, and I'll leave a note for

144

my relief, too.'

Saracen returned to Accident and Emergency to speak to Tremaine. 'Does Garten know about this?' he asked.

'He was out when I called,' replied Tremaine. 'How is Chenhui?'

'Bad,' replied Saracen.

'Will she make it?'

Saracen shook his head. 'I doubt it.'

Tremaine made a face. Saracen pulled up the collar of his coat and said, 'I'm off.'

Saracen poured himself a whisky and sat down wearily in front of the fire. He hoisted his feet up on to a stool and let out his breath in a long sigh, before massaging his eyelids with thumb and forefinger. Things could not go on like this, he concluded. The sight of Chenhui lying in Intensive Care so close to death had just been too much coming on top of everything else. What had she been trying to do when she had fallen. Could she even have been pushed? Saracen baulked at the thought of Garten being involved in murder, but still clung to his original suspicion that Garten had been keeping Chenhui out of the way at Morley Grange. Perhaps she had been trying to escape? If only he could speak to her, but that seemed a remote possibility in view of her condition. The other option was to confront Garten directly. Saracen drained his glass and decided that that was exactly what he would do. He poured out more

145

whisky and started to think about how he would do it, when fate preempted him and the telephone rang; it was Garten.

'I've just heard about Chenhui. Tremaine told me you'd been up to see her?'

'Yes,' said Saracen flatly.

'Well?' The irritation showed in Garten's voice. 'How is she?'

'Multiple skull fractures. Looks bad.'

'My God, what was she trying to do?' muttered Garten.

'Escape?' ventured Saracen, jumping in with both feet.

The silence seemed to go on for a long time before Garten said, in a voice that had been filtered clean of any emotion, 'Would you care to explain that remark?'

Saracen took a deep breath and said, 'I don't think Chenhui should have been admitted to Morley Grange in the first place. I think you arranged it in order to keep her quiet.'

'Have you taken leave of your senses, Saracen?' spluttered Garten. 'Quiet about what, for God's sake?'

'I don't know,' confessed Saracen. 'But it has something to do with the deaths of Myra Archer and Leonard Cohen. What happened to them, Nigel? What are you up to?'

'You must have gone mad, Saracen! Stark staring mad!'

'I don't think so,' replied Saracen. 'But we'll let the police decide that, I think.'

Garten's tone changed. He became conciliatory. 'Look Saracen, I don't know what's troubling you but I'm sure that there's a perfectly rational explanation for whatever it is. Why don't we have a talk about this in the morning? You can get things off your chest. We'll sort it all out and then we'll both feel better.'

Saracen considered his position and then concurred. 'All right,' he said, 'but if I'm not satisfied with your explanation I'm going to the police.'

'In the morning, then,' soothed Garten.

Saracen put down the receiver, knowing that there was no going back. A knot of fear and foreboding settled in his stomach and he felt certain that it would remain there for the forseeable future. When Saracen came on duty at eight o'clock in the morning to relieve Alan Tremaine, he told him what he had done.

'Want me to stick around?' Tremaine asked.

'No, keep your head down for the moment.'

Garten was expected to arrive at nine, but by nine thirty there was still no sign of him. At ten Saracen grew edgy and called Garten's home. There was no reply. Ten thirty came and went, and still no Garten.

At eleven the duty phone rang; it was the Medical Superintendent's secretary. 'Dr Saithe would like to see you in fifteen minutes, Dr Saracen.'

'I can't leave Accident and Emergency, Dr

147

Garten hasn't come on duty yet.'

'Dr Garten says Accident and Emergency will be covered.'

'Garten's up there?' exclaimed Saracen.

'Dr Garten is with Dr Saithe at the moment.'

Saracen hung up. Garten and Saithe together? What was going on? Saracen felt the knot tighten in his stomach. He found Sister Lindeman and told her that he would have to go out for a while. 'I understand that cover's on the way.'

'Who?' asked Lindeman.

'Search me,' replied Saracen distantly.

Saracen was in the locker room getting changed when Alan Tremaine came in looking annoyed. 'I'd just got into bed and Garten rings telling me to get right back here. What the hell is going on?'

'I'm just about to find out,' said Saracen. 'I've to be in Saithe's office in five minutes. Garten's already there.'

'Where does Saithe fit into all this?' asked Tremaine.

Saracen shrugged and said, 'I don't know, but I've got a bad feeling.'

'Good luck,' said Tremaine, as Saracen opened the locker room door. Saracen smiled weakly in reply.

Saracen turned off the main corridor and started to climb the stairs to the administration block. He spun round at the sound of a metallic crash behind him and saw that a porter had caught the bottom step with a kitchen trolley. The man cursed loudly as he wrestled it back on course, and the smell of boiled potatoes reached Saracen up on the landing. He turned back and continued to climb.

'Take a seat, please,' said Saithe's secretary without smiling. Saracen took this as a bad sign. Secretaries were always a dead give-away, an advance warning of what was to come. He wondered if they mirrored their bosses' attitudes dutifully or whether they managed to contrive at some kind of personal agreement. He watched the woman as she returned to her typing, the gold chain attached to her spectacles quivering slightly on the purple plain of her twin set. His attention wandered to the picturre on the wall behind her. The bows of the clipper *Tae Ping* were dipping into spray frozen by the artist for ever. A buzzer sounded. 'Ask Dr Saracen to come in.'

Saracen had been prepared for two men in the room, but there were three.

'I don't think you know Mr Matthew Grimshaw, chairman of the health board,' said Dr Saithe.

Grimshaw, a small thickset man with little in the way of neck or forehead, and a nose the colour of a ripe tomato, did not hold out his hand. Instead he gave a barely perceptible nod. Saracen nodded back and Saithe indicated that he sit down.

Saithe removed his spectacles and held them on the desk in front of him. 'Dr Saracen,' he began, 'we are given to understand that you authorized the giving of blood to one Matilda Mileham before statutory permission had been obtained.'

Saracen was taken aback. This was not what he had expected. 'The girl was a Jehovah's Witness. Her parents refused permission,' he said, feeling puzzled.

'You are aware of the hospital's policy in such cases?' asked Saithe.

'Of course,' replied Saracen. 'I did apply for her to be made a ward of court.'

'But you did not wait for the order to be granted?'

'I couldn't. The child would have died.'

'In your opinion,' said Garten, speaking for the first time and sounding hostile.

'In my opinion,' replied Saracen, rising to the bait. 'And I was the one there at the time.'

'The child has subsequently developed hepatitis from the transfusion,' said Saithe.

'It can happen. It was just bad luck, that's all.'

'Or bad judgement,' said Garten.

'Your precipitate action has laid the health board open to a serious court action,' said Saithe.

'Precipitate action!' repeated Saracen, unable to contain himself any longer. 'What are you

150

talking about? The child needed blood or she would have died! This is ridiculous!'

'Lawsuits are not ridiculous, Doctor, they are a very serious matter indeed,' said Saithe.

'What lawsuit?' exploded Saracen. 'There isn't a court in the country would find against measures taken to save a child's life.'

'The question is were those measures necessary, Doctor? Or were they the headstrong actions of a doctor with little or no regard for authority?'

'Of course the transfusion was necessary!' stormed Saracen. 'The girl was close to death.'

'Dr Garten disagrees.'

So that's it, thought Saracen, Garten's gone on the attack. 'Dr Garten was not there,' he said coldly.

'I am quite satisfied that Dr Garten has had access to all the relevant information and notes I—we,' Saithe turned to Grimshaw, 'are confident of his judgement in this matter.' Saithe put his glasses back on and looked directly at Saracen. He said, 'Dr Saracen, you have by your irresponsible action placed this hospital and its health board in an embarrassing and potentially damaging situation. You are accordingly suspended from duty pending a full inquiry.'

Saracen was stunned and for a moment there was silence in the room. Then, recovering himself he said, 'This is ludicrous!'

'You will have the opportunity to defend

151

yourself at the inquiry,' said Saithe evenly, as he gathered together his papers from the desk.

Saracen was furious. He looked at Garten and said, 'I see, you keep Chenhui quiet by locking her up under sedation and now you get me out of the way with this lawsuit nonsense. Well, it won't work! I'm still going to go on asking questions about Myra Archer and Leonard Cohen.'

Saithe interrupted Saracen saying, 'Dr Garten has told us something of your outrageous allegations. Just what is it that you are suggesting, Doctor?'

'I am suggesting,' said Saracen slowly and making a conscious effort to keep his temper under control, 'that there were serious irregularities over the deaths of two patients admitted to Accident and Emergency.'

'And what were these "irregularities"?' asked Saithe scathingly, his forehead creasing into a well-practised frown that was meant to imply a superior intelligence in action.

'The first case, a woman named Myra Archer, was recorded in the book as being dead on arrival at Skelmore General. She was not. I know for a fact that she was alive when the ambulance brought her in.'

Saithe looked at Garten, who adopted an air of mild exasperation before smiling, as if about to correct the foolish notion of a child. 'There is a perfectly simple explanation,' he began.

'Mrs Archer was indeed alive when the ambulance arrived—the first time—but not when she was admitted.'

Saithe adopted his frown again. Grimshaw pulled out an exceedingly large handkerchief and blew loudly into it, causing Garten to pause before continuing, 'Dr Tang, who was the medical officer on board, came and told me that she suspected the patient might be suffering from an infectious disease. Under the circumstances, I thought it wiser that she be taken on to the County Hospital.'

'What infectious disease?'

'A Salmonella infection.'

'How did Chenhui diagnose that?' asked Saracen.

'From her initial interview with the patient,' replied Garten.

'But she was unconscious when Medic Alpha got to her,' protested Saracen.

'Dr Tang says different, and she was there,' said Garten with a cutting edge to his voice.

'What happened next?' asked Saithe.

'The patient died shortly after leaving the hospital grounds. Dr Tang radioed for advice and I told her to return here, whereupon Mrs Archer was then classified dead on arrival.'

'Why did you bring her back?' asked Saithe.

Garten smiled conspiratorially at Saithe and said, 'I'm sure you are only too well aware, Martin, that the County Hospital believes we send them too many of our cases already. I thought it wiser to re-call Medic Alpha and do the paperwork myself.'

Saracen glanced up at the ceiling in frustration. Not only was Garten sounding plausible, he was beginning to sound like a saint.

Saithe grunted his approval. Saracen parked his tongue in the side of his cheek.

'Any more "irregularities"?' asked Saithe, his voice tinged with distaste.

'Lots,' replied Saracen, making the word sound like an expletive. 'When Myra Archer's husband arrived at A&E he was told that his wife had been taken to the County Hospital.'

'A regrettable misunderstanding,' said Garten smoothly.

'Then he was refused permission to see his wife's body.'

'I thought it wiser in view of the post-mortem that the request be denied,' said Garten.

'What post-mortem?' asked Saracen, playing his ace. It failed to have the effect he anticipated. Garten exchanged an exasperated glance with Saithe, then he looked at Saracen and shook his head. Saracen felt his stomach go hollow. Something was wrong. He had played his trump card and Garten hadn't even flinched.

'Surely you know that there has to be a PM on all sudden deaths, Doctor?' said Garten. 'Why should Mrs Archer be an exception?'

'I would like to see the report,' said Saracen feeling like an automaton and fearing the worst.

Garten remained motionless for a moment, like a spider surveying a fly caught in its web, then he delivered the *coup de grâce*. He picked up his briefcase from the floor and took out a document. He slid it over the desk towards Saracen.

Saracen read the heading on the paper: *Findings of the Post-Mortem Examination on Myra Louise Archer*. His heart sank as he leafed through the preliminaries to look for the pathologist's signature. His eyes followed every curl in the ink as he read, *Cyril. A Wylie*. Cause of death was given as myocardial infarction. Listed as a complicating condition was *Salmonella otangii type IV*. Saracen looked up to meet Garten's eyes.

'How else could I have signed the death certificate?' said Garten with such quiet menace that Saracen felt transparent.

'Can I ask a question?' asked Grimshaw.

'Of course,' replied Saithe.

'What exactly is this infection that was mentioned?'

'Salmonella? It's a serious form of food poisoning. It's related to the bacterium that causes typhoid,' said Saithe.

Garten added, 'Dr Tang's suspicions were quite right, which was just as well, as it happens. On the strength of her diagnosis we requested British Airways to contact Mrs Archer's fellow passengers on the flight from Zimbabwe and arranged for them to have some

155

covering treatment.'

'So you think it was something she caught on the plane?' asked Grimshaw.

'It was a possibility I could not overlook,' replied Garten.

'Of course not,' Grimshaw concurred.

Saracen found himself holding a grudging admiration for Garten. The man had had a busy night, preparing a line of defence against every conceivable line of attack.

Saithe looked at his watch pointedly and said, 'We are all busy men. Unless you have something sensible to say, Dr Saracen, I suggest we terminate these proceedings.'

'Where is Leonard Cohen's body?' said Saracen.

'I beg your pardon?' said Garten.

'I think you heard,' said Saracen. 'I asked where Leonard Cohen's body was.'

'You know very well that Mr Cohen's body was taken to the premises of a local undertaker when our refrigeration system failed,' replied Garten. 'You went there yourself yesterday to examine the body, though for what reason I cannot imagine.'

So Dolman had been in touch with Garten, thought Saracen. He took comfort in the slight look of unease that had appeared in Garten's eyes as he failed to follow Saracen's line of questioning. It was something he had not been prepared for. 'I did go there yesterday,' he said, 'and I did examine a body, but it was not that

156

of Leonard Cohen.'

'What are you saying, Doctor?' asked Saithe.

'I am saying that I went to the premises of Maurice Dolman and Sons yesterday to examine the body of the patient Leonard Cohen, whom Dr Garten had transferred immediately after his death. The undertakers showed me a body, but it was not that of Leonard Cohen.'

'What do you mean it wasn't Leonard Cohen?' snapped Garten.

Saracen told him his reasons and saw the first hint of fear on Garten's face.

'I'm sure there must be a perfectly rational explanation if what you say is true,' said Garten. 'Perhaps the attendant showed you the wrong body.'

'He showed me the only male corpse they had,' said Saracen, driving home his advantage.

'What time was this?' asked Garten.

Saracen got the impression that Garten was stalling. He told him what time it was when he went to Dolman's.

'Ah, that explains it,' said Garten, with feigned relief. 'Cohen's body would have been away for autopsy by that time.'

'And you have the report,' said Saracen quietly, seeing that Garten had recovered the initiative. The man had had a busy few hours.

'Of course,' replied Garten, pulling out another document from his case.

Again Saracen saw Cyril Wylie's signature on the report. He handed it back and said, 'I'd still like to see the body.'

'Really Dr Saracen, this is all becoming too much,' protested Saithe.

Garten gave an apologetic smile and added, 'And rather academic, I'm afraid. In the absence of any next of kin Leonard Cohen's remains were sent for cremation after the post-mortem this morning.'

Saracen felt the numbness of defeat. Liquid lead flowed in his veins. Saithe got to his feet and said to Saracen, 'Doctor, I must remind you that you are suspended from duty until further notice.'

Saracen returned to the flat feeling angry and impotent. His worst fears were becoming reality. This was no minor skirmish with authority; this was his exit from medicine unless somehow he could turn the tables on Garten. He called Moss at the County Hospital and told him what had happened. Moss agreed to meet him for lunch in Skelmore rather than talk further on the telephone. They met, as arranged, outside the Green Man pub at twelve thirty.

'I thought you said that there was definitely no post-mortem done on Myra Archer,' said Saracen, unable to keep the accusation out of his voice.

'That's right. There wasn't.'

'Garten had a PM report on her signed by Cyril Wylie. He's just crucified me with it.'

'Has he?' said Moss quietly. 'What date?'

'The thirteenth.'

'I checked Wylie's schedule from the twelfth right through to the fifteenth. Myra Archer wasn't on it. He simply didn't do it, unless of course he took his work home with him.'

Saracen did not feel like laughing. 'Can you prove that Wylie did not carry out a PM on Myra Archer?' he asked Moss.

The smile faded from Moss's face. 'Do you know what you are asking?' he said seriously.

Saracen nodded and said, 'It's my only chance.'

'All I have to go on is the schedule. Even if he hadn't done it he could simply say that there had been a change in the listings and he had done the Archer woman instead of somebody else.'

'I think it has happened twice.'

'What do you mean?'

'Garten showed me a PM report on Leonard Cohen that Wylie was supposed to have done this morning. I don't believe he did it.'

'I can check,' said Moss. 'I'll call you this afternoon.' Moss got to his feet and said, 'I'll have to go.' Saracen was left with an empty feeling in his stomach as he realized that he himself had nothing to hurry back for.

Saracen started to walk back to the flat in the watery sunshine that had broken through after a morning of mist and drizzle, but the looming prospect of brooding in silence made him change his mind. He opted instead for a walk. He needed distraction and noise and the unwitting camaraderie of the streets would make him feel less vulnerable.

The sun broke from behind its thin filter of cloud and warmed Saracen's cheek as he turned off the main thoroughfare to enter Coronation Park. He held the iron gate open for a young mother pushing a pram before letting it bounce back on its post and continuing down the central path to its junction with a riverside walk. The people he saw on the way were either young women with children or old men, and it made him wonder about the lack of old women. What did they do while their menfolk followed the meandering trails of the park? Was it just that, after a lifetime of going out to work, the men felt a greater compulsion to be out and about while women were more used to the confines of the home? There did seem to be an artificial sense of purpose about the way the men moved. Even the oldest of them, their backs bent as if some unseen hand were pushing them into the earth, never seemed entirely aimless in their choice of direction.

Saracen stopped as he came to a willow tree. It arched out from the embankment and hung over the river, boughs heavily pregnant with the new season's leaves. He wondered what would have happened to him by the time it was full and green. At the moment it seemed that his only hope of professional survival lay in

Moss being able to offer some kind of proof that the PM examinations on Myra Archer and Leonard Cohen were never carried out. But what would that mean? That the reports were forgeries? Surely not. Garten would not be that crude. But if Cyril Wylie had prepared them without actually doing the autopsies what did that mean? Why would he do such a thing? If the worst comes to the worst, thought Saracen as he threw a pebble into the river, I'll ask him.

The telephone was ringing in the flat when Saracen finally got home. He had the feeling that the caller would hang up just as he reached it but, for once, it didn't happen. It was Jill. 'James? I've been trying to get you for ages. Where have you been?'

'I went for a walk.'

'I heard what happened, you must be feeling awful.'

'Not good,' agreed Saracen, with a half-hearted attempt at a laugh.

'Oh, James,' sighed Jill, recognizing the resignation in Saracen's voice, 'they can't possibly make it stick. Everyone knows the girl would have died. Dr Tang knows it; Sister Lindeman knows it. You'll be cleared, you'll see.'

In his heart Saracen could not share Jill's conviction. Chenhui was in no position to back him up and Sister Lindeman's opinion would not be sought in a purely medical dispute. But he did not say so. He said simply, 'We'll see.'

'Can I come round tonight or would you like to come round here? I'm still at the flat.'

Saracen hesitated while he thought what he had to do. 'Can I leave it open at the moment? I'm waiting for Dave Moss to call.'

'Of course,' said Jill. 'If you want to come round, just come. I'll be there.'

Moss called at three thirty. 'Sorry I took so long. I had to wait my chance. It's as you suspected, there's no record of Wylie doing a PM on Cohen this morning. He did carry out an examination but it was on an eighty-three-year-old woman named Isabella Leith.'

Saracen felt relief flood through him. 'I can't thank you enough, Dave.'

'There is one thing...' Moss began.

Saracen thought he detected a note of uneasiness in his voice. 'Yes?'

'There's really not much more I can do. I'd appreciate it if somehow you could leave me out of things from now on?'

'Of course, I understand,' said Saracen, and thanked Moss again before putting down the receiver. He smiled wryly. Perfect friends were for books and films, real ones were human.

Saracen took a moment to compose himself before dialling the number of the Pathology Unit at the County Hospital, but his pulse rate rose while he waited for an answer.

'Pathology.'

'Dr Wylie, please.'

'One moment. Who's calling, please?'

'Dr Saracen.'

A lengthy pause.'

'Yes, what is it?' snapped Wylie's voice.

'I wonder if I might talk with you, Dr Wylie?'

'Who is this?' demanded Wylie, making no attempt to disguise his irritation.

'James Saracen. I am, or rather, I was Nigel Garten's registrar at Skelmore General.'

'Garten, you say,' said Wylie, his tone of voice changing, although Saracen could not tell whether it was from surprise or something else. 'What do you want to see me about? I'm a busy man.'

'Myra Archer and Leonard Cohen,' said Saracen bluntly.

There was a pause before Wylie asked quietly, 'What do you mean?' This time Saracen had no difficulty in interpreting the nuance in Wylie's voice. It was fear. Hearing it filled him with confidence. Wylie was going to be Garten's Achilles heel, the weak link that he was going to break.

'I want to know why you signed post-mortem reports for these patients without carrying out the autopsies,' said Saracen. He heard Wylie swallow hard at the other end of the phone before he replied, 'This is preposterous!'

'I agree,' said Saracen evenly. 'The trouble is, it is also true.' He endowed the words with the slow but irrestible momentum of an ocean liner nudging the quayside.

'You're Garten's registrar, you say?' Wylie stammered.

Saracen could almost see the sweat on his brow. 'Garten won't save you,' he said. 'I know all about Garten's involvement. He is in it up to his neck. I just thought I would ask for your side of things before I went to the police. It would be a pity if you had to take all the blame on your own.'

The words had the desired effect. Wylie started to panic. 'The police? Surely there is no need for the police. I mean, there must be some alternative?'

'I don't think so,' said Saracen, turning the screw.

'Look, can't we discuss this?'

'I don't see that there is anything to discuss, really,' said Saracen coldly.

'But you don't understand. At least give me the chance to explain. That's all I ask.'

'Go ahead.'

'No, not over the phone. I'll stay on in Pathology this evening. Come round here at about nine. I'll tell you everything you want to know.'

Saracen could hardly believe his luck. The bullying, blustering Cyril Wylie had collapsed like a house of cards and it had been so easy.

He concentrated on keeping a hard edge to his voice when he said, 'I'll be there, and one more thing.'

'Yes?'

'Don't go calling Garten or anyone else for that matter. If you do I'll know about it and go straight to the police.' Saracen put the telephone down before Wylie had a chance to reply, confident that Wylie would not call his bluff. He was too scared.

Jill rang at four thirty. She said, 'I don't really have a good reason for calling you again. I just wanted to know how you were.'

'That was nice,' said Saracen softly, 'I appreciate it. I've got to go out tonight to see Cyril Wylie.'

'The pathologist?'

'That's right, but I should be through by nine thirty or so. I'll come round then, if that's all right with you?'

'Of course it is.'

Saracen had no sooner replaced the receiver than it rang again. It was Sister Melrose from the Intensive Care Unit at the hospital. 'You asked to be kept informed about Dr Tang, Doctor?'

'She's come round?' asked Saracen.

'No, she died ten minutes ago.'

'I see,' said Saracen hitting the flat calm of depression. 'Did she recover consciousness at all before she died?' asked Saracen.

'Briefly.'

'Did she say anything?'

'Most of it was Chinese but there were a few English words. The nurse wrote them down.' There was a rustle of paper before Sister Melrose read out, 'Six days, more than six days, too long, not Myra Archer.'

'That's all?'

'Yes.'

'Thank you, Sister.'

Saracen thought about what he had just heard but could make no sense of it, although he did remember that the words were similiar to those Sister Turner had reported hearing when Chenhui was ranting at Garten during her 'breakdown'. Six days? Too long for what, he wondered, and what was 'not Myra Archer?' Perhaps after seeing Wylie he would understand. He looked at his watch.

SEVEN

When Saracen left the flat shortly after eight thirty in the evening it had started to rain. It was light at first, but before he had reached the County Hospital it had become the kind of deluge that emptied the streets of people and only the hiss of the car tyres broke the persistent rattle of the rain.

166

The County Hospital stood on the southern edge of Skelmore and comprised a collection of chalet-like buildings in red sandstone connected by glass-windowed corridors that had obviously been added at a later date. It had served originally as a sanatorium for consumptives before streptomycin had all but wiped out the scourge of tuberculosis, and at that time the hospital had stood at a discreet distance from the town. Passing years and spreading housing estates had brought the town right up to its boundary fence.

Saracen drove through the entrance and turned left to head for the Pathology Unit, which was situated well away from the main hospital and lay in a slight dip in the grounds screened from view by a ridge of poplar trees. A notice at the turn-off said, simply, 'Private'. This was to deter any wandering patients and their visitors from approaching the circle of buildings that included the hospital mortuary.

Saracen drove slowly past the sign and turned into the courtyard. Only one other car was there, a dark blue Rover that Saracen took to be Wylie's. He parked close to the back door so that he would be exposed to the rain for as short a time as possible in his dash to the entrance.

Warm air and the smell of formaldehyde greeted him as he entered the building and immediately evoked memories of the incident at the mortuary in Skelmore General. He had been to the Pathology Unit before, but always in daylight. At night it was unpleasantly eerie.

All the lights were on but there was no sign of anyone. This was not unexpected, for he knew that Wylie would be alone, but he also thought that Wylie would have heard him arrive. As it was, he found himself looking into rooms at empty benches and dust-covered typewriters. Not wishing to relinquish the psychological advantage he believed that he had over Wylie, Saracen refrained from calling out the pathologist's name.

Halfway along the passage he heard something metallic fall on to what sounded like stone, but he knew instinctively that it would be marble because the sound had come from the turret room at the end of the building: the post-mortem examination suite. Saracen walked deliberately towards the tall doors, clenching his teeth slightly for he had not bargained on this. He pushed open one of the doors and stood there as if unwilling to cross the threshold.

Wylie looked up from the table and smirked when he saw Saracen standing there. Saracen looked at him but did not say anything. He found the scene bizarre. Wylie and the cadaver he was working on were caught in the bright light from the huge, saucer-shaped overhead lamp like actors on some hellish stage. Something viscous dripped from Wylie's gloves as he removed his hands from the chest cavity and straightened up. 'Come in,' he said, 'and shut the door behind you. Don't want this bloody smell pervading the whole building.'

Saracen closed the door quietly and walked towards the table, stopping some feet away to avoid being splashed. 'Thought you'd be used to the smell by now,' he said.

Wylie gave a bitter laugh and said, 'Thirty-four years and I still hate it.' He threw a used scalpel on to the tray beside him and cursed as it missed the intended container and clattered on to the floor. Saracen noticed the slur in Wylie's voice.

'Where the...' Wylie muttered, as he looked about him in irritation before rummaging through a pile of instruments and extracting the one he wanted. He looked up at Saracen and gesticulated with the knife in his hand. 'Tell me, Doctor,' he demanded, 'have you any idea —have you any bloody idea—what it's like to spend thirty years of your life doing this?' he looked down at the cadaver in disgust. 'Have you?'

Saracen had no wish to imagine but he was learning a lot about Wylie. His drinking made some kind of sense now, even his bitter, abrasive personality. The man hated his job; he had spent his entire career doing something he loathed. With thirty years of resentment and disgust inside him, how else could he be? It took a few moments for the full horror of Wylie's position to become apparent to Sara-

169

cen. Many people in life found themselves doing things for a living that they had little heart for, but when the thing happened to be pathology? It didn't bear thinking about. 'But, why?' he asked, incredulously.

Another bitter laugh from Wylie. 'Why Why? What does it matter why, anymore? How many of us ever have any control over what we end up doing?'

'But this...' Saracen looked at the almost hollow cadaver and then at Wylie, but Wylie had no wish to pursue the subject any more. He stripped off his gloves and threw them into the chest cavity. He nodded to the corpse and said to Saracen in a voice that had recovered its old arrogance. 'Do you know what he died of, Doctor?'

Saracen shook his head.

'Old age,' said Wylie. 'Like the last one I did and the one before that and probably the next one. But no one is allowed to simply die of old age in our society. Oh no, society insists that I cut open anyone who dares to, and then I'm obliged to come up with something suitably scientific sounding to stick on the death certificate. The public are encouraged to think that senility is some kind of medical condition that can be cured if you throw enough money at it. Clowns! And do you know what this chap's relatives put in the local rag death notices? ''Sleeping, only sleeping.'' Christ! Does he look only sleeping to you? ''Donations, please,

170

to heart research.'' That's what did it! Not the fact that his heart was worn out like the rest of him. Christ! He was blind, deaf and crippled with arthritis, but they figure that with a bit more heart research he could have been ''saved''. Christ!' Wylie hung his head over the corpse and shook it as though some deep inner frustration were struggling to free itself. Saracen watched in silence.

After a few moments Wylie recovered and looked up at Saracen. 'Mark my words,' he said, 'They want to hang on to these tower blocks. Ten years from now they are going to need them to store psychogeriatrics, all plugged in to their little machines. Beeping, only beeping.'

Wylie broke into raucous laughter and Saracen could not make up his mind whether the man was just drunk or mentally unbalanced. Either way, he felt uneasy and wanted to put a stop to things. He said, 'I came here to discuss something else, Doctor.'

The sneer returned to Wylie's face. He said, 'Of course you did. You came here to find out why I signed for two of the buggers without doing the butchery first.'

'There was more to it than that,' said Saracen. 'You didn't even see the bodies, did you?'

All the aggression seemed to disappear from Wylie. He sagged at the shoulders and said quietly, 'I had no choice.'

'Garten?' asked Saracen.

'Garten,' agreed Wylie. 'He made it clear that if I didn't go along with what he wanted and provide him with reports, he would have me dismissed and then struck off for gross professional misconduct. The shame, my wife, my daughter—she's just become engaged. I had no choice, you must see that. He would have ruined me!'

Saracen nodded, unwilling to say anything in case he broke the flow from Wylie. Even by alcoholic standards Wylie's changes in mood and demeanor were dramatic and emotionally confusing for Saracen. He felt anger, disgust, pity, sympathy, all in the space of a few short minutes, but now, as a strange calm seemed to settle over Wylie he felt something else, something very close to fear.

Without the trace of a slur in his voice Wylie said, 'I couldn't let him do that, no more than I can allow you...'

The threat was plain enough and Saracen felt his adrenalin begin to surge. The immediate problem was that he could not identify where the threat lay. He had expected Wylie to lose his temper, bully, bluster and in the end threaten, but with what? He had envisaged loud, empty threats but here was Wylie, very calm, very confident and very frightening.

Wylie reached under his instrument tray and pulled something out from underneath. He asked, 'Do you know what this is?'

Saracen drew in his breath as he saw the gun

172

appear in Wylie's hand, but almost immediately his alarm changed to bemusement when he saw the tiny hole in the muzzle. 'It's an air pistol!' Saracen exclaimed, with a mixture of relief and ridicule in his voice.

Wylie did not flinch. He waited a moment and then pulled the trigger. The metallic slap of the report echoed in the quiet of the high, tiled room.

Saracen felt a sudden sharp pain in his thigh and looked down to see the dart protruding from his trousers. 'What the, you idiot, Wylie? What the hell do you think you are playing at with that bloody toy?' He started towards Wylie but stopped because his leg felt numb and he almost lost his balance. The feeling filled him with panic as he realized there must have been something special about the dart. 'What? What did you...?'

Wylie was staring at him dispassionately. He said, 'The dart was loaded with a muscle relaxant, Doctor, courtesy of our veterinary friends who use it to pacify large animals. In a moment you will be totally paralysed, in fact, if I have inadvertently used too much your heart will stop, but that would be inconvenient. Let's hope I got it right.'

By now Saracen had sunk to the floor, unable to combat the fatigue and growing numbness in his limbs as the poison spread. He pressed his palms against the cold marble but his elbow joints remained useless. He could still think clearly but his body would not respond to the fevered signals that his brain was sending. Everything, including breathing, was becoming laboured and difficult.

'Don't waste your time,' said Wylie, who was now standing over him. The words made sense inside Saracen's head but they sounded as if he were inside a cathedral. He could see Wylie's wellington boots only inches from his face as he lay on his left cheek. They were splattered with blood from the cadaver he had been working on.

Saracen tried to speak, but the muscles in his face would not respond. Wylie seemed to read his mind. He rolled Saracen over on to his back with his foot and looked down at him. 'You must be wondering what is going to happen to you now,' he said.

The words echoed in Saracen's head as he struggled to move his mouth but only succeeded in moving his lower jaw to bring his teeth together. He repeated the action like a wooden puppet as he looked up at Wylie's face above the long, blood-stained gown.

'Your death will be painless,' said Wylie, matter of factly. 'You are about to commit suicide in a state of deep depression following your suspension from your position at Skelmore General.' Wylie's eyes hardened; they were bloodshot and moist with anger as he hissed. 'I did not spend thirty years in the slaughterhouse for some busybody to come along and destroy it all.' He started to remove his gown, turning his back on Saracen to walk over to the laundry bin. 'Carbon monoxide,' he announced. 'That's how it is going to happen. We are going to go for a nice drive in the country in your car, then we'll find a quiet spot and I'll connect up the exhaust pipe to the interior. I'll turn the engine on and leave you. Nice and simple. A routine, everyday kind of suicide that the police will hardly take notice of.'

Wylie had replaced his wellingtons with worn, suede shoes and had returned to stand over Saracen who was still moving his mouth like a fish out of water. Wylie gave a short laugh and said, 'Do you know what the final irony is going to be?' He paused for an answer that could not come and then said, as if confiding a secret, 'I will be detailed to carry out the post-mortem examination on your body! I will be asked to slice open your flesh, turned pink with carboxy-haemoglobin, and asked to give my professional opinion. Now, there's a scene to conjure with!'

The feverish activity inside Saracen's head remained locked there, for all communication to his limbs had been severed, save for the small degree of movement afforded to his lower jaw. He felt Wylie grip his ankles and pull him across the smooth floor to the door, pausing to turn out the lights before dragging him out into the corridor. Saracen's head lolled helplessly to the side so that his face received an agonizing friction burn that he could do nothing about.

As they reached the back door Wylie stopped pulling and bent down to search through Saracen's pockets for his car keys. He found them and then cursed as he noticed the red weal that had sprung up on Saracen's face. He gripped his cheek harshly and turned his head to examine it further. 'Careless,' he muttered, 'must be more careful.'

Saracen felt a blast of cold air when Wylie opened the back door and left him for a moment while he went to open up the car. Somewhere above him the rain hammered against the skylight and the echo in his head made it sound like a roll of drums. Wylie returned and pulled him first up into a sitting position, and then into a position where he could get his shoulder under his armpit and half-walk, half-drag him out to the car.

Saracen felt himself being pushed into the back of his own car before Wylie left him again to return to the lab for a few moments. He came back and Saracen was aware of him manoeuvring something into the car. An object passed in front of Saracen's face as he lay there completely paralysed. It was the end of a long piece of plastic tubing.

As the car drove off through the rain, Saracen was still working desperately at trying to move his muscles. The fact that he was now having less difficulty breathing encouraged him in the thought that the effects of the drug might be lessening. It was important to keep trying, he reasoned. The faster his metabolism worked the quicker the stuff would be cleared from his system.

They had been travelling for about fifteen minutes when Saracen heard the car slowing down. His initial hope that they might be reducing speed for traffic lights or some road signal faded when he felt the wheels bump off the road and they began to travel along some rough track. The car came to a halt and there was silence for a few moments before Saracen heard Wylie get out and felt the plastic tubing being dragged out from the back. He was still totally paralysed except for the jaw movement and maybe the slightest hint of power returning to his neck, but it was academic. There was nothing he could do to help himself. He had to lie there in silence, listening to the contracting sounds made by the engine as it cooled, aware of a slight rocking movement as Wylie forced the tubing over the exhaust pipe.

The rear door opened and Saracen was manhandled out into the cold, wet night. He harboured a hope that his thirteen-stone weight might give Wylie some trouble and create more delay, for time is what he needed most; but Wylie manipulated him expertly through the front door and into the driver's seat.

'There we are,' said Wylie, speaking for the first time since they had left the Pathology

Unit and sounding pleased with himself. He arranged Saracen's arms across the steering wheel and gently allowed Saracen's head to come down and rest on his right cheek. When Wylie was satisfied that the pose seemed natural he made a few final adjustments to the plastic tube that he had fed into the car through a quarter-light, and came round to open the passenger door. He reached across Saracen to turn the key. 'Goodbye, Dr Saracen,' he whispered, 'and good riddance.' The engine sprang into life and settled down to a steady idle.

The passenger door slammed shut and Saracen, from his fixed position, could see Wylie, through the window, take a flask from his pocket and put it to his mouth. He took a long swig and then walked off into the night.

Saracen screwed his eyes shut in despair, for his limbs were still useless and unconsciousness and death could only be minutes away. The horn! If only he could manoeuvre his jaw over the horn ring, perhaps he could draw attention to his plight; but the idea was stillborn as Saracen faced the fact that he would be long dead before anyone came to investigate. If he could stall the engine that would be a different matter! If he could somehow get the car into gear so that it would move forward and hit something, making the engine stop. But how? There was only one way: he had to make himself fall on to the gearstick. Desperately he worked his lower jaw against the cross member of the steering wheel, levering his head against his useless left arm.

As the seconds passed Saracen was tortured by the thought that what he was attempting had been doomed to failure from the start. The likelihood of him getting the car successfully into gear by falling on the stick was remote. The reality was that he was going to die, but he had to keep trying. He succeeded in forcing his left arm off the steering wheel where it fell and dangled uselessly only inches from the stick, then he levered his chin down over the wheel rim and felt a momentary elation as he realized that he was about to fall.

The fall stopped abruptly and agonizingly as his head pitched forward and hit the fascia. Ironically it left him staring down at the gearstick that he had failed to make contact with. Despair briefly threatened to overwhelm him before he became aware or a new sensation. His head was becoming fuzzy as if the pain and worry were beginning to dissipate. There was a suggestion of warmth, even comfort on the horizon...

Saracen recognized the symptoms of carbon monoxide poisoning and panicked. The fear of death flowed through his neck muscles and allowed him to turn his head slightly against the fascia in an attempt to break the deadlock, but suddenly he stopped struggling as he realized that the knob directly below his mouth was the choke control.

The choke! The bloody choke? Why hadn't he thought about it before? If he could pull the choke out on a warm engine he would stand a good chance of flooding the carburettor and stalling the motor!

Saracen dropped his lower jaw and worked his mouth round the knob until he had it firmly between his teeth. Then, gripping it tightly, he used it to lever his head away from the fascia. He was on the verge of unconsciousness when he succeeded and fell down into the foot well of the car. Still not sure how far he had managed to pull the choke out, he lay blindly in the darkness that surrounded him. He felt consciousness slip away, and was only vaguely aware that the engine had started to splutter.

Saracen woke up in agony. His calf muscles had gone into cramp and he did not yet have enough muscular control to be able to flex them. Worse still, his arms were useless and he could not push himself up from the foot well where he lay with grit grinding into his grazed cheek and the smell of rubber rapidly inducing nausea. But he was alive; he was going to survive; the car itself was beautifully silent.

Sweat broke out on his face as one of his calf muscles again locked in spasm, making him bite his lip in a vain attempt to divert attention from the pain in his leg. He felt a tingling

180

sensation in his neck and shoulders telling him that his upper body was beginning to recover from the effects of the paralysing drug. It enabled him to move his body by pressing his forehead against the floor and twisting his shoulders. He could now see a red glow in the fascia above him where the ignition light was still on. Below it he could see the silhouette of the choke control; it was half-way out: two centimetres that had saved his life.

Muscular control was now returning fast. Saracen found that he could move his left arm, then shortly afterwards his right. He got back up into the seat and clumsily forced the door open to take great lungfulls of the cold night air, completely oblivious to the rain. He massaged his legs as well he could with his weak hands and then got out of the car, using the top edge of the door for support. He lay with his arms across the roof of the car, thinking how wonderful the smell of grass was, how sweet the night air. He even looked up hoping to see the stars, but there was nothing but darkness under invisible rain clouds.

The car's interior light was on because the door was open and in the dim light Saracen could see the plastic tubing trailing along the ground from the exhaust pipe to the window. The sight of it filled him with anger, so much so that, even in his unsteady state he took a kick at it, then another and another. He worked his way along it to the tail pipe, where he supported himself on the boot lid while he kicked at the joint until the plastic fell free.

Saracen's chest was hurting from the exertion. He got into the driving seat again and sat there with the door open until he had got his breath back. His thoughts turned to Wylie, and the anger that rose inside him brought on a fit of coughing. Trying to curse at the same time did not help matters until, finally, he got out of the car again and walked around it for a few minutes until the coughing had stopped and he could think clearly.

How had Wylie got back to town, Saracen wondered. He must have walked, either that or taken the bus. No, he would not have done that. He would not have risked being seen anywhere near the area of the car. Come to that, what was that area? Saracen had to admit that he had no idea where he was. All he knew was that they had driven for about fifteen minutes after leaving the Pathology Unit. But in which direction?

Saracen thought back to the moment when they had turned off the road to come along the track: it had been a left turn. If he were to drive back along the track and turn right then surely he would be heading in the right direction. He might even come across Wylie on the road. He looked at his watch. It told him that it was eleven fifteen but little else, for he had no idea what time it was when they had arrived or for that matter how long he had been unconscious.

Saracen started the engine and, despite the fact that it was still raining heavily, he wound down the driver's window. Fresh air had assumed a new importance in his life. He turned the car with some difficulty in the restricted space between the trees and eased his way back along the track, swearing as the nearside front wheel nose-dived into a pot-hole whose depth had been disguised by the rain water in it. It was to happen once more before the car was back on smooth tarmac and gathering speed.

Within minutes Saracen had picked up a road sign and knew that he was seven miles south of Skelmore and heading towards it. Wylie had driven out on the old Atherton road, which was still an A road, but relatively quiet since the opening of the nearby motorway. The thought of catching up with Wylie was uppermost in Saracen's mind and, for the moment, nothing else mattered. His eyes followed the sweep of the headlight beams with absolute dedication, searching the hedgerows and trees for any sign of a walking figure. But as he rounded a bend it was a police warning sign that the lights picked out. It was followed by two others: SLOW. ACCIDENT.

Saracen had slowed down to a crawl by the time he reached the first sign of activity. A policeman in reflective clothing was waving him down with a long-handled torch.

'There's been an accident, sir,' said the

officer, looking in through Saracen's open window.

Saracen's priorities changed. 'I'm a doctor. Can I help?' he asked.

The policeman looked rather surprised for a moment and it made Saracen realize how dishevelled he must be. His hair was soaking wet, his face, he thought, must be filthy and he had congealed blood on his cheek from the graze.

'You'd have to be Jesus Christ to do something for the poor sod who got hit, sir, but perhaps you could take a look at the driver of the car. He's elderly and a bit upset. You know how it is.'

Saracen got out, more than ever aware of the policeman's appraising looks.

'Been in a bit of an accident ourselves, have we sir?' the man asked.

Saracen was expecting this question. 'Puncture,' he said, 'Had to change a wheel in this damned rain, then the wheelbrace slipped and I hit my face on the side of the car.'

'Always the way, sir,' laughed the policeman, 'you never get punctures on sunny afternoons.'

Saracen saw the body lying on the side of the road; it was covered by a tarpaulin. Two policemen were standing beside it waiting for the ambulance to arrive. One was stamping his feet and swinging his arms across his body to keep warm. Saracen went across and was aware of the sound of the rain on their plastic jackets as he bent down to draw back the cover. It was Wylie! His eyes were open and lifeless.

'You old bastard,' said Saracen under his breath.

'Can I take it you know this man?' asked one of the policeman.

There was a long pause before Saracen said flatly, 'I know him. This is Dr Cyril Wylie, consultant pathologist at the County Hospital.'

'I thought he looked vaguely familiar,' said one of the policemen to the other. 'I've seen him in court.'

Saracen pulled back the tarpaulin a bit more and saw that Wylie's chest had been completely crushed where the car had gone over him. He put back the cover and stood up.

'Was Dr Wylie a friend of yours, sir?' asked the policeman who had flagged Saracen down. He was puzzled at Saracen's behaviour.

'No,' replied Saracen, unable to take his eyes off the crumpled heap on the ground.

'You wouldn't happen to know what Dr Wylie would be doing out here on foot on a night like this?'

'Perhaps his car broke down,' said Saracen.

'Had a puncture, you mean, sir?'

Saracen heard the inflection in the policeman's voice and read scepticism about his own story in it. It put him on his guard. 'Possibly,' he said.

'We've put out an alert for his car,' said one of the other policemen, but Saracen's man was

185

reluctant to let the moment go. 'The driver of the car that hit him says that Dr Wylie weaved out in front of him as if he were drunk, or had been in a fight or something?'

So that was it, thought Saracen. PC Super Sleuth had come to the conclusion that he and Wylie had been fighting because of the state of his clothes and the mark on his face. He said evenly, 'It was common knowledge that Dr Wylie had a drink problem. He was due to retire soon.'

'I see, sir. I dare say the post-mortem will reveal all.'

Post-mortem? thought Saracen. He looked down at Wylie again and said softly. 'The final irony was even more bizarre than you thought, old man.'

'What was that, sir?'

'Nothing.'

Saracen did what he could for the distressed occupants of the car until the ambulance arrived, and then continued his own journey back to Skelmore. It was only then that the full implication of Wylie's death became apparent and it made a depressing thought. Any chance of implicating Garten had gone. The post-mortem reports on Myra Archer and Leonard Cohen could not now be shown to be false. He was back at square one.

Saracen looked at his watch; it was a quarter to midnight. Too late or not, depression made him head for Jill's place.

'I thought you'd changed your mind,' said Jill as she opened the door cautiously. 'Good God, what happened to you?' she added, as she undid the chain and opened the door so that the light fell on Saracen's face.

'It's quite a story. Can I clean up first?'

Jill finished cleaning Saracen's graze and said, 'I'm all ears.' Saracen told her all that had happened and watched as Jill's eyes grew wider. 'This is incredible!' she protested.

'But it's true,' said Saracen.

'But if Wylie is dead, surely that means that...'

Saracen interrupted her, 'I've got nothing against Garten.'

Jill poured two whiskies and handed one to Saracen. She squatted down at his feet in front of the fire. 'What about the death certificate?' she asked.

'Garten has a PM report that can't be challenged now. He had every right to sign it.'

'Of course, I forgot. What about Cohen's body?'

'It was cremated this morning. Garten told me.'

'Do you believe him?'

Saracen looked down at Jill and confessed that he had not thought to doubt it.

'Perhaps he was just trying to stop you looking for it?' suggested Jill.

187

'Now there's a thought.'

'How could you find out?'

Saracen thought for a moment. 'I could go up to the crematorium and check the records. I could do that in the morning. I've nothing else to do.' Saracen ran his fingers through Jill's hair and thanked her for the idea.

'Do you have to go?'

Saracen smiled and said softly. 'No.'

It rained all night and it was still raining when Saracen left Jill's flat to set off for Skelmore Municipal Crematorium. It had now been raining for so long that storm drains had failed to cope and several sections of the road were flooded. The worst was only a few hundred metres from the crematorium, where the road dipped and then rose sharply to approach the granite walls and black iron gate of the crematorium itself.

Saracen had to wait while the vehicles in a funeral procession took turns to cross the lake in the dip with caution and high engine revs to keep the water out of their electrics. When he did finally reach the gates, he had to wait again when the hearse up ahead spluttered to a halt and blocked the entrance. The drivers of three black limousines behind got out to help but, after failing to re-start the engine, they resorted to pushing the hearse the final few metres up to the chapel entrance. Saracen watched the pathetic sight impassively through flicking windscreen wipers.

Saracen had no idea how to go about checking crematorium records; he would have to play it by ear. He parked the car well away from the funeral party, waited until everyone concerned had entered the chapel and the polished wooden doors were closed behind them, then he got out and made for the door in the building opposite that said, 'Administration'. He knocked once on the frosted glass door and entered immediately, wanting to be out of the rain.

A middle-aged woman looked up from her typewriter and said, 'The chapel is across the courtyard to your left.' She suffixed the remark with the kind of tight-lipped smile that people behind desks reserve for the 'general public'.

Saracen shook the rain from his hair and said, 'Thank you. It's not the chapel I'm interested in. I want to inquire about the cremation of a man called Leonard Cohen.'

The woman was instantly on the defensive. 'All our files are confidential,' she said, with smug complacency.

'Why?' asked Saracen.

The woman appeared to take the question as a personal insult. 'They just are, that's all,' she said, bristling with indignation.

Saracen took a deep breath and said, 'All I want to know is, was Leonard Cohen cremated here yesterday? Surely there can be nothing confidential in that?'

'I am not at liberty to divulge any information at all,' recited the woman primly.

'Then can I see the manager?'

'Do you have an appointment?'

'Of course I don't have a blood...No, I don't have an appointment.'

The woman picked up one of her two telephones and pressed a button. Saracen looked at the other one and thought it was probably a direct line to Washington.

'Mr Posselthwaite? There's a man here asking questions about our files. I've told him they are confidential but he won't accept it. Yes sir, thank you, sir.' She replaced the receiver and turned to Saracen. 'Mr Posselthwaite is coming out,' she announced. She said it as though Saracen should be filled with awe.

A door opened behind the woman and a small, rotund man wearing pinstripes emerged. 'Now then, Miss Bottomley, what's all this about?'

'This is the man, sir,' said Miss Bottomley in triumph.

The little man pretended to notice Saracen for the first time and said, 'May I be of some assistance?'

Saracen saw all the signs he associated with lesser officialdom in Posselthwaite, and knew that the majesty of the little man's position was about to be maintained by sheer bloody-mindedness, but he went through the motions anyway and explained what he wanted to know.

'Are you a relative?'

'No, I'm not.'

'Then what, might I ask...?'

'Leonard Cohen's body was transferred to the premises of Maurice Dolman and Sons two nights ago from Skelmore General Hospital. I understand that it was then brought here for cremation. I would like to know if the cremation has been carried out yet. If not, I would like to see the body.'

'See the body?' repeated Posselthwaite.

'I'm Dr Saracen from Skelmore General.'

'I see,' said Posselthwaite slowly, his face registering disapproval of Saracen's appearance in faded jeans and jerkin. He rubbed his chin and pretended to be deep in thought, but Saracen suspected that he was thinking up some other way to be obstructive. 'I think perhaps I should see some formal identification.'

Saracen had reached the limit of his patience. 'Identification? What for? All I want to know is did you cremate a man called Leonard Cohen yesterday? Where's the problem? Watch my lips, YES or NO!'

'This is intolerable!' stormed Posselthwaite. 'Never in my career have I been spoken to in this fashion. Just what do you think I am!'

'You don't want to know that,' said Saracen. 'Let's just forget the whole thing.'

All the frustration of the past twenty-four hours welled up inside Saracen as he hurried back to the car, bending his head against a wind that drove rain into his face with relentless accuracy. Although many factors were involved, Posselthwaite was the immediate target of his anger. 'Stupid little man,' he muttered, as he gripped the steering wheel tightly and stared out at the rain through the windscreen. He noticed a flight of steps leading down behind the chapel and could see from the position of the chimney nearby that they must lead to the furnace room. It gave him an idea.

Saracen got out of the car and ran across to the steps. At their foot he came to a door marked. 'NO ADMITTANCE' but he went in anyway. The room was long and dark for there were no windows. Two men were working there and both held long-handled fire rakes. They were removing the ash contents from one of the ovens. One turned in surprise as Saracen entered.

'What's your game then?' he demanded.

Saracen reached inside his jacket for his wallet and drew out two five pounds notes. 'All I want is the answer to a simple question,' he said, holding the money up.

'Here, you're one of those reporter blokes,' protested the smaller of the two men. 'We don't know anything about any racket! All of the coffins get burned, understand? All of them! Now bugger off!'

The other man put a restraining arm on his colleague and said, 'Wait a minute, George.

He hasn't asked us anything yet.' He looked towards Saracen.

'Did you or did you not cremate the remains of a man called Leonard Cohen yesterday? That's all I want to know.'

The two men looked at each other. 'That's all?' asked one.

'That's all.'

'From Dolman's, a man with no relatives?'

'That's the one.'

'Yes, we did.'

Saracen handed over the money and left. At the head of the steps he came face to face with Posselthwaite. There was no mistaking the anger in the little man's face, although it made him look more ridiculous than impressive as he stood there, his hands deep in the pockets of an oversized raincoat and his spectacles splattered with rain.

'Just what do you think you're playing at?' he fumed, his hands shaking with fury. Saracen, with disappointment now added to his frustration, brushed past him without saying anything.

'You haven't heard the last of this!' shouted Posselthwaite as Saracen got into his car. Saracen drove off as though he had not even noticed that the other man was there.

EIGHT

'I wish I had never suggested it now,' said Jill, when Saracen told her what had happened at the crematorium.

'It's not your fault, it was a good idea.'

'I hate to keep asking this,' Jill began tentatively, 'but what are you going to do now?'

'The theory is simple,' replied Saracen. 'If I can't see Leonard Cohen's body, I have to see Myra Archer's.'

Jill looked astonished and said, 'But surely she was cremated long before Cohen?'

Saracen shook his head. 'No, Garten was about to have her cremated when her husband turned up and insisted that she should be buried. She was interred in St Clement's churchyard.'

'But could you get an exhumation order?' asked Jill, as if she already knew the answer.

Saracen smiled wryly and said, 'I said the *theory* was simple.'

'Surely there must be another way of exposing Garten,' said Jill.

'If there is I can't think of it,' said Saracen. 'As far as I can see, the only chink in Garten's armour lies six feet under the earth in St

Clement's graveyard; a body that never underwent post-mortem examination, a body that holds the key to this whole affair.'

'But if you can't get an exhumation order I don't see what you can do about it,' said Jill.

'There is another way,' said Saracen.

Jill looked at him strangely and said, 'You can't be serious?'

'I can and I am.'

Jill was speechless for a moment, then she shook her head in disbelief. 'But you can't!' she exclaimed. 'That would be positively ghoulish. People don't dig up graves any more! That stopped with Burke and Hare!'

Saracen waited until Jill had calmed down a little, then said, 'Look at it from my point of view. If I don't come up with something against Garten he is going to get away with it and I am never going to practise medicine again. I have to prove that a PM was never carried out on Myra Archer. I have to!'

Jill still had no stomach for the notion, but she could understand Saracen's predicament. She said, 'And what happens when you open up the grave? Do you call the police?'

'No, I call Peter Clyde at the Pathology Unit. I'll have a copy of the death certificate and the false PM report with me. I'll show him the body and the papers. He, as senior forensic man for the area, will be able to get a legal exhumation order authorized.'

Jill nodded silently. 'When?' she asked quietly.

'As soon as possible. All that rain must have made the earth soft.'

'I, I don't think I can offer to help,' said Jill.

'Of course not,' said Saracen softly, 'this is something I'll do alone.'

Saracen had lunch with Jill before driving her to the hospital to begin her duty shift at two o'clock. He then drove round to St Clement's church and parked the car in a cobbled lane that ran along the back of it. He had to see where Myra Archer's grave actually was before he could formulate any plan for the disinterment. He entered the churchyard by a small wicker gate about fifty metres west of the main church entrance, which was flanked on either side by juniper trees.

Saracen walked slowly through the oldest part of the burial ground where moss-covered stone slabs guarded ancient lairs and rusted railings protected body vaults from intruders of another age. To his relief he found that modern day burials were carried out in land well to the rear of the church and out of sight of the road. He found Myra Archer's grave in front of a little copse of pine trees. A temporary headstone said, simply, Myra Archer. In front of it, in a little glass jar, were a few spring flowers, but the mouth of the jar was too wide and the flowers lay almost horizontal.

Saracen looked around to get his bearings and to determine the best way to get there at night. He decided on parking in the lane again. From there he could climb over the back wall and reach the grave through the pine trees without having to walk through the churchyard at all.

There was a small wooden hut just past the pine trees. When he was sure that no one was about, Saracen went over and had a look inside. He saw three spades, a tarpaulin and various sections of wooden shuttering. It was the gravediggers' hut. He would not have to bring his own shovel.

There were times during the afternoon and early evening when Saracen himself could hardly believe what he was about to do. These moments passed, but only to recur with growing frequency as the time neared. He was relieved when night fell and the waiting was over.

The lane behind the church was deserted, just as he hoped it would be. He parked the car on the concrete apron of a bank of old lock-up garages, hoping that a car standing there would not look out of place, although the condition of the lock-ups suggested that they were no longer used. As he walked along the lane he had the constant feeling that he was being observed and accordingly invented a series of casual reasons for looking round. Each time he did he saw no one. The feeling was born of guilt.

The top of the cemetery wall was wet and covered with moss. Saracen could smell the green dampness as he rolled over its rounded crown and dropped down on the other side to crouch there for a moment, listening for any sign that he had been seen. All was quiet. He was about to get to his feet again when a sudden movement up on the wall made him freeze. Iron fingers clutched at his stomach until he saw with relief that it was a cat, its green eyes burning in the dark. Saracen swore under his breath and moved away from the wall to court the shelter of the pine trees as he made his way to the gravediggers' hut.

Wet rust from the hasp came off on his hands as he pulled the door open and took out what he needed: two blocks of wood, a tarpaulin and a spade. He closed up the hut again and opened out the tarpaulin on the ground. In addition to what he had taken from the hut, Saracen had brought with him a torch, a screwdriver and a tyre lever. There was too much to carry along to the grave so he placed everything on the tarpaulin and dragged it along the ground behind him like a sledge. A cold wind touched his cheek; it rustled the needles of the pines, disturbing the sepulchral silence and making him feel a little less vulnerable.

The earth, as he had hoped, was soft after all the rain, a..d put up little resistance after he had removed the top layer of turf. As he dug down he piled the wet earth up on the spread out tarpaulin, occasionally cursing as wet clods stuck to the face of the shovel, forcing him to shake it free and thereby induce painful protests from his back. After twenty minutes he stopped suddenly as the spade hit wood. He had reached the coffin.

All the pangs of guilt and self-doubt of the afternoon came flooding back to make the sweat on Saracen's forehead go quite cold. His conscience screamed at him: This is desecration! Stop this madness! But there was no going back now. He cleared away the earth from the coffin lid and shone the torch down on the brass plate: 'Myra Archer RIP', *Requiescat in Pace* —*in pace*—*in pace*—repeated itself in his conscience as his pulse rate climbed ever higher. He worked on the screws holding down the lid until his trembling fingers had extracted the last one and pushed it clumsily into the pocket of his jerkin with the others. Saracen paused to steel himself for the sight of Myra Archer's shrouded body before levering up the lid.

All feelings of guilt, remorse and the accusing finger of a long-lost faith disappeared in an instant. The coffin contained four sandbags and nothing else. Saracen stared dumbly at the dirty hessian sacks, unable to make sense of it all.

Surely Garten could not have beaten him to it? No, that was ridiculous, he decided. That left the other possibility. Myra Archer's body had never been there in the first place! The burning question now was whether or not an empty grave would be enough to nail Garten. He could not be sure. It would certainly be enough to instigate all sorts of official investigations, but where would they lead? He could reach no firm conclusion.

Becoming increasingly anxious at his own indecision, Saracen decided he must seek a witness to what he had found. He would telephone Jill and ask her to come down. He left everything as it was and climbed back over the wall into the lane where there was a telephone box at the end. He ran towards it, only slowing to a walk when reaching the junction with the main road so as not to attract attention. The phone seemed to ring for an age before Jill answered.

'Is it over?' she asked, before Saracen had had a chance to say anything.

'No, I need you here.'

'James, I couldn't face it.'

'It's nothing like that. The coffin is empty. I need a witness, that's all.'

'You did say empty?'

'Yes. There isn't much time. Can you get over here now?'

'Claire Tremaine is here at the moment. She invited herself over.'

Saracen cursed softly.

'We could both come. She knows all about the goings-on at the hospital, her brother has told her.'

Saracen thought for a moment then saw he had no option. 'All right,' he said. 'Quick as you can.'

Ten minutes later the girls arrived in the lane. Claire was driving and she parked her green Metro next to Saracen's car in front of some disused garages. From where he was waiting by the wall, Saracen could see that Jill seemed nervous but noted that Claire was her usual confident self. They hurried towards him and he helped them over the wall and led the way through the pines to the open grave.

Jill just nodded when Saracen shone the torch down into the coffin. Claire grinned and said, 'Not much doubt about that.'

'That's all I wanted you to see,' said Saracen. 'You can go now, if you want.'

To Saracen's surprise it was Jill who said, 'We'll wait for you. Is there anything we can do to help?'

Claire looked at her and added, 'Good idea. I like all this spooky stuff. It's like some black magic ritual.' She qualified her assertion by dancing a few steps round the edge of the grave, to Jill's embarrassment and Saracen's annoyance. Saracen lowered himself into the hole and replaced the lid of the coffin before climbing out again to begin filling in the earth.

'Shouldn't you call the police or something?' asked Claire.

'I'm going to confront Garten first,' said Saracen. 'It will short-circuit a lot of red tape.'

'There's a car coming!' whispered Jill, as headlights swung into the lane and lit up the middle branches of the pines. The three of them crouched and froze as the car passed slowly along Church Lane, its engine murmuring quietly.

'It's gone,' whispered Claire.

'No,' cautioned Jill, holding up her hand. 'It's stopped!'

Saracen closed his eyes briefly and swore.

'I'll take a look,' whispered Claire, and made for the wall before anyone could stop her. She was back within moments. 'It's the police!' she whispered. 'They've stopped beside the cars.'

'They're going to start looking for us shortly,' said Saracen.

There was a moment's silence before Claire said, 'Leave it to me.' She got to her feet and ran off across the churchyard to leave by the gate. A few moments later the sound of Claire's voice came from the other side of the wall. 'Good evening, Officer. Is anything wrong?'

The policeman's reply was muffled and Saracen guessed that Claire had deliberately spoken loudly to let them know what she was doing.

'Not at all, Officer. I've been visiting friends

in Trinity Road. It seemed sensible to park round here rather than on the main road. That's all right, I hope?' Claire's Oxford accent was suffused with solicitous concern. Once again Saracen and Jill failed to hear the reply.

'Oh I see!' exclaimed Claire loudly, 'The warehouse! You thought we were burgling the warehouse!' She burst out laughing. 'No, things aren't quite as bad as that!'

Saracen heard the policemen join in the laughter and then heard Claire say, 'Yes, that car too. I just had to leave the party early.'

There was some more laughter before the sound of slamming car doors told Saracen that the crisis was over. Claire's Metro drove off, followed moments later by the police car.

Saracen continued with the filling in of the grave while Jill held the torch. He finished by trampling down the surface as hard as he could before replacing the turf. There was a pile of earth left over on the tarpaulin because of the lack of ground compaction. He dragged it over to the trees and scattered it evenly before returning the borrowed implements to the gravediggers' hut and fastening the door. 'Right, that's it,' he sighed. 'Let's go.'

As they walked back to the car Jill said, 'I still don't understand why you didn't call the police and let *them* see that the grave was empty.'

'If I had to start explaining everything from

the beginning and things start going through official channels it will take forever, but if I confront Garten directly and tell him that I have two witnesses to the fact that Myra Archer's grave is empty then he will see that the game's up and he will have to tell me everything.'

'If you say so,' said Jill, far from convinced.

They returned to Jill's apartment and found Claire sitting outside in her car. 'Everything all right?' she asked.

'Thanks to you,' said Saracen. Jill agreed with him.

'Anyone want a drink?' asked Jill, closing the door of the flat behind them. Saracen and Claire said yes without hesitation.

'Can I ask what you are going to say to this man Garten?' asked Claire.

'I'm going to tell him exactly what we found out tonight, and make him tell me what's been going on,' said Saracen.

'Garten isn't going to like it,' said Jill.

Saracen's silence said that she was stating the obvious.

'I mean, you might be pushing him too far. It could be dangerous.'

'Depends on how awful his secret is, I suppose,' said Claire.

Saracen had not seriously considered the possibility of being in any physical danger from Garten, but he could see that Jill and Claire had a point. If the secret was big enough there was no way of telling how far Garten would go to protect it. The actions of a man under extreme pressure could be wildly unpredictable. The spectre of the drunken, embittered Cyril Wylie standing over his own paralysed body flitted through Saracen's mind and chilled him to the marrow.

Saracen phoned Accident and Emergency at nine-thirty in the morning, to be told by Tremaine that Garten was probably at home, for he was not due on duty until two in the afternoon. 'Claire told me about last night,' said Tremaine. 'Good luck.'

Saracen put down the telephone and considered for a moment whether or not he should wait until the afternoon. The alternative was to go round to Garten's house and have it out with him there and then. He decided against waiting.

Nigel Garten and his wife lived in the Croft Valley district of Skelmore. Every town has its Croft Valley, where the influential and wealthy tend to flock together for solidarity and reassurance. Such areas usually have nicknames given them by the more humble inhabitants of the town and Skelmore was no exception. In the pubs and clubs Croft Valley was known as Toffee Town.

The population living inside Croft Valley was further stratified into 'Just Money' and 'Real Class'. Despite the strenuous efforts of Matthew Glendale to elevate his daughter to the latter category, Mildred Garten had consistently failed to gain acceptance to the top echelons of Skelmore society. This was construed bitterly by Mildred's father as blind prejudice against a lass from an honest working background and, by Mildred herself, as a result of what she believed was her basic shyness and over-sensitivity. People just did not understand her. In truth, they understood her only too well. That was why they detested her. Mildred's capacity for antagonizing people was quite unbounded and totally independent of race, creed and colour. From the milk-boy to the Mayor of Skelmore, she was universally loathed.

Saracen walked up the path to the front door, his feet crunching on the gravel. The house, a red sandstone town house, had a pleasing air of solidity about it, as though it knew that people would come and go but it would go on for ever. He was about to ring the bell when he heard Mildred's voice. It sounded angry, but then, as Saracen mused, it usually did. Angry, whinging or disgruntled. The sound was coming from the back garden, so Saracen opened the little wooden gate that led round the side of the house.

'I wanted them over there!' screeched Mildred's voice.

Saracen could now see that it was the gardener she was berating.

'But it makes more sense to plant them over here, Mrs G.'

'I want them over there!' insisted Mildred. 'And what's more, if I've told you once, I've told you a hundred times, that I do not wish to be called "Mrs Gee!" '

'Yes, madam,' said the man.

'Excuse me,' said Saracen.

Mildred turned abruptly. 'Oh, it's you,' she said, with distaste.

'Yes it's me, Mildred, or should I say madam?'

Mildred's face darkened. 'What do you want?' she snapped with her characteristic lack of charm.

'I'd like to see your husband.'

'You can't. He's busy.'

'I still want to see him.'

'Are you stupid? He's busy, I told you.'

'Tell him it's about sandbags. He'll see me.'

'Sandbags? Did you say sandbags?'

'Yes, deceased sandbags.'

'Diseased sandbags?'

'No Mildred, deceased as in dead.'

Mildred Garten looked at Saracen as if he had taken leave of his senses and backed away into the house, leaving him alone with the gardener. The man winked at Saracen and whispered, 'You wouldn't think I used to go supping ale with her old man, would you? A proper Lady Muck, that one turned out!'

'Fur hat and no drawers,' said Saracen.

The old man cackled and got on with his

raking before pausing again to say, 'Tell you one thing. Them bloody plants are stopping where they are!'

Mildred returned and Nigel Garten was with her. 'You had better come in,' he said to Saracen. Saracen followed him inside and up the stairs to his study on the first floor. He closed the door behind him, leaving Mildred standing at the foot of the stairs, wondering what was going on.

Garten cleared away a pile of political leaflets from a chair and invited Saracen to sit down. Saracen could see with some satisfaction that Garten appeared to be very nervous; he noticed that he was deliberately taking a long time to clear his desk, as though he was unwilling to face him. He waited patiently until he finally had Garten's attention and then said, 'What have you done with Myra Archer's body?'

Garten's shoulders visibly sagged and he seemed to have aged ten years. 'What do you know?' he croaked.

'I know that she is not in the ground at St Clement's, and I have witnesses to prove it.'

Garten closed his eyes as if in prayer, and then sighed with resignation. 'I had her cremated,' he said.

Saracen said nothing but kept looking at Garten, who took this as a sign of disbelief. 'It's true,' he said, 'I had her cremated. I had to!'

'Had to?'

'She died of plague.'

Saracen felt his eyes open wider. 'You did say *plague?*' he asked softly.

Garten nodded. 'Chenhui recognized the symptoms when Medic Alpha brought her in. She had seen it before in China. She told me and I persuaded her to say nothing after the woman died in the ambulance.'

'But why cover it up for God's sake?'

'Isn't it obvious? Black Death in the town! How long do you think Skelmore's bubble will last with rumours of that kind of outbreak in the offing? We aren't the only development area in the land, you know. Scotland suddenly could seem a very attractive alternative to the Japanese.'

'But this isn't the Middle Ages!' protested Saracen.

'Some diseases still scare people witless.'

'But the fuss would die down.'

'Do you know what happens to a business at full stretch when something like this happens? When housing developments lie empty and the bank still demands payment?'

'You mean your father-in-law would go bust?' asked Saracen, determined to introduce a personal note to Garten's altruism.

'If you like,' admitted Garten, 'But not just Glendale's. Lots of small firms would go to the wall. Any suggestion of even short-term labour difficulties on the horizon, and the Japs would pull out. With their muscle they can set up almost anywhere they like, and get the same concessions.'

Saracen shook his head and said, 'But to cover up an incidence of plague...'

'It's not as bad as you make it sound,' said Garten. 'It's obvious that the damned woman picked up the disease in Africa before she came here. She's just an isolated case, that's all, and her contacts in this country were minimal. She had no friends or relations here, apart from her husband. There was just too much at stake for the town to notify the case to the authorities. I thought if we just kept it quiet, that would be the end of it.'

'But what about the contacts she did have?' asked Saracen.

'I invented a Salmonella infection so that hospital staff and passengers on the plane she came over on could be given appropriate antibiotic cover. The risk to anyone was minimal.'

'You hope,' said Saracen. 'It should have been done properly.'

'I keep telling you, there was too much at stake.'

'And Leonard Cohen?' asked Saracen.

'The whole affair seemed to be fading, and then Cohen was admitted. He died of plague, too.'

Saracen raised his eyes to the ceiling and swore softly.

'But it was just an oversight,' protested

Garten. 'Cohen lived in the same block of flats as the Archer woman. We just didn't realize that he knew her; the caretaker told us that she didn't associate with anyone in the building.'

'So you wanted to cover up that one too and Chenhui disagreed?'

'More or less. Her nerve seemed to snap when she saw Cohen's body and she started screaming at me. I tried to convince her that it was just a case of one contact having slipped through the net and that, as he lived alone and didn't go out much, there was still no danger of an epidemic, but she wouldn't have it. She practically went berserk.'

'So you drugged her?'

'I didn't really mean her any harm. I thought that if I could just keep her quiet until she saw I was right and everything was back to normal then everything would be fine.'

'But now she's dead.'

'Don't think I don't feel badly about it, but it was an accident, that's all, just an accident.'

'Just one of those things, eh?' said Saracen, pointedly.

'Well, if the silly bitch hadn't gone off her rocker and listened to reason instead, she would still be alive today, wouldn't she?' snapped Garten.

Saracen kept his temper but the urge to strike Garten was strong. 'You were behind the affair at the mortuary when I got hit over the head?' he asked.

Garten nodded. 'You stumbled across Dol-man's men removing Myra Archer's body.'

'And then they disinfected the place with formaldehyde?'

'Yes. Now I suppose you are going to call the police?'

Saracen did not get the chance to reply for Mildred, who had been listening at the door, burst in and she was holding a double-barrelled shotgun.

'Please Mildred, put the gun down,' said Garten softly. 'This isn't going to help matters.'

Mildred ignored her husband and moved towards Saracen, hugging the gun into the folds of fat around her stomach. Saracen remained absolutely still. He could see from the look in Mildred's eyes that any false move on his part could precipitate disaster. Mildred stopped with the gun only inches from Saracen's face. She hissed, 'If you think that you are going to destroy everything we have worked for, you are very much mistaken.'

'Mildred, please!' insisted Garten. 'You are overwrought, dear. Please put down the gun.'

Saracen still did not say anything, hoping that Garten could calm his wife down. He did not believe that Mildred was capable of cold-blooded murder, but there was a very real chance that the gun could go off by accident, especially when it was in the hands of some-one so blessed with incompetence as Mildred. Mildred began to listen to her husband but still chose to argue. 'Nigel, I will not let him take away everything that Daddy has planned for us. He's just a cheap trouble-maker. You did nothing wrong. Everything you did was for the benefit of the town.'

Saracen looked back to Garten, expecting him to continue the argument, but was puzzled to see Garten's hand sneak casually across the desk to the buttons on the intercom. Who could he be alerting? There was no one else in the house as far as he knew. Garten gave a fake cough and Saracen suddenly realized that he had done it to cover the sound of a recorder being switched on. A shiver of fear ran up Saracen's spine as he tried to fathom what Garten was up to. Why in God's name did he want this scene recorded?

Garten said, 'Mildred, my dear, I appreciate your loyalty, but I have done wrong and must take the consequences. Please put down the gun.'

Mildred looked doubtful.

Garten continued softly. 'It's not the end of the world, dearest. I know that I shouldn't have covered up for Cyril Wylie but I did, out of regard for an old friend, and now I must face the music.'

Saracen frowned. What was all this nonsense about covering up for an old friend? He had been blackmailing Wylie. Even Mildred looked puzzled, but then the world continually puzzled Mildred.

'After all, dear, when I get out of prison,' continued Garten, pausing after the word prison, 'we'll still have each other, so please put down the gun.'

'Prison!' squawked Mildred.

'But not for too long, dear,' soothed Garten. 'I'll probably be struck off, of course, but...'

'Struck off!' echoed Mildred.

Saracen could see what Garten was doing. He *wanted* Mildred to shoot him. He was pretending to dissuade her while all the time he was inciting her with bleak pictures of their future. If the gun went off by accident, they might both get away with it. If not, then he would have the tape to prove that Mildred was the murderer and that he had tried everything possible to stop her. The nonsense about covering up for Wylie would give him a chance to invent some story to account for the missing Archer body, something that laid the blame at Wylie's door and diminished his own involvement to little more than misplaced loyalty. Garten could come out of this smelling of roses.

'You little shit,' said Saracen, unable to contain himself any longer, 'You devious little turd!' He turned to Mildred and said, 'Can't you see what he is doing, you silly bitch? How can you be so stupid! Your precious husband is responsible for covering up an outbreak of plague in this town. He is responsible for the death of Dr Chenhui Tang, and for blackmailing a consultant pathologist into falsifying records.' Saracen was vaguely aware of Garten switching off the recorder.

'You're lying!' screeched Mildred.

'It's the truth!' insisted Saracen.

'Nigel is a gentleman! He is going to be a Member of Parliament one day, Daddy said so.'

'Members of Parliament don't have wives who shoot people, Mildred,' said Saracen. 'Put the gun down before someone gets hurt.'

'Yes dear,' said Garten softly, 'Being a Member of Parliament isn't everything...'

Mildred clutched the gun tighter and Saracen pushed himself back into his seat in trepidation.

'No! You are not taking this away from us,' she screamed. She struggled with the gun and Saracen realized that she intended to shoot. He threw himself sideways to the floor.

There was an agonizing silence in the room broken only by Mildred's grunting as she struggled with the weapon, unable to fire it for some unknown technical reason. As Saracen poised himself to make a bid for the gun Mildred swung it to the side to look at the triggers, not realizing that both barrels were now pointing at her husband.

Garten opened his mouth to protest but Mildred, now satisfied that she could pull the right thing instead of the trigger guard, did so and emptied both barrels into her husband's chest. The force of the blast lifted Garten clean out of his chair and nailed him momentarily to the wall before he slid to the floor, his chest a hollow, crimson crater. The recoil of the weapon drove the walnut stock of the gun back into Mildred's stomach, making her retch violently as she fell to her knees. Saracen looked at the scene from his kneeling position on the floor and whispered to no one in particular, 'Christ Almighty.'

NINE

It was four thirty in the afternoon before the police had finished questioning Saracen. He himself had called them, Mildred being incapable of doing anything other than scream hysterically. Garten's name and the fact that he was Matthew Glendale's son-in-law ensured that the most senior police officers in Skelmore were in attendance; in fact Saracen had noted that officers of junior rank seemed to be markedly absent during the proceedings. This raised a question in his head that might have developed into paranoia had Mildred not already conceded that she had fired the weapon.

The confession, however, had been made amidst loud protests that 'it really hadn't been her fault,' that the gun had 'gone off', and that 'if it hadn't been for that swine', meaning Saracen, her husband Nigel would still be alive. Saracen feared that the police might lean towards the welfare of the establishment and so it proved to be. Rest and sedation were prescribed for Mildred, while open hostility was the order of the day for him.

As the seemingly endless round of questions proceeded, Saracen could sense that the police were determined to interpret Garten's death as being accidental, the tragic outcome of a domestic accident while he himself was an interloper who had somehow precipitated the whole sorry affair. Saracen found himself becoming more and more annoyed. He would not allow himself to be rail-roaded along that particular path and determinedly stuck to the truth. Mildred Garten had been trying to kill him when the gun had gone off and killed her husband instead. She had been trying to stop him reporting Garten to the police over irregularities in the handling of two deaths at Skelmore General. Saracen was further annoyed that no one seemed to be writing anything down. 'I thought that I was making a statement,' he protested.

'All in good time, sir,' said the superintendent, with a smile that bore no humour.

'Can I ask what you are going to do?' said Saracen.

'We are going to gather all the facts together and then make our report, sir,' said the superintendent with a condescension that put Saracen's teeth on edge.

'I understand that you are presently under suspension from the General Hospital, sir?' said one of the other policemen.

'Is that relevant?' snapped Saracen.

'It might be,' replied the policeman. 'Further, I believe that it was Dr Garten himself who instigated your suspension?'

'Yes it was, but that has nothing to do with...'

'Quite so, sir.'

The senior policeman present leaned back in his chair and folded his hands across his ample stomach. He regarded Saracen with a world-weary gaze. 'Now then, let's see if I have got this right,' he said. 'This woman, this Myra Archer, was not buried in St Clement's Churchyard. She was cremated because she died of plague, which she caught in Africa before coming here. She gave it to one of her neighbours, who also died and he was cremated too. You say that Dr Garten covered up the true nature of these deaths in order to avoid public alarm and loss of business confidence in the area?'

'It's not just a case of covering up,' replied Saracen, alarmed that the policeman had made it sound so unimportant. 'There should have been a full scale epidemiological investigation of the outbreak.'

'Epi...?'

'He should have notified the public health authorities so that one of their teams could have identified the exact source of the outbreak, traced and isolated all the contacts, and placed quarantine orders if necessary.'

'But I thought we had established that this Archer woman brought the disease with her from Africa?' said the policeman.

'Well, yes, but...'

'Then what you are really quibbling about is Dr Garten's failure to do the paperwork?'

'No, I'm not,' retorted Saracen angrily. 'We are talking about plague! Black Death! Not influenza! You don't take anything for granted and you never take chances with it!'

Saracen could see from the glances that passed between the policemen that he had been cast in the rôle of meddling busybody. He considered for a moment telling them the full story of Cyril Wylie's involvement in the affair, and of Wylie's attempt to murder him, but found that he had no heart for it. There was no point, he decided. What he really wanted to do was to go home.

Saracen poured himself a large whisky and slumped into a chair facing a window in the flat. He looked up at the sky and the passing clouds and, for once, was glad of the silence; it was exactly what he needed.

As the minutes passed the whisky did its bit in blunting his nerve ends, and it was tempting to climb into the bottle for the rest of the evening, but there was something else he had to do.

He felt he had to go and see Timothy Archer and explain personally about his wife's death and why she had not been buried where they had always planned. There would be no pleasure in it, but then there was no pleasure to be taken in any of it.

Feelings of self-recrimination began to arise in Saracen. Perhaps it would have been better all round if he had never thought to interfere in the first place. 'Damnation!' he said out loud, before throwing back the whisky. How he envied people who could tell right from wrong so easily. Oh for a black-and-white world instead of the universal greyness that was his! He got up and ran a bath. Too much quiet could be a bad thing.

Saracen decided on a suit and tie for his visit to Timothy Archer; he needed all the props of social nicety to tell the man what he had to. As he straightened his tie in the mirror he wondered how Archer would take the news. He had had time to get over his initial grief, but there were more factors to consider than might otherwise be the case. His wife's death had come at a time of great upheaval and disorientation for them both, for they had just given up what had been their whole life style for twenty years in order to come back to Skelmore. That in itself must have been a considerable strain. True, Skelmore had once been home to Archer but twenty years is a long time and seeing gaps where familiar buildings used to stand could not have been comforting. In strange surroundings and with nothing familiar to cling to, the tide of grief could come perilously high.

When Saracen turned off the engine in the residents' car park at Palmer's Green, he was struck by how quiet it was. It was only seven thirty in the evening and the weather was fine, but there were no children's voices to be heard, no sound of balls bouncing on concrete, no jangling bicycle bells. Only the sound of birds singing disturbed the quiet. He got out and walked across the spotless courtyard to the double-glazed front doors, where he had to wait for the caretaker to open them.

As he waited he smiled at his own naïveté. Of course there would be no sounds of children at Palmer's Green. The apartments here cost the earth. No young families could possibly afford them. They were the prerogative of the well-heeled and, in Skelmore, that automatically meant the elderly.

The door slid back and Saracen approached the hall desk. 'I'd like to see Mr Archer.'

'Is Mr Archer expecting you, sir?'

'No.'

'What name, please?'

'Dr Saracen.'

'One moment.'

The man picked up the green telephone and

Saracen turned away, unwilling to eavesdrop on someone else's conversation, however mundane. He casually examined the large mosaic that occupied an entire wall in the entrance area and recognized Greek helmets, spears and rocks that appeared to have elephants' trunks protruding from them. Leaning his head first to the right and then to the left he still failed to establish an overall theme and gave up with a slight shrug of the shoulders.

'Mr Archer will see you, sir. Flat number fourteen,' said the caretaker.

Saracen followed the direction of the man's outstretched finger and made his way to Archer's apartment. He knocked gently on the door and it was opened almost immediately. 'Come in, Doctor. It's good to see you.'

Saracen noticed that Archer's tan had faded a good deal since the last time they had met and his hair was more unkempt than it had been. An open bottle of whisky stood on a small table by the armchair, a half-filled glass beside it.

'Can I fix you one?' asked Archer, nodding to the bottle. Saracen agreed and Archer poured a generous measure into a tumbler. 'Anything in it?'

'A little water.'

Archer went to the kitchen to fetch the water, giving Saracen time to appraise his surroundings. There was an impersonal, almost hotel-like ambience about the place, with no books, ornaments, photographs or letters lying around.

Through an open door he could see a half-full suitcase lying open on the floor. He guessed that time had been standing still for Archer.

Archer returned and said, 'I'd like to think that this is a social visit, Doctor, but maybe not?'

'It's about your wife,' Saracen began tentatively. 'There are some things I think you should know.'

When Saracen had finished. Archer sat forward in his chair and cradled his head in his hands.

'I'm sorry,' said Saracen softly.

Archer shook his head and said, 'Plague? My wife died of plague?'

'I'm afraid so.'

'But surely that faded out centuries ago?' protested Archer.

'In Britain, but it's endemic in some areas of the world, including parts of Africa.'

'But I haven't got it!'

'No,' agreed Saracen. 'But did your wife leave to come to Britain directly?'

Archer shook his head. 'No, she went around the country visiting some of our old friends for a week or so before she left, saying goodbye, that sort of thing.'

Saracen nodded and said, 'Well, somewhere along the line she must have come into contact with an infected source.'

Archer shivered and rubbed his arms briskly. 'God, it's cold in here,' he said and got up.

He went over to the heating controls on the wall and fiddled with the dials before complaining that it was no use, the place was always cold.

Saracen smiled and sympathized. He was relieved that his task was over and Archer had taken it well. 'Have you any idea what you will do now?' he asked Archer.

'I thought I might take one of these sea cruises, get some sun, new places, new faces, start picking up the pieces.'

'Good idea,' said Saracen.

'But not just yet,' said Archer. 'First I'm going to spend the summer here in Skelmore. I'm going to do all the things that Myra and I said we'd do if we came back.'

Saracen smiled and nodded. He put down his empty tumbler and got to his feet. Archer got up with him and held out his hand. 'Thank you for coming; thank you for telling me.'

There were two police cars parked outside his apartment when Saracen got back. One was a marked Panda car and the other a large black saloon, its identity only betrayed by its communications aerial. There was a third car parked well behind the police vehicles and Saracen thought that he recognized it. As he got nearer, the BMA sticker on the windscreen confirmed it; the car belonged to Martin Saithe.

Saracen entered the building and met his would-be guests coming back down the stairs. Saithe was at their head and saw Saracen.

'Ah, James, there you are.'

Saracen was rather taken aback at Saithe addressing him as 'James'. It inferred a familiarity that had never existed between them.

'James, this is Superintendent Carradyce. We were wondering if we might have a word.'

'Of course,' replied Saracen. He led the way back up the stairs and invited his visitors inside. The fixed smile on Carradyce's face and Saithe's false manner told Saracen that they wanted something from him. He wondered what.

Carradyce and Saithe sat down facing Saracen and the policeman said, 'It's about this awful business with Dr Garten, sir.'

'I thought I'd told the police all I could about that, Superintendent,' said Saracen.

'A tragedy, an absolute tragedy,' said Saithe, as if he were auditioning for the National Theatre, thought Saracen.

'You were very helpful, sir,' said Carradyce, shifting uncomfortably in his seat. 'It's just that I'm sure we would all like to minimise the after effects of this tragic affair. Wouldn't you agree?'

'Minimize?' said Saracen unhelpfully.

Saithe leaned forward solicitously and said, 'We do realize of course that it must have been very unnerving for you, James.'

Saracen had never seen Saithe pretend to be nice to anyone before; it had all the fascination of watching an unnatural act. 'But?' he said.

'Mildred was very upset at the time, James, and the aftermath for the poor woman, well that doesn't bear thinking about. She has lost everything, absolutely everything...'

So that was it, thought Saracen. Matthew Glendale had been pulling strings to get his daughter off the hook and avoid a family scandal.

'The gun did actually go off by accident, sir,' Carradyce reminded him.

Saithe leaned forward in his seat and said to Saracen, 'What the Superintendent is getting at, James, is...'

Saracen had had enough of this game. He said, 'I know what the Superintendent is getting at. You would like Nigel Garten's death to be recorded as a tragic accident. You would like there to be no mention of the plague cases and no mention of any attempt on my life by Mildred. Correct?'

'More or less,' agreed Saithe with a slight air of embarrassment. The policeman looked even more embarrassed.

'Don't misunderstand us, James. We know that what Mildred tried to do was unforgivable but...'

'Matthew Glendale could do without the scandal,' said Saracen.

'The whole town could do without a scandal, James,' Saithe corrected.

Saracen got up, turned his back on his guests and walked over to the window. He hated to admit it, but Saithe was right. A public scandal was not going to do anyone any good and possibly a lot of harm. The affair was best forgotten as quickly as possible. 'Very well, I agree,' he said, and turned round.

Saithe and Carradyce were visibly relieved. Saithe gave a genuine smile. It looked quite different from the one he had previously been affecting. He said, 'There is, of course, the matter of an apology to you, James, over your unfortunate suspension. I'm sure I will speak for everyone at Skelmore General when I say that the sooner we have you back in harness the better. Indeed, I think that I can safely say that when it comes to the matter of selecting a new consultant for A&E we won't have far to look.'

Saracen felt uncomfortable, even unclean. He felt as though he had just been bought. 'If you will excuse me now?' he said.

'Of course,' said Saithe, getting to his feet. He held out his hand and Saracen shook it. The policeman did likewise. Saracen felt even worse.

'Do you mean she's getting away with it?' asked an incredulous Jill, when she heard the news.

'It's for the best,' said Saracen. 'The sooner we get back to normal, the better.'

Jill sipped her drink. She seemed angry. Saracen ran his fingers lightly through her hair and she put her hand up to hold his. 'It just doesn't seem right,' said Jill.

'The main thing is that it is over,' said Saracen.

'I suppose you're right,' conceded Jill, but her voice still harboured doubts. 'What about your suspension?' she began.

'It's over. I'll be back on duty tomorrow.'

Jill smiled for the first time and said, 'Well, that's one good thing.'

'Maybe we should celebrate. Go out to dinner?'

'Chinese or Italian?' asked Jill.

'Neither. How about the Station Hotel?'

Jill's eyes widened. 'Little ol' me at that big ol' Station Hotel,' she mimicked. 'Won't I have to dye my hair blue and dress up like a Christmas tree?'

'It might help,' agreed Saracen. 'But if we talk posh they might let us in.'

'I'll have to change.'

'I'll run you round. But first I'll phone for a table.' Saracen walked over to the phone but it started to ring before he had reached it. It was Dave Moss at the County Hospital.

'I know this is going to sound ridiculous, but I must talk to someone,' said Moss.

'Shoot.'

'One of my patients died this evening.'

'Go on.'

'He died of pneumonia only four hours after admission.'

228

'Old people often succumb quickly, you know that,' said Saracen.

'But he wasn't old. He was a strong, thirty-year-old man. I gave him a million units of penicillin on admission and expected him to be stable by this evening, but he went downhill like a lead balloon. The cyanosis was something to behold. By the end his skin was almost black.'

Saracen felt the hairs on the back of his neck begin to rise. He had an awful sense of foreboding. 'I agree, it's unusual,' he said slowly.

'I know it sounds crazy and I know you will laugh, but I think he died of—pneumonic plague!'

Saracen closed his eyes. It wasn't over after all. Plague was still in Skelmore.

'James? Are you still there?'

'I'm here. Did your patient live in Palmer's Green?'

'One moment.'

Saracen heard the receiver being laid down and paper being shuffled.

'No, he didn't. Why do you ask?'

'Where did he live?' asked Saracen.

'Madox Road. But why?'

'Christ Almighty!' said Saracen softly, on hearing an address that was on the other side of town from Palmer's Green.

'What are you not telling me?' demanded Moss.

229

'Myra Archer and Leonard Cohen both died from plague. Garten covered up the deaths believing that they were isolated cases and that would be the end of it. They both lived in the flats on Palmer's Green. If you've had a case from the other side of Skelmore we could be in real trouble.'

Moss spluttered in disbelief. 'How in God's name did we come to get plague in Skelmore?' he exclaimed.

'Myra Archer had just arrived here from Africa. She must have brought it with her. Cohen was one of her neighbours at Palmer's Green.'

'And Garten covered it up?'

'He thought the press coverage would destroy the Skelmore development plans. He thought the Japs might pull out and his father-in-law would go bust over his housing investments.'

'Good old Nigel,' said Moss. 'Self, self, self.'

'Have you told anyone else of your suspicions about your patient?' asked Saracen.

'I wanted to try it on a friend first.'

'Lab tests?'

'I sent them off in the usual way, giving severe pneumonia as the provisional diagnosis.'

'Maybe you should warn the lab about the specimens?' suggested Saracen.

'I will do. I'll arrange for the staff to have cover, too. Any idea what the recommended drugs are?'

'I think it's streptomycin and tetracycline,

but we had both better check. All I can remember for sure is that penicillin is no use at all against plague.'

'That would explain my patient's failure to respond,' said Moss quietly.

'You weren't to know. We would all have gone for penicillin in the circumstances,' said Saracen.

'Thanks.'

'Will you notify the health authorities or will I?' asked Saracen.

'I will. We will have to get to the family quickly.'

'I'll inform the powers that be at the General and then I'll get back to you.' Saracen put down the telephone, then picked it up again and called Saithe.

'And Moss is quite sure?'

'He doesn't have the results of the lab tests yet but it sounds like the real thing.'

'Damnation!' muttered Saithe. 'But we must be careful not to cross our bridges until we come to them. We don't want to cause unnecessary panic.'

'No, sir, but Dr Moss is calling the public health people anyway.'

'I see,' said Saithe distantly, as if he were thinking about something else. 'I think what we must do,' he said slowly, 'is set up an *ad hoc* committee to monitor the situation.'

Saracen raised his eyes to the ceiling. 'If you say so.'

'Now, who should we have on it...' continued Saithe, as if Saracen were no longer there.

'An expert on plague,' interrupted Saracen.

'What was that? What did you say Saracen?'

'I suggested that we find an expert on plague for your committee. None of us knows anything about it, bar what we read in our text books years ago.'

'Good point,' said Saithe. 'There can't be too many experts on plague around.'

'And certainly not in Skelmore,' added Saracen.

Two hours later Saithe called back to say that an emergency committee had been decided upon. Saracen was invited to join. The committee was to comprise Saithe himself, Braithwaite, the medical officer for the county, Chief Superintendent Carradyce, David Moss, John Laird, the medical superintendent at the County Hospital, the hospital secretaries of both the General and County Hospitals and their senior nursing officers. In addition, and more important to Saracen's way of thinking, a man named MacQuillan would be coming up to Skelmore from the government's research establishment at Porton Down. He was due to arrive in the town at around eight fifteen. The first meeting of the committee was scheduled for nine pm. Saracen said that he would be there.

At ten minutes to nine Saracen left Accident and Emergency, where he had called in to see Alan Tremaine and inform him that he would be coming back on duty in the morning. He was thinking about Tremaine as he pulled his collar up against the drizzling rain and waited for an ambulance to pass before crossing the quadrangle to the east wing of the hospital. Tremaine was looking tired, too tired thought Saracen; unless anything came up at the meeting to prevent it, he would go back to Accident and Emergency and work the night shift. Tremaine could go home and get some sleep. Saithe had said something about getting locum housemen for the unit: Saracen made a mental note to remind him; the matter was now urgent.

Dave Moss was getting out of his car as Saracen reached the east door. He held it open for him and asked, 'How are things?'

'Not good. The dead man's wife has been admitted.'

'Same thing?'

'Looks like it.'

Saracen cursed softly.

'It gets worse,' said Moss. 'She worked as a cook at Maxton Primary School.'

They had reached the east wing lecture theatre where the meeting was being held. Moss opened the door and allowed Saracen to enter first.

'Good evening,' said Martin Saithe, looking

over his glasses and then at his watch. 'I think we are all here now.' He exaggerated the act of looking at everyone present to confirm it.

Saracen disliked the lecture theatres in the General, for there never seemed to be enough light in them, especially at night when single bulbs hanging beneath metal shades seemed to provoke more shadow than illumination. Apart from the installation of projection equipment, no concession at all appeared to have been made to the modern era. The dark wooden bench seating rose steeply to the ceiling and curved in a hemisphere round a central podium, as it had done when Victorian medical students had filled it. Saithe was standing behind a table that, in its time, had witnessed a continual stream of embarrassed and hapless people, there to display their afflictions for the education of the 'young gentlemen'.

Saithe said, 'I must apologize for our surroundings this evening, but Dr MacQuillan has some slides for us; we need the projector.'

A small, balding man with a dense black moustache who was wearing a tweed suit took this as his cue and got to his feet. He joined Saithe behind the table and picked up an automatic slide-changer. Saracen thought he recognized a slightly aggressive air about the man in the way he stood with his feet well apart and held the slide changer at a distance from his body.

Saithe said, 'Dr MacQuillan is an expert on Yersinia pestis, the organism that causes plague. He has kindly agreed to fill in the gaps in our knowledge.'

MacQuillan gave a little grunt of acknowledgement and took the floor from Saithe. He picked up a pointer from the table and clicked on the first slide. 'First the culprit.'

MacQuillan's Scottish accent and clipped words matched his stance, thought Saracen, who had now classified him as a pugnacious, no-nonsense Scotsman. Good, he thought, the absence of bullshit should speed things up considerably.

MacQuillan slapped the pointer against the screen and said, 'This is Yersinia pestis, a rod-shaped bacterium less than two thousandths of a millimetre long. It looks like any other bacterium, you might say, and you would be right but, in the fourteenth century, this little fellow wiped out one quarter of the entire population of Europe.' MacQuillan paused, but found his audience too sophisticated to gasp out loud. 'Ironically,' he continued, 'man is infected as an unwitting interloper between infected rats and their fleas. An infected rat dies, its fleas look for a new host. A human being is nearby, bingo, he gets plague.'

MacQuillan clicked the slide-changer and a monster from science fiction leapt on to the screen. 'Xenopsylla cheopis,' said MacQuillan. 'The rat flea. The cycle is as follows: flea bites infected rat and picks up the organism. The bacteria multiply inside the insect's gut. It regurgitates them and, mixed with its saliva, it passes on the disease to its next victim, usually another rat, but not always.'

'But surely plague can be transmitted in other ways?' said Phoebe Kendal, the General's senior nursing officer.

'Indeed it can,' replied MacQuillan. 'The process I have described is for the transmission of *bubonic* plague. There is another form of the disease, termed *pneumonic* plague which is what we are seeing here in Skelmore. In advanced stages of the illness the patient produces copius amounts of bloody, frothing sputum containing a myriad of plague bacteria. This gives rise to highly infectious aerosols, produced when the patient coughs or sneezes. People in the vicinity inhale the infected particles and contract pneumonic plague.'

'Thank you, Doctor,' said Phoebe Kendal.

MacQuillan changed the slide. 'This is the bubonic form,' he said. 'The patient shown here is close to death. Note the swollen lymph glands and here,' he slapped the pointer once more against the screen, 'in the inguinal region is the primary bubo, the most common site for it.' Another click of the changer and a different patient appeared. 'This man has pneumonic plague; he is about three hours from death. Note the skin colour; he's almost black, hence the nickname, Black Death.'

'What's the mortality rate?' asked Moss.

'In untreated cases of pneumonic plague, mortality is almost one hundred per cent. In untreated bubonic cases, it's between fifty and seventy-five per cent.'

'You said "untreated",' said Saracen.

'Yes, the use of modern antibiotics can alter things dramatically. Tetracycline therapy will reduce bubonic plague fatality to around one per cent. It is also extremely effective against the pneumonic form if the time factor is right.'

'Time factor?'

'After twelve hours nothing will save you.'

Saithe asked about incubation time for the disease.

'One to six days, depending on the infecting dose,' said MacQuillan.

Saracen was beginning to wonder why Braithewaite, the county medical officer, was saying nothing, and was about to say so to Moss when MacQuillan answered his question for him.

'I have spoken to Dr Braithewaite and his people are currently taking appropriate action to contain the outbreak. I don't think I am being too optimistic when I say that this should be all over in the very near future.'

'Can I ask what "appropriate action" means?' said Moss.

'Over to Dr Braithewaite,' said MacQuillan, and sat down.

Dr Braithewaite got to his feet with the

237

usual difficulty of a very fat person and turned to face his audience. He wrinkled up his nose and eyes as though he had suddenly been exposed to light, and thrust his hands deep into the voluminous pockets of his trousers. 'Well, basically,' he began, pausing to clear his throat unnecessarily, 'it's a question of tracing contacts quickly and treating them.'

'With what?'

'Tetracycline.'

'And if they are children?' asked Moss.

'I know what you are getting at, Doctor, but in this case I think we have to overlook the deposition of the drug in growing bones and teeth and give the children tetracycline too.'

No one chose to disagree.

'What about protection for hospital staff?'

'Anti-plague vaccine and serum is on its way,' replied Braithewaite.

'For my men too?' asked Carradyce.

'Of course.'

'But not the public?' asked Saracen.

Braithewaite screwed up his face still further. 'No, not at this stage,' he said. 'We don't want to encourage any unnecessary panic and I feel that this unfortunate incident can be adequately contained without mass vaccination.'

'Then you have established the link between the man who died at the County Hospital and either Archer or Cohen?' said Saracen.

Braithewaite shifted uncomfortably on his feet and cleared his throat once more. 'I think we have come as close as we can,' he said. 'The man was employed on the development at Palmer's Green. I think it reasonable to suppose that he must have come into contact with either Mrs Archer or Mr Cohen.'

'It would have to have been Cohen,' said Saracen.

Braithewaite looked bemused; MacQuillan stepped in to save him. 'By the incubation time, yes, you are quite right, Doctor. Mrs Archer has been dead too long for it to have been she who infected the man. The deceased must have been infected within the last six days; that makes it Cohen.'

'Are you taking steps to prove it?' asked Saracen.

Braithewaite was dismissive. 'Inquiries will be made, but it is purely academic,' he said.

Moss said, 'Am I right in thinking that what we are aiming for is six clear days without a case of plague?'

'Better say eight, to be absolutely sure,' said MacQuillan. 'Eight days without a case and Skelmore will be in the clear.'

'Assuming all the presumptions are right,' said Saracen.

'I don't think I understand,' said Braithwaite coldly.

'I said assuming all the presumptions are correct and A gave it to B who gave it to C, et cetera.'

'Do you have a better idea, Doctor?'

'The point I am trying to make is that we must take nothing for granted with something as dangerous as plague. Every detail must be checked.'

'Very commendable, I'm sure,' said Braithwaite. 'After only thirty years in the profession I'm grateful for your advice.'

Saracen was aware of one of the senior nurses hiding a smile behind her hand and felt embarrassed and annoyed at the put-down.

'What was that all about?' whispered Moss, as one of the hospital secretaries changed the subject to ask about ward accommodation.

'I don't know myself,' confessed Saracen. 'I just think they are taking it a bit too lightly. There's something wrong somewhere.'

'But what?'

Saracen shrugged. 'I don't know. I wish I did.'

'Finally,' annouced Saithe, 'the Press.' He paused to allow time for groans and head shaking. 'I think we must insist that no one other than our official spokesmen should say anything at all to the newspapers.' There was a murmur of agreement and Moss asked who the spokesmen were to be.

'Both hospital secretaries and Dr Braithwaite as medical officer for the county,' replied Saithe. 'But the less we say the better. If we can stall all questions for a week, or eight days to be precise,' Saithe looked at MacQuillan, 'we can speak about all this in the past tense.'

TEN

Saracen returned to Accident and Emergency and told Alan Tremaine what had been going on.

'I trust we can all sleep safely in our beds now that a committee has been formed,' said Tremaine, in a tongue-in-cheek tone.

'You certainly can,' said Saracen. 'The county medical officer says so.'

'Then maybe I'll emigrate,' said Tremaine.

'No respect, the younger generation, none at all. Now, if you want to give me the report you can go home and get some sleep.'

'Are you serious?' exclaimed Tremaine.

'I'm serious.'

'Then I'm not going to argue,' said a delighted Tremaine. He picked up a clip board and started to read out facts and figures. 'Road accident, two admitted, man with skull fracture, three broken ribs and broken left femur. He's in ward twelve. Woman, severe facial lacerations, broken left wrist, admitted to ward thirteen. Kid knocked off his bike, cuts and bruises, bad sprain to left ankle. He's presently at X-Ray but I don't think it's broken. One drunk with a four-inch cut on his face from a beer glass. Singh is stitching him up in cubicle four. Lastly, a woman with a rash all over her body. It came out while she was dining in a restaurant with her husband. I think it's an allergy rash, most likely from something she was eating. She's responding well to anti-histamines.'

'That's it?'

'That's it.'

'See you in the morning,' said Saracen. 'By the way, have all the staff had their tetra-cycline?'

'To a man. How about you?'

'I'm just about to.'

'Don't forget,' said Tremaine, and with that he left.

Saracen took his tetracycline and then started looking for the day book. He failed to find it and went to ask Sister Lindeman.

'I put it on Dr Garten's desk; I thought you would be using that room from now on.'

'Of course, thank you, Sister,' said Saracen, who had overlooked that side of things. He discovered that Lindeman had moved some of his other books and papers into Garten's old room and it made him think about her. He had often tried to define what made a good nurse, but had never fully succeeded. Whatever it was, Moira Lindeman had it in abundance; she was quite simply the best. Quiet, unob-trusive, competent and smoothly efficient. But there was more to it than that. She had the capacity not only to act, but to anticipate what would be required in any given situation. In many other professions she would have been highly rewarded for that quality, but here in Accident and Emergency she was taken for granted.

Saracen finished scanning through the day book and closed it as there was a knock at the door and a nurse put her head round. 'Dr Saracen? The pubs are closing. We need you.'

Saracen joined the rest of the team in the treatment room as the first casualties of 'the Happy Hour', as Tremaine termed it, arrived at Accident and Emergency. This was the hour immediately after closing time, when arguments fuelled by too much booze were settled by violence.

'What happened?' Saracen asked a burly man with blood pouring from a head wound. He was holding a dirty handkerchief against it.

'It were this other bastard, see, it were all his fault. There I was, mindin' me own business when this...'

Saracen switched off. He had heard it all so many times before. He concentrated on stitching the cut, but just before he started the man put a hand on his arm and asked thickly, 'Is this gonna hurt?'

'Hope so,' said Saracen.

There was a welcome lull between one and

243

two in the morning, by which time the town had settled its differences and gone to sleep. Saracen grabbed the chance to drink some tea and eat the digestive biscuits that had gone soft through lying too long on the plate. In the quiet of the small hours he started doing the *Guardian* crossword, and was pencilling in the word ARCHIMEDES when the phone rang; it was Dave Moss.

'The woman died and we've had four more admissions.'

'From where?' asked Saracen.

'From the Maxton estate. A woman and three kids.'

'Known contacts?'

'Don't know yet. Braithwaite's people are investigating but there's more to worry about at the moment; I've got the lab results back.'

'And?'

'It's plague, all right. They've isolated Yersinia pestis, but there's some kind of problem with the drug tests.'

'What kind of a problem? MacQuillan assured us that the treatment was cut and dried,' said Saracen.

'Well, the lab think so too but they are not too happy with the readings they've been getting. They'd like Porton Down to check them out.'

'What's to check? The strain is either sensitive or resistant to tetracycline, and plague is always sensitive. MacQuillan said so.'

'I know that's what MacQuillan said, and that's what the book says too, but the lab found that although tetracycline slowed the bug down, it didn't kill it.'

'Maybe some problem with the potency of the drug used in the test,' suggested Saracen.

'Maybe,' said Moss, hesitantly.

'So what drug do we use in the meantime, until they check it out?' asked Saracen.

There was an uneasy pause before Moss said, 'Trouble is, all the drugs the lab tested behaved in the same way. They slowed the bug down, but they didn't kill it.'

Saracen's head reeled with the implications of what Moss was saying, 'But that means we can't treat it!' he said finally.

'Yes it does,' agreed Moss.

'If tetracyline slows it down, what are the chances of the patient's own body defences coping?' asked Saracen.

'That's the big money question,' agreed Moss. 'We won't know until we've tried it. So far all the patients have been well into fever before we've seen them; they probably would have died anyway. The only people treated with tetracycline have been the staff and the known contacts, and they seem all right so far, touch wood.'

'When will we hear from Porton Down?' asked Saracen.

'Two days, they reckon. It has top priority.'

'So we just sit tight and hope,' said Saracen.

'Nothing else for it,' agreed Moss.

Saracen put down the telephone and sat staring into space for a moment. Sister Lindeman interrupted him. 'I'm sorry, we've got a right mess coming in,' she said.

'Tell me,' said Saracen wearily.

'Glue sniffers. Four kids. The police found them on the Palmer's Green building site.'

Saracen could smell the solvent on the breath of the children. Like a lot of other smells, tar, petrol, disinfectant, it was not unpleasant in small doses, but when you put the stuff in a polythene bag and clamped it over your nose and mouth as the four boys in front of him had been doing, it was a different story. He looked at the blistered mouths and rolling eyes and shook his head as he examined each child in turn.

One of the four, a streetwise youngster with a mop of curls in a grubby T-shirt and jeans, seemed less affected than the others, so when everything was under control Saracen came back to ask him some questions. He asked the boy his age.

'Twelve,' came the sullen reply.

'Why do you do it?'

'Nothing else to do around here.'

'Crap!' said Saracen.

The boy seemed taken aback. 'It's true,' he mumbled.

'And I'm telling you it's crap! Don't you

246

think I've got enough to do without dealing with a bunch of cretins who stick plastic bags over their heads?'

'You can't say that! You're a doctor!' protested the boy.

'I just did,' said Saracen. 'Where did you buy the glue?'

'Ain't sayin'.'

Saracen looked at the police constable who had brought the boys in, but the man shrugged his shoulders.

'I asked you a question,' said Saracen, turning back to the boy.

'An' I said I ain't sayin'!' replied the boy aggressively.

Saracen eyed him up for a moment and then said, 'In that case, my son, I think a nice enema is called for.'

'What's that?' demanded the boy.

Saracen leaned over and whispered in the boy's ear. 'First the nice nurse will take this big tube and then...'

The explanation had the desired effect. The boy's eyes opened wide and aggression changed to panic. 'No one ain't gonna do that to me!' he spluttered.

Saracen nodded gravely. 'Oh yes they are,' he said, 'And with ice cold water, too.'

The boy began to shrink away but was restrained by the constable's hand.

'Now, perhaps if you were to answer my question I might just be able to reconsider your treatment,' said Saracen, calmly looking at his fingernails.

The truth dawned on the boy. 'This is blackmail!' he stammered.

'I believe it is,' agreed Saracen.

The boy gave in. 'Bartok's in Weaver's Lane,' he said. 'He said we weren't to tell anyone.'

'I'll bet,' said Saracen quietly. He looked at the policeman and asked, 'Mean anything?'

The officer nodded and said, 'We know old Bartok. Tight as a cat's arse.' Realizing too late what he had said, the policeman began to colour and offer his apologies to Sister Lindeman. 'We've heard worse,' she said.

'You'll have a word with him?' asked Saracen.

'We'll lean on him a bit but he'll swear blind that he thought the kids were building model aeroplanes.'

'See what you can do, anyway.'

The constable got to his feet and replaced his helmet. 'Can I take it these four rogues are going to be all right?' he asked Saracen.

Saracen nodded and said, 'This time.'

'Are you keeping them in?'

'These three had better stay overnight, this one can go home,' said Saracen, lightly shaking the shoulder of the boy who had provided the information.

'Right then. You come with me,' said the policeman to the boy. 'I'll take you home and

248

have a word with your dad.'

'Don't do that, mister. He'll kill me!' said the boy.

'Where do you live?' Saracen asked the boy.

The boy gave an address in the roughest part of the Maxton estate and Saracen looked at the constable. His shrug was a plea for mitigation. The policeman smiled and said, 'Perhaps in view of the help this young man has given us and taking into account the fact that he is never going to do anything like it again...'

'Never, I promise, mister.'

'Right then. Wait here while I get their details from Reception.' The officer left the room.

'What were you doing on the building site anyway?' Saracen asked the boy.

'Playing.'

'You came all the way down from the Maxton estate to play on Palmer's Green.'

The boy hung his head and Saracen played the waiting game. 'A bloke at school said you could get treasure at the site.'

'Treasure?'

'That's what he said.'

'What kind of treasure?'

'Gold.'

'Gold, on a building site?' asked Saracen.

'It's true!' said the boy defiantly. 'Edwards had a cross, a gold cross; he got it on the site.'

'Whereabouts on the site?'

'He wouldn't tell us.'

'So you thought you would investigate on your own?'

The boy nodded.

'Find anything?'

'Not yet.'

Saracen smiled at the defiance. 'Building sites are dangerous places. If Edwards found a crucifix there, it probably belonged to one of the workmen; he should have handed it in.'

'No, it was different. It was *treasure!*'

'Treasure or no treasure, you stay away in future. Understand?'

The boy said he would, but avoided Saracen's eyes when he said it. The constable returned.

Saracen was called to a special meeting of the emergency committee on Thursday morning and guessed rightly that this was to discuss the results from Porton Down. The meeting was delayed while they waited for Dave Moss to arrive from the County Hospital, but when ten minutes had passed, still with no sign of Dr Moss, Saithe decided to start without him and handed over to MacQuillan immediately.

'Not to beat about the bush,' said MacQuillan, 'Porton Down agrees with the findings of the local laboratory. There is, in fact, a problem.' MacQuillan paused to let the murmur die down. Saracen was only too aware of the inflection that MacQuillan had put on the

250

word 'problem'. It made him uneasy.

'The plague bacterium appears to have undergone some alteration to its outer membrane, affecting both passive and active diffusion.'

Saithe said, 'Perhaps for the benefit of those among us who are not scientists?'

'Of course, I'm sorry,' said MacQuillan. 'The outer wall of the bacterium has changed, mutated in some way, so that it has become impervious to certain agents.'

'Does "certain agents" include antibiotics?' asked Saracen.

'Among other things, yes,' replied MacQuillan quietly. The buzz in the room grew loud and Saithe had to ask for quiet.

'So there is no way of treating the disease?' said Saracen.

'Antibiotics do have some effect,' said MacQuillan. 'Tetracycline in particular slows the growth rate of the organism markedly.'

'But in the end?' persisted Saracen.

'In the end, the outcome is inevitable. The prognosis for treated cases will be the same as for the untreated; a one hundred per cent fatality rate can be expected.'

Braithwaite interrupted. 'This is all academic, of course,' he said. 'If my people have moved quickly enough to isolate the contacts, as I believe they have, there is nothing at all to worry about.'

'I disagree,' said Saracen flatly.

The room fell to awkward silence before Saithe said, 'Perhaps you had better air your views, Dr Saracen.'

Saracen stood up and said, 'We must not be complacent. I suggest that steps be taken immediately to isolate Skelmore from the rest of the country.' Even before he voiced the last word Saracen was aware of the murmurs of disapproval. These murmurs spawned a small, supercilious smile on Braithwaite's lips. He said, 'I am sure the good doctor should be commended for his caution, but this is *not* medieval England. Isolating a modern day town is not a matter to be taken lightly. It would do untold damage to the economy, not to mention putting an end to Skelmore's development hopes for the future. I think most of us here would agree that there is certainly no call for such a drastic measure at this juncture.'

Sounds of agreement greeted Braithwaite's words.

Saracen continued his losing battle and said, 'This may not be medieval England, but what we have here in the town is medieval plague, and from what Dr MacQuillan has said we are no more equipped to deal with it in this age than we were then.'

Silence met Saracen's comments until MacQuillan said, 'I'm afraid that there is a deal of truth in what Dr Saracen is saying.'

'But surely you don't think that we should isolate the whole town too?' said Braithwaite.

MacQuillan adjusted his spectacles and said, 'As always in these cases, the crux of the matter lies in the source of the outbreak. In this case we think we know the source; it was the Archer woman and she brought it in with her from Africa. That being the case, I see no need to quarantine the town.'

'There we have it then,' said Braithwaite, pleased that MacQuillan had backed him up.

'I take it that the relevant African medical authorities were informed about Myra Archer?' asked Saracen.

'Of course,' replied Braithwaite, content to leave it at that but Saracen persisted. 'Have you heard back from them yet?'

'No, but then I really don't expect to,' said Braithwaite, with more than a trace of irritation. 'The simple fact is that the disease is endemic in areas of that continent. I suggest you read the World Health Organisation's report on the subject, Doctor.'

'I don't doubt it,' replied Saracen. 'But I would like to know if any case of plague has been notified in the area relevant to Myra Archer in the past few months.'

'Africa isn't England, Doctor,' snapped Braithwaite. 'People come and go, live and die without the state ever being aware of it, let alone writing it all down. Official records are scanty if they exist at all.'

The meeting fell into thoughtful silence until Saithe said, 'Is anyone other than Dr Saracen in favour of taking steps to isolate the town?'

No one spoke.

'Very well then,' said Saithe. 'We carry on as we have been doing for the time being.'

Saracen telephoned Moss at the County Hospital as soon as he got back to Accident and Emergency. He wanted to find out why he had not attended the meeting.

'The anti-plague vaccine arrived this morning,' said Moss. 'I thought it more important to start vaccinating the staff. Anything interesting come up?'

Saracen told Moss of the Porton Down findings.

'So the lab was right,' said Moss. 'The bug is resistant to tetracycline.'

'Worse than that. MacQuillan says that its altered cell wall makes it immune to just about everything.'

'All things bright and beautiful...' intoned Moss.

Saracen had a chilling thought. He said, 'I wonder if Porton Down checked the bug's antigenic structure.'

'What do you mean?'

'If our bug has a different cell wall, it may not be susceptible to antibodies produced against different strains,' said Saracen thoughtfully.

'Christ! You mean the vaccine we have may not be any good against the Skelmore strain?' said Moss.

'Just a thought,' said Saracen.

'That would be all we need,' groaned Moss.

'I'd better check with MacQuillan,' said Saracen. 'Can you give me the batch number of the vaccine you are using?'

'Hang on.'

Saracen waited for Moss to return to the telephone and used the time to uncap his pen and flick over his desk pad to a new page. He was absent-mindedly drawing a clover leaf in the top right hand corner when Moss came back on the line. 'It's WHO 83 YP 761. Got it?' Saracen confirmed that he had, and said that he would contact MacQuillan immediately.

As he was about to dial MacQuillan's number Saracen saw Jill Rawlings pass the glass door-panel. She was walking along the corridor with another nurse. Saracen opened the door and called her back. 'Do you have a moment,' he asked.

'Of course,' replied Jill, indicating to her companion that she should carry on without her.

'I haven't seen you for ages. I'm sorry,' said Saracen, closing the door.

'Don't be. I know how things are but I'm here if you need me.'

'I need you,' said Saracen.

Jill seemed taken aback. She said, 'Well, Doctor, it took something for James Saracen to say that, didn't it?'

255

'Maybe,' conceded Saracen. 'Can I see you tonight?'

'I'm on duty until eight thirty. I'm free after that.'

'Good, perhaps we can go out to dinner and...'

Jill put a finger on his lips. 'No,' she said. 'You were on call last night in A&E.'

'Yes, but...'

'And the night before?'

'I'm fine, really I am,' insisted Saracen.

Jill would have none of it. 'Stay at home,' she said. 'I'll come round when I've finished and we'll eat in, then we'll relax with a drink and then we'll make love and then, my dear doctor, you will go to sleep. Understood?'

Saracen looked down at Jill's smiling eyes and said, 'You are a very special lady.'

'See you later,' said Jill backing out of the doorway.

Saracen telephoned MacQuillan and told him of his worries about the vaccine. 'Could you ask Porton Down to check it?' he asked. 'I've got the serial number of the batch.'

'The check is already being done,' said Mac-Quillan. 'Our people thought of it as soon as they discovered the altered cell wall.'

'I should have realized,' said Saracen, feeling foolish.

'I'll let you know when I hear the result,' said MacQuillan.

'There is one other thing,' said Saracen tentatively.

'Yes?'

'If the vaccine should turn out to be ineffectual, what then?'

'A new antiserum and vaccine would have to be prepared from the Skelmore strain,' replied MacQuillan.

'As simple as that?'

'Yes. It would take a little time of course, but preparing a bacterial vaccine is no great problem. We can be grateful that plague is caused by a bacterium and not a virus. Viral vaccines are a different ball game.'

'You said antiserum as well as vaccine?'

'Now that we have a problem with antibiotics we can innoculate animals with the Skelmore strain and then use their serum to treat human cases. There's always a risk of serum sickness of course, even anaphylaxis, but it's a lot better than nothing.'

'Quite.'

Saracen left Accident and Emergency at six o'clock and despite a threatening sky decided to leave his car and walk home, for he felt the need for fresh air. Jill would not arrive much before nine, so there was no reason to hurry. He took a detour through Coronation Park and sat for a while beneath the trees, feeling depressed. There was no specific reason for the feeling, he just had a sense of foreboding;

it was almost as dark as the sky. Perhaps it was the weather, he reasoned, heavy, still air, trees absolutely motionless, as though holding their breath while they waited for something to happen. The sky grew even darker; the clouds were almost black and the failing light made the grass seem a much richer green than usual. What few people there were in the park at that time started to scurry away as the first large drops of rain speckled the path.

Saracen was soaked to the skin by the time he got back to his flat but showed no irritation, for he had taken no steps to avoid it. True, his first impulse had been to run for cover when the rain had started, but tiredness in his limbs and the general feeling of despondency had changed his mind. He had opted instead to walk through the rain, knowing that a warm bath and a change of clothes were to come. In the event, he discovered that the timer on the water-heater in the flat had failed to trigger and there was no hot water. He switched it on manually and towelled himself dry while he waited in front of the gas fire for it to heat up. After twenty minutes or so he settled for a lukewarm bath with large whisky propped up on the soap bar.

At eight-thirty Jill phoned; she seemed distraught. 'It's Mary Travers,' she said, 'she collapsed on the ward.'

'What's the matter?'

'They don't know yet but I want to stay with

her until they find out.'

'Of course,' said Saracen. 'Is there anything I can do?'

'I don't think so. I'll still come round later, if that's all right?'

'Whenever,' said Saracen.

Saracen turned on the television and flicked through the channels until a programme about the Amazon River caught his attention, but after a few minutes drowsiness began to compete with his interest and the soporific hiss of the fire colluded with the slow monotone of the narrator to induce in him an overwhelming desire to sleep.

He was rudely awoken by the telephone, and the crick in his neck when he sat up told him that he had been asleep for some time. The clock confirmed it; it was a quarter past ten.

'James? It's Jill; I'm still at the hospital.'

It took Saracen a few seconds to clear his head and gather his thoughts. 'What's the problem?' he asked.

'Mary is very ill and Dr MacQuillan thinks it would be a good idea if I didn't leave the hospital right now.'

Saracen was suddenly wide awake. 'What's MacQuillan doing there?' he asked in alarm. He was aware of Jill breathing quickly as though she were very upset. 'What's going on?' he asked. 'Take a deep breath and tell me.'

259

'They think Mary has plague!'

Saracen felt his stomach go hollow. His mind started to race, but he kept a tight rein on his tongue while he considered the implications. Mary Travers had been the nurse on Medic Alpha on the night it had brought in Myra Archer. She, like the others, had been given tetracycline cover. It seemed that all the drug had done was slow down the development of the disease. An outbreak among the other contacts could be imminent.

'James, are you still there?'

'Sorry. You say that you are staying at the hospital?'

'Dr MacQuillan thinks it would be a good idea if those of us who have been in contact with Mary stay here for the moment. They're opening up ward twenty as an isolation unit and asking for volunteers to staff it. I thought that as I was here anyway...'

'You volunteered.' Saracen closed his eyes for a moment. 'Take care,' he said softly.

'You too,' said Jill.

'Can I speak to MacQuillan before you hang up?' asked Saracen.

'Hang on.'

After a few seconds MacQuillan's voice came on the line. 'Dr Saracen?'

'Staff Nurse Rawlings told me about Nurse Travers,' said Saracen. 'It looks as if the contacts are beginning to go down with the disease.'

260

'I wish I could disagree,' said MacQuillan.

'That means that there could be half a dozen or more people scattered over Skelmore about to develop plague. It's like having incendiary bombs in a woodpile.'

'Braithwaite's people are bringing them in and isolating their families.'

'But will they be in time?'

'It's touch and go. It could go either way, that's why I've requested a government order.'

'Government order?'

'From 6 am tomorrow morning nothing moves in or out of Skelmore.'

'Can the police cope?'

'It will be a military affair,' replied MacQuillan. 'The town will be under martial law.'

'Good God!' said Saracen. 'That has an unpleasant ring.'

'There's no other way.'

'Staff Nurse Rawlings said that ward twenty is being opened and staffed with volunteers.'

'And you are wondering about the volunteer angle?'

'Yes.'

'There's a moral dilemma involved,' said MacQuillan. 'We know that the patients admitted to ward twenty will almost certainly die, but they have to be cared for. On the other hand there is some doubt about the efficacy of the vaccine offered to staff as protection. While that doubt persists, I feel we must make the job voluntary.'

'About protection for the staff...' Saracen began.

'I've placed an urgent request for respirator suits from the Ministry of Defence. They will be here by tomorrow morning. In the meantime we have isolated Nurse Travers in a plastic cocoon.'

'Is there anything I can do,' asked Saracen.

'Get some sleep while you can,' replied Mac-Quillan. 'And if you're a praying man, now's the time to do it.'

At the sound of the National Anthem Saracen woke up. He got up from his chair, rubbing his neck, and turned the television set off before padding over to the window to look out at the rain. Something told him that he had just had all the sleep he was going to get.

The telephone rang at two am; it was Moss.

'Where are you?' asked Saracen.

'At home. The hospital has just rung to say that four of the other Archer contacts have developed full-blown plague.'

'Which ones?'

'The two ambulancemen, the police constable who attended the incident and one of the porters.'

'How about their families?'

'The public health people are working at full stretch trying to reach them in time.'

'I don't envy them.'

'Braithwaite is beginning to fray at the edges.'

'Have they established any link between the dead workman and the other three cases from the Maxton estate?' asked Saracen.

'The woman was having an affair with the dead man. Braithwaite isolated the man's family but no one told him about the other woman. Just about everyone knew, but no one liked to say. You know how it goes.'

'And the kids?'

'Two belonged to the woman, the other was a school friend who happened to be staying.'

'God, what a mess.'

'I believe "tangled web" is the expression.'

'You've heard about the quarantine order?'

'From 6 am, yes.'

'Do you know when the public are going to be told?'

'In the morning, when the road blocks are in place and it's too late to decide on a snap visit to Auntie Mabel in Birmingham.'

'Makes sense.'

'The police have had a meeting with the heads of local radio and television. It's been decided to present the situation as a sensible precaution and a chance for Civil Defence bodies to have a major practice. Appeals will be made to British common sense, and so on.'

'It's still hard to believe this is happening,' said Saracen.

Moss murmured his agreement.

263

Saracen lay back on the headboard with his hands behind his head and listened to the sound of the rain outside in the darkness. There was no way that he was going to be able to sleep. He swore softly and got out of bed.

ELEVEN

Tremaine looked surprised when Saracen walked into Accident and Emergency. He looked at his watch and saw that it was five am.

'Couldn't sleep,' said Saracen.

'Things that bad?'

'And getting worse. How was the locum?'

'No problems. He's just having a cup of tea.'

Saracen was checking up on Malcolm Jamieson, one of two locum housemen appointed to compensate for the loss of Chenhui Tang and Nigel Garten.

'When does the other chap arrive?' asked Tremaine.

'Tomorrow, if they let him in,' replied Saracen. He told Tremaine about the quarantine order on the town.

'Claire is going to love that,' said Tremaine. 'She was planning to go to London for a few days.'

'Can't be helped. I'll just take a shower and then I'll have a chat with Jamieson.'

Saracen showered in the locker room under the pitiful trickle that eventually emerged from the sprinkler head after a noisy journey through endless overhead piping. The room, like all the others in the General, was at least fifteen feet from floor to ceiling and decorated with white tiles, so crazed that they appeared brown. The ventilator fan had been broken for some months, so on days when it rained, the window pane acted as a condenser for the steam and water streamed down it.

Saracen watched the stream drift up past the metal lightshade and hang in a pall round the electrics. If Legionnaire's disease doesn't get you in this place the wiring probably will, he thought. He dressed and returned to the unit to speak to Jamieson.

Jamieson, a tall young man with ginger hair and a serious expression, got up when Saracen came into the duty room and seemed uneasy at having been caught drinking tea. Saracen put him at his ease and asked, 'Have you had your vaccination?'

'Dr Tremaine gave it me last night,' replied the houseman.

'And you know why?'

Jamieson nodded and said that Tremaine had told him. 'This is all a bit of a surprise,' he added.

'Wishing you hadn't come here?' asked Saracen.

'I didn't say that,' replied Jamieson.

'No, you didn't,' Saracen agreed. He told the houseman about the isolation order on the town.

'It's that serious, then?'

'It could be,' said Saracen. 'That's why I wanted to have a talk to you. Be on your guard at all times. Think plague. Every apparent drunk that you see puke on the floor: think first! Every apparent junkie with cramps and cold sweat: think first! Things might not be what they seem. None of us is too familiar with the disease.'

'I thought that plague could be cured easily these days,' said Jamieson.

'That's what the books say but this isn't the book, this is for real and there's a problem.'

'What kind of a problem?'

'At the moment we can't treat it.'

The houseman's eyes opened wide. 'Are you serious?' he asked.

'Very.'

Jamieson seemed to pale slightly. He covered his discomfort with an embarrassed grin. 'Well, this really is something,' he said, flicking some imaginary dirt from the knees of his trousers.

'In practice we are going to set up a separate reception area for potential plague cases, but the odd one could slip through under the guise of something else.'

266

'I'll be on my guard,' said Jamieson.

Saracen covered Accident and Emergency on his own until Prakesh Singh joined him at half past seven. There had been only one patient in the interim, a Gas Board worker who had fallen off his bicycle on the way to work and fractured his wrist. The man was leaving as Singh arrived. Saracen gave Singh the same warning that he had given Jamieson and satisfied himself that the man had understood it before leaving him in charge of admissions. He himself retired to his office to start making plans for the new reception area.

The immediate problem was to find a route between reception and ward twenty that avoided all contact with the rest of the hospital. His attention was drawn to a room beneath ward twenty itself that was currently being used as a store room for empty gas cylinders awaiting collection. According to the hospital plan, there existed a staircase that led from the room up to the ward above. If access were restored then the location of the room would make it an ideal reception area for plague patients. Ambulances would be able to take their patients directly to it. Saracen decided that he would have to check with the hospital secretary whether or not the connecting staircase was wide enough to permit the passage of stretchers. He would do this at the next meeting of the emergency committee, which was scheduled for eleven o'clock.

Saracen was surprised when he got to the lecture theatre. There were a great many people there that he had not seen before. Two of them were wearing army uniform, and the others were introduced by Saithe as being heads of department in Skelmore's administration.

'And now,' said Saithe, 'I am going to hand you over to Lieutenant Colonel Beasdale who, from six o'clock this morning, is technically in command of Skelmore.'

The officer smiled and cleared his throat. 'Let me begin by saying that this situation gives me no pleasure at all.' He smiled again as if to reinforce his statement, but no one smiled back. Beasdale continued. 'Nothing would give me greater pleasure than to see an end to this business and the restoration of the town to the proper civil authorities. In the meantime, however, my orders are clear and simple. No one is to enter or leave Skelmore without my say-so. Second, I am charged with the maintenance of law and order.' Beasdale looked round at his audience but no one spoke. He continued, 'In practice we would all hope that things will continue pretty much as normal. The civilian authorities will continue to operate as usual, and my men will maintain a low profile. They will stay outside the town, in fact, except for transfer duties.'

Someone asked what transfer duties were.

'Essential goods coming in to Skelmore will be transferred to military vehicles outside the town and delivered by my men. Civilian delivery drivers will not be permitted to enter.'

'What happens if someone absolutely insists on leaving the town?' asked the County Hospital's senior nursing officer.

'My men would explain the position to them and politely turn them back,' said Beasdale.

'And if they still persisted?'

'They would not be allowed to leave.'

'Meaning?'

Beasdale rubbed his forehead in a nervous gesture of frustration and said, 'We would be obliged to use as much force as was necessary to maintain the integrity of the cordon.'

'Thank you, Colonel.' The woman sat down again with an air of self-satisfaction that Saracen found hard to fathom, for Beasdale did not seem to be an unreasonable character at all. If anything, he seemed to be rather embarrassed by the situation and was deliberately playing down his authority rather than flaunting it.

Beasdale continued. 'This, of course, is not a routine military operation in that the problem is not one of civil unrest but of medical necessity. For that reason, all of us concerned with administration of the town will be heavily reliant on medical advice, not just for situation reports but for forecasts as to how things may develop.'

The more Beasdale said, the more Saracen liked him. Never a great fan of the military mind, he was relieved to discern in Beasdale a great deal of common sense which was a rarer commodity than most people imagined. It did not necessarily come with intelligence and you could not be taught it at university or military academy. It had to be innate.

'Before I hand over to Doctors Braithwaite and MacQuillan, I must tell you that this will be the last meeting of the emergency committee in its present form.'

'Why?' demanded the nurse who had forced Beasdale into admitting that he would use force if necessary.

'It has served its purpose,' said Beasdale. 'It makes no sense to have the centre of administration here in the hospital, one of the areas most likely to be affected by the problem.'

'Do you mean that you are afraid, Colonel?' asked the woman.

Silly cow, thought Saracen.

'On a personal level I suppose you could say that I was, Miss...?'

'Williams.'

'Miss Williams. Like most lay people, I know nothing at all about plague save for the horror that the word implies. I depend on you and your colleagues to provide me with more realistic information. But my decision has nothing to do with personal considerations. Should the worst happen and God forbid that it does, Skelmore must not be left without effective administration.'

'So where will your headquarters be, Colonel?' asked one of the civilian administrators.

Beasdale smiled and said, 'I am afraid my colleague here has something for you all to sign before I say anything else.' The other army officer took some papers from his briefcase and started handing them out.

'What on earth?' exclaimed someone in the front row.

'The Official Secrets Act,' said Beasdale.

With the formalities over, Beasdale said, 'Headquarters will be at Skelmore municipal waterworks.'

The sense of anticlimax in the room was unanimous. Beasdale said, 'One or two of you here will already know the reason for this. For the rest of you it will come as a surprise to learn that sixty feet below ground at the waterworks there is a series of well-equipped chambers designed as a regional seat of government for the area.' Beasdale paused to let the noise die down.

'But surely that sort of thing is for nuclear attack and the like?'

'It does sound a bit overly dramatic, I agree,' said Beasdale, 'but the powers that be thought that this would be a good opportunity to put the facilities to the test.'

'So we all meet there in future?' asked one of the administrators.

'No, not all,' said Beasdale. 'None of the medical personnel will be permitted to enter the administration centre. Instead, my men will install extra communication facilities between the waterworks and the two hospitals, so that we can communicate at any time and in complete confidence. There will be no need for any of the medical people to come to the centre. Any questions?'

There were none.

'In that case I will now hand you over to Dr MacQuillan for a progress report.'

MacQuillan got to his feet and switched on the overhead projector. He placed a transparency on it and picked up the pointer. 'This,' he announced, 'is an epimid, short for epidermiological pyramid. It is a chart that records the spread of a disease during an outbreak. As you can see, we have the patient Myra Archer at the top of the pyramid the source of the outbreak in Skelmore.' MacQuillan slapped the pointer unnecessarily against the name Myra Archer and then slid it down to the next line. 'She in turn gave it to her neighbour Leonard Cohen, and he gave it to Moran, a workman on the Palmer's Green site; this makes a nice, narrow vertical line, just what we like to see. But yesterday things began to change. Moran not only passed it on to his wife, he gave it to a woman he was having an affair with and, more importantly, whom we knew nothing about. This woman gave the disease to her children and another child who happened to be staying in her house, and this makes the base of the pyramid spread out.'

MacQuillan swept the pointer horizontally along the screen. 'To compound an already-worsening situation, four of the hospital staff who attended the original case have gone down with the disease and none of them has been in quarantine.' MacQuillan added lines to the transparency with a felt tip pen and then returned to the screen to run the pointer all the way along the bottom. He said, 'Each of these people has a family, a circle of friends and in three cases a classroom full of contacts. The situation is, to say the least, volatile and this is why the quarantine order was invoked.' Mac-Quillan invited Braithwaite to take the floor. Saracen thought that Braithwaite looked tired and drawn as he got to his feet and shuffled to the table. There was little trace of the self-assurance, almost arrogance, that he had displayed at the previous meetings.

Braithwaite said, 'My staff have been working all night to isolate known contacts of the patients admitted to hospital yesterday. We hope that we have got them all in time, but we can't be sure.'

'What exactly do you do when you get to them?' asked Beasdale.

'In the case of families we simply instruct them to stay indoors and wait for further instructions. The social services see that they get everything they need in the way of supplies. It's just a matter of keeping them out of circulation. Our biggest headache, of course, has

273

been the school. We've had to close it and put in quarantine all the families of children in one particular class.'

'How long will the quarantine be maintained?'

'Eight days. The incubation time for the disease, plus a safety margin.'

'So we wait and see.'

'Yes.'

'Suppose any of the contacts do develop the disease. Does that mean we are in real trouble?'

'Not necessarily,' interjected MacQuillan. 'It's rogue contacts we really have to worry about, people that we don't know about, like Moran's woman-friend. These are the people who can spread the disease all over the place before we get to them. If that happens, the base of the pyramid will broaden until we can no longer hope to trace and isolate contacts.'

'And if that should happen?'

'Then we close all factories, schools and non-essential shops and tell people to stay at home.'

There was a long pause before Saracen asked, 'Has the protective clothing arrived?'

'This morning,' replied MacQuillan. 'The staff on ward twenty already have it. Everyone else should have it by lunch time.'

'The army, too?' asked Saracen.

'My men do have it,' replied Beasdale. 'But, as a matter of policy, will not don it unless the situation deteriorates markedly. The sight of soldiers in spacesuits is not one to encourage public optimism.'

'The same goes for my men,' said Chief Superintendent Carradyce.

The meeting broke up and people began filing out of the lecture theatre until there was only a handful left; Saracen was among them. He leaned forward in his seat and rested his elbows on the wooden rail in front of him while he looked at MacQuillan's epimid, which was still up on the screen. MacQuillan noticed him and came over.

'Well, what do you think?' he asked.

'You're the expert,' Saracen smiled. 'What do you think?'

MacQuillan kept his voice low. He said, 'There are too many imponderables to be able to say with any certainty what is going to happen. We are riding a roller-coaster that isn't secured to the rails. Whether we stay on or fly off is entirely in the lap of the gods.

'Maybe we should co-opt a vicar?' said Saracen.

'Or an astrologer,' replied MacQuillan.

Saithe closed the door of the lecture theatre and said to the members of the General's staff who had stayed behind, 'Is there anything we should discuss before we go about our duties?'

'Admission arrangements for plague cases,'

said Saracen. He made his suggestion about the room below ward twenty.

'Sounds eminently suitable,' said Saithe. 'What is it being used for at the moment.'

Saracen told him and voiced his one qualm about the suitability of the stairs for stretcher bearers.

'That's no problem. They are wide enough,' said the hospital secretary Jenkins, a small, dapper man with gold-rimmed spectacles and a penchant for wearing shirts with collars in contrasting colours. Today's was dark red with a pristine white collar.

Saithe asked Jenkins to see to the room's conversion. MacQuillan asked about ambulance access.

'That's partly the reason for choosing it,' replied Saracen. 'It faces on to the courtyard; ambulances can drive right up to the door.'

'What about ambulance crews?'

'Two crews have volunteered for special duties and have been equipped with respirator suits. Two vehicles have been taken out of routine service and will be used exclusively for the plague emergency. They will be decontaminated after every call.'

'Sounds fine,' said MacQuillan, getting to his feet to leave. 'Up to the number of cases that two ambulance crews, two vehicles and a handful of volunteer nurses can deal with.'

Saracen returned to Accident and Emergency

and telephoned Jill at ward twenty. He had to try twice before he finally got through and asked to speak to Staff Nurse Rawlings.

'Who is speaking?'

Saracen recognized the voice; it was Sister Lindeman. I might have known it, he thought, Lindeman in the thick of things as usual. 'It's James Saracen, Sister,' he said.

'One moment, Doctor.'

'James?'

'Hello, how are you?' Saracen asked softly.

'Not so good. It's all so hopeless,' replied Jill. 'There's so little we can do for them.'

'How is Nurse Travers?'

'Mary died two hours ago.'

'God, I'm sorry. You really shouldn't be on duty.'

'There's no point in sitting around moping about it when I can be of more use up here. I just wish there was something more positive we could do other than try to make people more comfortable while they wait to die.'

'They're all bad, then?'

'Without exception. The three kids died in the early hours of this morning, then Mary died, and the others will die before nightfall. If there are no admissions today the ward will be empty by tomorrow. All dead.'

'What are the duty arrangements for the nurses?'

'We have divided into two twelve-hour shifts. We've been given our own quarters in the side rooms outside the ward where we can watch television and play Scrabble. You know the sort of thing.'

'I'll come up later on.'

Jill paused before saying, 'That's probably not a good idea.'

'Why not?' said Saracen.

'As yet you haven't been exposed to the disease. In the interests of what could conceivably happen in this town, perhaps we shouldn't take any silly chances?'

Saracen had to agree reluctantly that what Jill said made sense. 'Take care,' he said softly.

'You too.'

No new cases were notified in Skelmore that day or during the following night, and while it was judged too early for optimism, the atmosphere at the medical committee meeting in the morning was certainly more relaxed. MacQuillan erased the names of the dead from his epimid chart and, more importantly, did not have to add any new ones. Beasdale sounded pleased when Saithe made his report and asked if this was a sign that they might be getting away with it.

'Too soon to say,' replied Saithe.

There had been stories of occasional arguments between Skelmore people and the military on the outskirts of town, but it had not gone beyond a little name calling. For the most part the quarantine order had been accepted with good humour and forbearance that the British extend to what they regard as government folly. 'Bloody daft if you ask me,' they would say, but they were smiling when they said it.

Saracen took time off to have dinner with Alan Tremaine and his sister, for the new housemen in Accident and Emergency had proved themselves to be reliable and knowledgeable enough to be left on their own, albeit with the instruction that they contact Saracen at the first sign of trouble. Tremaine's flat was well within bleeper range.

Claire Tremaine greeted Saracen with a drink and a tirade against the officialdom that had prevented her from visiting London to 're-charge her batteries'. 'Being stuck in Skelmore is going to drive me mad,' she maintained.

'C'mon. You know you love it,' her brother teased.

Claire took the bait. 'Love it!' she exclaimed. 'My friends get jobs in Greece, Egypt, Colombia, and I end up digging in the rain in Skelmore! Yuck!'

Saracen smiled and asked her how her work was going.

'It's not,' she replied. 'We are beginning to think that the map might be some kind of fake. We haven't found a trace of the legendary abbey.'

'Give it time, sister dear. Patience was never your strong point,' said Alan Tremaine. Claire made a face at him.

Saracen's bleeper went off as they were having after dinner coffee. He phoned the hospital.

'Bad news?' asked Tremaine, when he came back into the room.

'A bus has mounted the pavement and ploughed into a bus queue in Church Road. The ambulances have just gone out.'

Claire looked disappointed. 'Oh dear, does this mean you'll have to go?' she asked.

'I think I'd better,' said Saracen.

'I have a better idea, you stay and I'll go,' announced Tremaine.

Saracen hesitated but Claire persuaded him to accept her brother's offer. As they heard Tremaine drive away Claire said, 'Delegation isn't your forte, James, is it?'

Saracen was taken aback. 'What made you say that?' he asked.

Claire smiled at his discomfort. 'It's written all over you,' she said. 'You're one of those people who has to do everything for themselves. Right now you are itching to be off to the hospital.'

Saracen had to admit to himself that Claire was right. 'They might need me,' he said defensively.

Claire shook her head slowly and said, 'No, it's not that. It would be the same if there were twenty doctors back there in A&E, you would still want to be there. Many people call it dedication but it's not, it's arrogance.'

'Arrogance!' protested Saracen.

'Yes,' continued Claire. 'You believe, subconciously or otherwise, that you are the best. No one can possibly do the job as well as you can. If you are not around there will be foul-up after foul-up.' She moved closer to Saracen and said, 'Is that not right?'

'I just think that...'

Claire moved even closer and said, 'Go on, admit it.'

Saracen started to protest, but then gave in and smiled. 'Perhaps there is a deal of truth in what you say,' he conceded.

Claire looked triumphant. 'More coffee?' she asked.

'Please.'

Claire returned with the coffee pot. 'Tell me,' she said, 'what are you doing in a one-horse town like Skelmore?'

'It suits me,' said Saracen, not wishing to pursue the matter any further.

Claire looked at him appraisingly, wearing a slightly amused smile and said, 'You are a funny one. There's much more to you than you ever let on. Tell me something else. Where does Jill Rawlings fit in to your life?'

'We are friends.'

'And lovers?'

'Mind your own business.'

Claire laughed, 'I asked for that.'

281

She sat down beside Saracen and ran her forefinger gently across the back of his hand. 'I didn't ask out of idle curiosity, you know,' she said softly. 'I am not entirely a disinterested party where you are concerned.'

Saracen looked at her with a puzzled expression. Claire kept up the massage on the back of his hand. She smiled and tilted her head to the right so that her hair fell away from her face. 'Well,' she said softly, 'what do you say?'

'You're playing games, Claire,' said Saracen. 'You're a bored London lady out to amuse herself with whatever is available in this "one-horse town" as you call it.'

Claire shook her head but did not stop smiling. 'You're wrong,' she said. 'I wanted you from the first moment I saw you.'

Saracen saw so much of his ex-wife, Marion, in Claire. She had the same easy self-confidence, the same will to get what she wanted and, what was more disturbing, she was generating the same excitement in him.

'Don't you find me attractive?' Claire asked.

'You know you are attractive,' said Saracen, feeling that the word was an understatement. He was only too conscious of the swell of Claire's hips in a tight-fitting, lemon silk dress.

'Well then, where's the harm?' Claire's voice had taken on the soothing reassurance of a hypnotist at work. She moved her head again so that her hair tumbled to the other side.

Saracen looked at her and said, 'If it didn't sound so bloody silly I'd say that I hated being used.'

Claire pouted and said, 'I'd still respect you in the morning.'

Saracen smiled.

Claire adopted a serious expression. 'I meant it,' she said softly. 'I want you.'

Saracen shook his head.

'It's Jill, isn't it?' said Claire.

'Maybe. I don't know myself.'

'You really are a strange one, aren't you.'

'I think I'd better go.'

Tremaine looked up and smiled when Saracen walked into Accident and Emergency but didn't say anything.

'How are things?' asked Saracen.

'Under control.'

'I thought I would just pop in on my way home.'

'Uh huh,' said Tremaine, with an amused look on his face.

'Are you going to tell me, or do I have to drag it out of you?' said Saracen.

'It wasn't as bad as it sounded,' smiled Tremaine. 'A number of the people lying on the pavement had just fainted. The most seriously injured patient is a sixty-three-year-old woman; she has fractures to both legs and her pelvis. One man has a hairline fracture of the skull, two people have concussion and three more have various cuts and bruises, like this chap here.' Tremaine was suturing a cut over the eyebrow of a middle-aged man dressed in dungarees.

'Good, I feared it would be a lot worse.'

'I would have called you if it had been,' said Tremaine, without looking away from his patient.

Saracen took Tremaine's point and said good-night.

The flat was cold when Saracen got in, but then it usually was. He lit the gas fire before he took his coat off and poured himself a drink before sitting down. He examined the whisky in the glass and considered for a moment that it might be playing an increasingly important rôle in his life, but then pushed the thought to the back of his mind. It would have to wait its turn with all the other problems.

Turning his mind to Jill and Claire he felt annoyed that he could not think clearly. The last thing he needed at the moment were personal problems, but he simply could not blot them out. Failure to do so made him angry. For God's sake, you're not a teenager, he reminded himself. Until tonight he had almost convinced himself that he was over Marion and was falling in love with Jill Rawlings, but tonight had brought new doubts. Even now the thought of Claire Tremaine's thighs occupied his attention for some minutes. The telephone rang and startled him.

'Dr Saracen? It's Malcolm Jamieson at A&E. The police have just called an emergency red at Palmer's Green.'

'What's happened?' exclaimed Saracen. The emergency red code was used to alert hospitals to the occurrence of a major civil disaster like a plane or a train crash, incidents when casualties could be expected to run into double figures at least.

'It's not clear yet,' said Jamieson. 'Emergency red was called fifteen minutes ago and then rescinded almost immediately. A few moments ago it was called again. I thought I'd better inform you.'

'And you've no idea what's wrong?' asked Saracen, puzzled.

'There was some talk of a gas leak at first, but now there seems to be confusion. We've had no patients as yet.'

'I'm coming in. Call Tremaine out, will you?'

'Will do.'

Saracen put down the telephone. It rang again almost immediately. It was Saithe. 'There's chaos down on Palmer's Green.'

'Jamieson's just phoned me. What's going on?'

'Apparently the police were called to the flats after people failed to get in all day. They had to force an entry and found everyone inside dead. Twenty-eight people in all, including the caretaker.'

'What in God's name happened?' asked Saracen.

'At first the police thought that it was a gas leak, but when the ambulancemen got there they knew immediately that it wasn't; the haemoglobin in the corpses hadn't been carboxylated—the bodies weren't pink—they were black!'

'Black!' exclaimed Saracen.

'Severe cyanosis in all cases.'

'Are you saying that they all died of plague?' said Saracen, his mind reeling.

'That's what it looks like, though God knows how. Luckily the ambulancemen had the presence of mind to radio back for instructions before they touched anything. The place has been sealed off to await medical confirmation.'

'From whom?' asked Saracen.

Saithe hesitated before saying, 'That's the thing, actually. Dr MacQuillan will be going down, of course, but I think perhaps one of us should accompany him. I haven't been able to get hold of Braithwaite and I'm a bit tied up at the moment. I wondered perhaps if you...?'

'All right. What's the arrangement?'

Saithe sounded relieved. 'The police have set up a mobile headquarters down at Palmer's Green. You and Dr MacQuillan are to meet there. A squad car is taking down protective clothing for you.'

'Understood.' Saracen put down the telephone abruptly. He did not want to talk to Saithe any more. He went to the bathroom and sluiced cold water up into his face and then dried himself roughly. He felt quite sober although he was aware that he had had quite a few drinks over the course of the evening.

MacQuillan was already sitting in the police caravan when Saracen arrived. He smiled when he saw who had been sent. 'How did you get the job?' he asked.

'I was always lucky,' replied Saracen.

'Your suits are ready, gentlemen,' said one of the policemen, looking round the door. MacQuillan and Saracen followed him through to an adjoining room where they donned their white protective clothing. Before fitting their respirator masks, MacQuillan gave instructions regarding their decontamination when he and Saracen came out of the building. Their suits were to be sprayed all over with the powerful disinfectant that had been brought down with them in the squad car.

'Ready?' asked MacQuillan.

Saracen nodded and made a final adjustment to his mask before following MacQuillan out of the door and across the courtyard. Saracen recalled the occasion on which he had last done this. It was on the night he had visited Timothy Archer to tell him about his wife. Would Archer be one of the dead? He wondered. It

287

seemed almost certain.

Services to the building had been cut off after the initial gas alert, so Saracen and MacQuillan carried powerful torches with them to use until such time as power was restored. There had been a certain reluctance on the part of the police to reconnect any services until it had been proved beyond all doubt that gas and toxic fumes were completely ruled out.

As MacQuillan pushed open the door to the building Saracen saw the damage to the smooth satin steel where the police had been obliged to force it. He allowed the door to swing slowly shut behind them, cutting out the sounds of the night as it came to rest on its seal. It was dark and eerily silent inside the building; just like a tomb, thought Saracen, but that's exactly what it was according to the reports. MacQuillan signalled that they should move to the right through the hall and Saracen signified that he had understood.

They stopped outside the door of the first flat and Saracen waited while MacQuillan found the pass key given him by the police. He opened the door and they went inside. There were two bodies in the apartment, a man and a woman in their sixties. Both were in bed. The woman's eyes were closed but her husband stared unseeingly at the ceiling through eyes that had turned to glass. MacQuillan pulled back the bedclothes to examine the bodies. The examination was perfunctory and swift. There was no doubt. It was plague.

TWELVE

Saracen inspected the flats on the first floor while MacQuillan went on with the remaining apartments on the ground floor. The scene was much the same throughout the building: darkness, silence and death. Many of the dead people were in bed, like the first couple; they had obviously taken to their beds on feeling unwell and had not risen again. A few, like Timothy Archer, had died elsewhere. One man had collapsed over the bath. Saracen was looking at him when the electricity supply was restored. The bathroom light came on without warning and made him step back involuntarily at the spectre of vomited blood splashed over white enamel.

Archer had died in the armchair he had been sitting in when Saracen had come to see him. He had obviously tried to fight the effect of his illness with whisky and a bottle lay on its side where he had knocked it over in his death throes. The contents had formed a dark stain on the carpet, and the smell reached Saracen through his respirator.

Saracen could see that Archer was holding something in his hand. He thought at first that it was a book but when he looked closer he could see that it was in fact a photograph, an old framed one. He freed it from Archer's grip and recognized a younger, slimmer Timothy Archer and knew that the smiling girl on his arm, the girl who had brought a nightmare to Skelmore, must be his wife, Myra. She looked young, carefree and—radiant was the word journalists used for brides—it would do, she looked radiant. He put the photograph back gently into Archer's stiffening hand and rested it in his lap. For the Archers, retirement to Skelmore was over.

Saracen and MacQuillan stood silent and subdued outside the building while policemen in boilersuits and wellingtons sprayed them all over with disinfectant. When they finally emerged from their plastic prison Saracen took great gulps of the night air and accepted the mug of steaming tea that was thrust into his hands. His sense of smell was heightened through having had the respirator over his face for so long. He could smell the night, the grass, the rain, aftershave, tea, boot polish.

'I never thought I would live to see anything like that in this day and age,' said MacQuillan, rubbing the back of his neck where the respirator straps had chaffed. Saracen swirled a mouthful of tea round his gums and spat it out.

'How the hell did it happen?' he asked.

'I don't know. All of them infected at the same time and dead within hours of each other. It doesn't make sense.'

'But it did happen.'

'It *has* to be down to the Archers,' said MacQuillan. 'This is where they lived. Anything else would be stretching coincidence too far.'

'I agree, but Myra Archer died three weeks ago and her husband never showed any signs of the illness at all.'

MacQuillan thought for a moment, then said, 'Suppose, just suppose that Timothy Archer *did* have the disease but had been taking tetracycline for, say, bronchitis. We know now that the drug would have slowed down development of the disease so, in theory, it could have been him who was spreading it around.'

Saracen looked doubtful. 'It's possible, I suppose,' he conceded. 'But I'm pretty sure he wasn't taking any medication. Besides, how could he possibly infect everyone else in the building at exactly the same time?'

MacQuillan thought for a moment and then said, 'Maybe the residents held a meeting about something which brought them all together at the same time. If they had done that when Archer was at his most infectious then it's just possible that they all could have contracted the disease at the same time.'

Saracen still looked doubtful but had to

concede the possibility. He could even suggest a reason for the proposed resident's meeting. He said, 'The residents were unhappy about the heating in the apartments.'

'There you are, then,' said MacQuillan, pleased that his suggestion had been made to sound more plausible.

'But that doesn't explain why they all got such a massive infective dose and all died within hours of contracting the disease,' said Saracen.

'No,' agreed MacQuillan. 'It doesn't.'

'Excuse me, gentlemen,' said the police inspector. 'About the bodies, we'll have to remove them.'

'The place will have to be fumigated first and the bodies sealed in plastic sacks before they are moved anywhere,' said MacQuillan.

'And then there are the funeral arrangements...'

'Too many corpses,' said MacQuillan, without enlarging on his assertion.

The inspector looked uncomfortable. 'I don't think I understand,' he said.

Saracen could sense that MacQuillan was on edge. He saw him turn on the inspector as if to snap at him and only restrain himself at the last moment. 'There are too many,' he said hoarsely. 'They will all have to go together.'

'A mass grave, you mean?' asked the inspector, obviously astounded at the suggestion.

'A mass cremation, to be precise,' said MacQuillan.

'But the relatives...' protested the inspector.

'Our priority lies in getting rid of these corpses as quickly and as cleanly as possible,' said MacQuillan. 'Nothing else matters.'

'Doesn't seem right,' mumbled the inspector.

Saracen could still sense that MacQuillan's nerves were taut, and stepped in to diffuse the situation. 'Perhaps some kind of memorial service could be arranged.'

The inspector was pleased at this suggestion but MacQuillan said, 'They can do what they like with their mumbo jumbo just so long as they burn these bodies first.' With that he disappeared into the caravan to collect his things.

'Cold bastard,' muttered the inspector.

'He's under a lot of pressure,' said Saracen. It wasn't MacQuillan's coldness that was worrying him, it was the look on his face when he had come out of the flats.

MacQuillan re-emerged. He said, 'I managed to contact Braithwaite. His people will deal with the fumigation; the army will remove the bodies.'

'The army?' exclaimed the police inspector.

'You don't have twenty-eight hearses in Skelmore,' said MacQuillan, with what Saracen thought was unnecessary brusqueness. 'A squad of soldiers will bag the bodies and take them away in trucks.'

'I don't know that we will have suitable plastic bags,' said the inspector.

'The army already have them,' said Mac-Quillan. 'Body bags, as used in the Falklands.'

'Where will they store the bodies?' asked Saracen.

'There will be no storage. They will take them directly to the crematorium,' replied MacQuillan.

The inspector indicated his disapproval by taking a deep breath and turning his head away. The gesture annoyed MacQuillan and pushed him too far. He said, 'Now understand this! This town is on the edge of disaster. You do not mess around with plague—if you do it kills you, your wife, your children and everyone else you ever knew—believe it!'

Saracen was alarmed, not at what MacQuillan had said but because of the way he had said it. The man wasn't just jumpy and on edge. He seemed genuinely afraid. The inspector backed down and slipped behind his professional front saying, 'Very good, sir. I'll keep my men here until the army arrives.'

MacQuillan nodded and then said to Saracen, 'There's no point in you hanging around. Go home. I'll see you in the morning.'

Saracen wanted a whisky when he got in, but he denied himself and switched on the electric kettle instead. He spooned instant coffee into an earthenware mug and let the spoon fall in with a clatter. He returned to the living room while the water boiled and flicked through his album collection, finally deciding on Schumann. He drank his coffee to the strains of Traumerei. Twenty-eight people dead and that look on MacQuillan's face. His stomach felt hollow. He got up and looked out of the window; it had started to rain again.

Within seconds of arriving at the morning meeting Saracen could sense that something was gravely wrong. Saithe looked drawn, Braithwaite looked as though he hadn't slept all night and MacQuillan seemed nervously preoccupied. Saithe said, 'In addition to the tragedy at Palmer's Green there were eight new cases of plague during the night.'

Saracen was surprised at the news, for he had left strict instructions that he should be called if any cases of suspected plague should arrived at the General.

Saithe continued and answered Saracen's unasked question. 'All the new cases were admitted to County Hospital's isolation unit. The County have agreed to accept all plague cases until the General's new reception area is fully operational, which will be some time later today.'

'Where did the new cases come from?' asked Saracen.

'All from the Maxton estate,' replied Saithe.

'Contacts of known cases?'

Saithe paused and took a deep breath before

saying, 'Four were, but the other four were not.'

'Four more wild cards,' said Saracen thinking out loud. 'What are the chances of getting to the new contacts?'

'In the circumstances, nil.'

'I don't understand,' said Saracen, totally bewildered by Braithwaite's air of hopelessness.

It was MacQuillan who replied. He said, 'We've had some bad news. Porton Down say that the vaccine we have been using is useless against the Skelmore strain.'

Braithwaite added, 'I cannot in all conscience ask my staff to continue working without any protection at all.'

'Of course not,' murmured Saracen.

'So what happens now?' asked the hospital secretary, breaking the ensuing silence.

'We start general quarantine measures. We close all schools, all shops and businesses that are not essential, and we tell people to stay indoors. We back it up with the police and the army if necessary.'

'Are Porton Down working on a new vaccine?' asked Saracen.

'Of course,' replied MacQuillan. 'And an antiserum, but it will take a little time.'

'Does Colonel Beasdale know about all this?' Saracen asked Saithe.

'I told him earlier. I'm awaiting his reaction. Why don't we all wait together?'

They did not have long to wait before Beasdale called over their special communications link to announce the new measures for the town; from noon Skelmore would be placed under conditions of generalized quarantine as advocated by his medical advisers. Schools, cinemas, businesses and non-essential shops would be closed as from midday. People would be requested to remain indoors, although not ordered to do so at this stage. Public gatherings of any sort would be forbidden.

Reports of the new measures would be given on local radio at eleven thirty, after which the radio station would be used exclusively for advice and information on the emergency situation. The public would be invited to telephone the station with their questions, which would be dealt with by a panel comprising an army officer, three civilian administrators and the medical superintendent of County Hospital. 'Are there any questions?'

'Have your men been told that their vaccination against the plague was ineffectual?' asked Saracen.

'Not in so many words,' replied Beasdale. 'But I will have to reverse my original decision about their wearing protective clothing. They will now wear it for all duties in the town. The public will be told that they are trying out the suits as part of an exercise.'

'Let's hope they are dumb enough to believe it,' said MacQuillan.

'You don't believe they will?' asked Beasdale.

'Would you?' retorted MacQuillan.

'Perhaps not,' conceded Beasdale evenly. 'But that's the way it's going to be.'

Saracen smiled at having discovered that the velvet glove was not empty.

'Now, gentlemen,' continued Beasdale, 'you have presented me with facts and figures. What I need now is an explanation. Twenty-eight people all die together and eight new cases appear during the same night. What's going on?'

MacQuillan said. 'The deaths at Palmer's Green were unexpected in an epidemiological sense in that they do not fit into the anticipated pattern of events. I think we have to treat it as a tragic, one-off occurrence. I would think that the Archers were almost certainly to blame, but the exact mechanism of the infection is for the moment unknown and, for that matter, academic. Our main concern must lie in the fact that four of the new cases were not on our list of contacts. This means that we can expect yet more cases.'

'Is the situation out of control?' asked Beasdale directly.

'No,' replied MacQuillan.

'Is it under control?' asked Beasdale.

'No.'

'Then things are still in the balance?'

'Very much so.'

'Thank you, gentlemen. Keep me informed and tell me when the General is ready to admit more plague cases, will you?'

'Of course,' said Saithe.

Saracen inspected the newly-completed reception area at two o'clock. He was accompanied by Jenkins, the hospital secretary. It was clean and functional, thought Saracen, and the whole area was bedecked with warning signs forbidding entry to the unauthorized. He examined the restored access to the stairs leading to the ward above and saw that Jenkins had been right, there was plenty of room for stretchers.

'It seems fine,' said Saracen.

'Then the General can go on line?' asked the secretary.

'We can go on line,' said Saracen.

When Jenkins had left, Saracen telephoned Moss at County Hospital to tell him personally.

'About bloody time,' said Moss.

'Knew you'd be pleased,' said Saracen. 'How are things going?'

'Three more this morning.'

'Known contacts?'

'Not on Braithwaite's list.'

'Not good.'

'To say the least.'

'You've heard about the vaccine?'

Moss said that he had.

At four in the afternoon, with the town stunned into enforced idleness, Saracen received the first plague alert for the General. An ambulance was on its way with a forty-five-year-old male suspect. Saracen checked the name against Braithwaite's list. It was not there. He swore under his breath.

Saracen donned his protective clothing and headed for the new reception area. One nurse accompanied him, also in full protective gear. They familiarized themselves with the details of the patient while they waited. The man was married with two children and worked for the Water and Drainage Department of the local council. He had no known contact with the Maxton estate. The sound of a siren in the distance indicated that his arrival was imminent. When the siren stopped, Saracen put on his face mask. There was a hospital rule about turning off sirens within a quarter of a mile of the hospital.

The ambulance pulled up outside and its two volunteer attendants, clumsy in their plastic suiting, unloaded the patient on to a trolley and brought him inside. They stood by while Saracen examined the man. It did not take long. Saracen's fear that he might be presented with an atypical case and have trouble reaching a firm diagnosis did not materalize. The patient presented a case of classic textbook pneumonic plague.

Saracen nodded to the attendants who, in contravention of normal working practice, had agreed to take all confirmed cases up to the isolation ward. This obviated the need for volunteers instead of the porters who would normally have done the job. In a way Saracen was glad that the patient was too ill to realize what was going on around him. Gowns and visors, gloves and scarlet danger signs would not have reassured him. By eight in the evening the General had admitted six patients to ward twenty, and the County had taken in another two.

The next day was Friday and at nine thirty, when the medical committee met, there were fourteen patients in ward twenty and twenty-two in the County's isolation unit.

MacQuillan was rattled. 'I don't understand it, I just don't understand it,' he complained. 'So many people are not on Braithwaite's list. It's as though there has been a spread of random contacts all over the town that we know nothing about at all.'

'Where is Dr Braithwaite this morning?' asked Saithe, looking at his watch.

'I understand he is not too well,' said Mac-Quillan. Eyebrows were raised around the room prompting MacQuillan to add, 'No, no, just been overworking, I think.'

'We have to decide what to tell Colonel Beasdale,' said Saithe. 'There is no doubt that the situation has worsened.'

No one thought to disagree.

'With the volunteer force as it stands, our capacity to cope stands at one hundred and ten patients between County Hospital and ourselves. It seems certain that we will reach this figure within three days,' said Saithe.

'There is the turn-over factor, of course,' said Saracen.

Jenkins started to ask what this meant when Saithe interrupted him. 'What Dr Saracen means is that nearly all of the patients admitted will be dead within three days. This helps keep the numbers down.'

'Are the dead going to be a problem?' asked Olive Riley, the senior nursing officer.

'If they are, Matron, it's nothing to do with us,' said Saithe. 'If the crematorium can't cope I dare say Colonel Beasdale has contingency plans.' Saithe repeated that they would have to agree on what to report to Colonel Beasdale.

'Tell him that the situation is worse but not yet out of control,' said MacQuillan.

'Is everyone agreed on that?' asked Saithe. There were no dissenting voices.

'If only I knew where these damned wild cards are coming from,' muttered MacQuillan, as he entered the latest details on his chart. He shook his head and Saracen noticed that his hands were trembling slightly as he wrote.

Saithe made his report to Beasdale and was asked for a prediction. 'Impossible to say,' replied Saithe. 'Things may get even worse before they get better.'

'How long before they start to get better?'
'I can't say.'

'How is everything else, Colonel?' asked MacQuillan, to get Saithe off the hook, thought Saracen.

'There was a sudden increase in the number of people trying to leave Skelmore yesterday after the quarantine announcement. My men turned them back, of course, but things got a bit nasty for a time. We lost a lot of good will but I'm afraid that was unavoidable; people are getting scared. It's a small town and word gets around fast. Tales of horrific deaths and mass funerals are now commonplace.'

'Perhaps the radio can be used to reassure them,' suggested the hospital secretary.

'Too much reassurance can be a bad thing,' said Beasdale. 'Apart from the fact that the rumours are basically true, an element of fear in the population works in our favour. Under these conditions people will police themselves. I don't want to have to ban people from the streets; it's impractical and we probably couldn't enforce it anyway. Voluntary co-operation is our best hope and that's where fear plays a part. But it's a delicate balance; too little and we'll have open defiance, too much and we'll have blind panic.'

'The whole bloody town is doing a balancing act,' said MacQuillan gruffly.

'Let's hope it can maintain it,' said Beasdale.

Saithe's theoretical limit of one hundred and ten patients was passed by seven o'clock that same evening. The volunteer ambulance crews finally broke under the strain of so many calls and Saithe had to request the assistance of the army shortly after eight. Saracen's heart sank as he saw the first military vehicle enter the grounds of the General carrying plague victims; four people all from the same street on the Maxton estate.

The soldiers, like alien beings in their white plastic suits and face masks, deposited their cargo and left without removing their masks to speak. Saracen watched them as they drove off, feeling like a castaway watching a ship pass by on the horizon. He gave an involuntary shiver and turned to his patients.

Tremaine was due to relieve Saracen at nine o'clock in the plague reception. At a quarter to, Saracen called ward twenty and asked to speak to Jill. She sounded tired.

'How is everything?' asked Saracen.

'The ward's full to overflowing, but I suppose you know that already. Seventeen deaths since I came on duty and there's nothing we can do except make people as comfortable as possible while they wait their turn. God, it's like living in a sea of blood and vomit!'

'Things will get better soon,' said Saracen softly. 'The antiserum should be here at any time.'

'I hope so. I don't think I can bear much...' Jill's voice broke off and Saracen tried to comfort her, but he had a lump in his throat. He asked about Sister Lindeman.

'She's an angel,' replied Jill. 'She never seems to rest. She's always with the patients, insists that no one must die alone. Even if a patient is hopelessly delirious one of us must be there to hold their hand and it's usually her. I don't know how she doesn't drop.'

'Try to persuade her to take more rest,' said Saracen.

'I have tried. It's no use.'

'Take care.'

'You too.'

When Tremaine took over in plague reception he said that he had called in on Accidental and Emergency on his way over.

'How was it?' asked Saracen.

'Quiet,' replied Tremaine. 'Fewer people on the streets means fewer fights and fewer accidents. Apart from that, people don't want to come anywhere near the hospital these days.'

Tremaine asked Saracen what the plague situation was like and listened in silence while Saracen briefed him. At the end he remained subdued and said quietly, 'Do you know, until this moment I hadn't considered the possibility that we might lose this fight. What *would* happen if things were to get out of control?'

Saracen had to confess to having had the same mental block. 'I don't know,' he said. 'I simply have no idea.'

Tremaine relayed a message to Saracen from

his sister. She suggested that he go round for dinner when he came off duty. It would save him having to cook for himself. Saracen nodded and went off to shower before leaving the hospital.

'You look tired,' said Claire, when they had finished eating.

'We're all tired,' said Saracen.

Claire played with her teaspoon and said, 'I know you don't think much of me, James, that I'm a silly London bitch and all that, but I would like to help in any way I can.'

Saracen shook his head and said, 'I don't think badly of you. Half the time I don't know what to think at all. I can make decisions at work but when it comes to my personal life I'm a mess.'

'Did your wife hurt you that badly?'

Saracen grimaced and said, 'That sounded like a bad line from a play.'

'You analyse everything too much,' said Claire. 'Every phrase, every word is scrutinized for ulterior motive. You should relax more, take things as they come.'

Saracen looked doubtful but did not protest when Claire moved round behind him and began kneading her fingers into his shoulders. 'You make it sound so simple,' he said.

'It is, if you would let it be.'

'I'm not convinced.'

'That's why you don't have any fun,' laughed Claire.

Saracen had to concede that there was some truth in what Claire was saying. It made him feel uncomfortable. 'I'm too old for fun,' he said.

'Nonsense! I think I know what the matter is with you,' said Claire. 'On the one hand you are afraid of falling in love in case you get hurt again like you did with what's-her-name. On the other you're afraid that you might not be able to fall in love again because of that same fear. That makes you very vulnerable, James. You could end up marrying someone you don't love and that would be like standing on the shore watching yourself drown.'

'If you say so,' said Saracen quietly.

'Now let's get this clear,' said Claire. 'You sure as hell do not love me but you want me as much as I want you, so where's the harm? Let's make life a little more bearable in this hell hole.'

Saracen still looked doubtful. Claire got up and walked over to the wall. She turned to lean against it and said, 'Don't worry. You don't have to pretend to love me. You don't have to say anything at all. No suburban foreplay is required. If you want me you can have me.'

Saracen swallowed hard as Claire, with a sudden movement of her hand, tore her blouse open. She smiled at the look of surprise on Saracen's face and started to hoist her skirt above her thighs.

'Call it rest and recreation if you like. If you want me, come and take me, right now.'

Saracen had not felt so sexually aroused since his teenage years. He moved towards Claire and pinned her to the wall while he tore away her underclothes.

'That's it, any way you want me.'

Saracen took Claire hard against the wall with a single-mindedness that could not be diverted. He felt an alien desire to hurt her for exposing in him such weakness and the cries from her throat only spurred him to greater efforts. But Claire's passion rivalled his own and her fingernails dug deeply into his back as he came within her and buried his face in her hair.

'Don't feel bad,' murmured Claire, as though reading Saracen's mind. 'I want you to enjoy me. I want to make all your fantasies come true, every schoolboy dream you ever had.'

Saracen's bleeper went off at three thirty when Jamieson called from Accident and Emergency to report that a number of people had been admitted with gunshot wounds.

'What happened?' asked Saracen.

'They were trying to leave Skelmore and the army opened fire.'

Saracen cursed.

'I've never dealt with this kind of injury, so

I thought I'd better call you,' said Jamieson.

'I'm on my way,' said Saracen.

Resentment against the military was rife in Accident and Emergency when Saracen arrived. 'Fascist bastards!' snarled one man who had been hit in the thigh. 'Good God, this is England!' protested another.

'They're Russians if you ask me,' added a fat woman, nodding her head wisely. 'We've been invaded. That's why they wear them fancy suits. It's to disguise the fact that they're Russians.'

Saracen did not attempt to interfere, for antagonizing an already incensed mob was going to be nothing but counter-productive. Instead he and Jamieson got on with the business of cleaning and dressing wounds. He knew little of arms and ammunition, but quickly saw that the wounds he was treating had not been caused by high velocity bullets. In addition they seemed to be confined to the lower limbs of the victims, indicating the intentions of the soldiers to do the minimum damage possible.

'If it's a bloody fight they want,' continued the man with the thigh wound, 'that's what they'll bloody well get. Next time we won't be empty-handed. My brother-in-law owns the sports shop in Griffin Street. We'll give them bloody guns! Two can play at that game. Fascist bastards!'

Saracen decided that things had gone far

enough. He told the man to shut up and added, 'You got what you asked for.'

The man was outraged. 'I'm an Englishman,' he said, 'I have a right to go where I please.' Murmurs of agreement ran round the room.

'The soldiers are Englishmen too,' said Saracen. 'They were only carrying out their orders.'

'That's what the SS said,' crowed the loudmouth. There were more sounds of agreement and Saracen had to wait until the noise had died down before saying, 'There's a world of difference. If there wasn't, you wouldn't be sitting here on your fat arse running off at the mouth.' The noise level rose again.

'Here, what kind of a doctor are you, anyway?' demanded the man.

'The kind who's fed up listening to all this twaddle. This town has a big problem and it's *our* problem. Spreading it to other towns and villages is going to help no one, so here we stay, all of us! Get used to the idea. Nobody leaves Skelmore until it's all over.' Saracen could sense that he had won over most of the crowd, perhaps all of them, with the exception of the loud-mouth who continued to mutter threats under his breath.

The trouble was over for the moment but Saracen was worried. He wondered how widespread the ill feeling was in the town. Local radio had taken to assuring people that the

310

arrival of an antiserum was imminent and had appealed for calm during the interim, but patience was being sorely stretched. Please God the loud-mouthed man was the exception rather than the rule, and please God there would be some news from Porton Down in the morning.

Saracen arrived early for the staff meeting and found MacQuillan unshaven and in his shirt sleeves. He was preparing filing cards and moving name tags around on a chart in front of him. He threw down his pen when he saw Saracen arrive and rubbed his eyes saying, 'It doesn't make sense. None of this makes sense. They don't know each other, they don't live beside each other, they don't work together and they have no common friends, and yet they all get plague. This whole bloody thing...,' he made a sweeping gesture towards the chart, 'is a complete waste of time.'

'Anything from Porton Down?'

'Nothing.'

'Damnation,' said Saracen. He told Mac-Quillan of the would-be escapers.

MacQuillan said, 'I'll call Porton Down after the meeting.' The others started to arrive.

'First, the figures,' said Saithe. 'Despite thirty-nine deaths during the night there are of this moment one hundred and twenty-nine confirmed cases of plague in the wards.'

MacQuillan let out a long sigh and let his head rest on his chest. Saracen remained

311

impassive although the numbers depressed him equally.

'Then the general quarantine order has made no difference,' said Jenkins.

Saithe replied. 'We don't know that yet and we won't for another four days.' In answer to Jenkins' puzzled look he said, 'The disease has an incubation period up to six days. The cases that were admitted yesterday were people who had picked up the infection before the quarantine order came into force. That will be true of the cases today and those we see tomorrow. Only after that can we expect to see a decline.'

'But the numbers by then...'

'Quite so,' said Saithe, cutting Jenkins off. 'I was rather hoping for some good news on the vaccine and antiserum front.'

Saithe looked to MacQuillan, who shook his head saying, 'Nothing yet.'

'In that case,' said Saithe slowly. 'I think we have to admit that things are slipping away from us. We have a serious space and staffing shortage and things look like they are going to get worse.'

'We could open up ward eight,' said Jenkins. 'It's been closed for redecoration but in the circumstances...'

Saithe shook his head and said, 'It's not just a question of space. Ward eight is in the heart of the main hospital.'

'I'm sorry, I should have thought. I'm afraid

312

there's nothing else.'

'I know,' replied Saithe. 'That's why I propose recommending to Colonel Beasdale that we open up two of the local schools as temporary plague hospitals. There are two that stand in their own grounds and are therefore isolated from the rest of the community.'

'Makes sense,' said Saracen, and MacQuillan agreed.

'But you will need staff,' said Olive Riley.

Saithe smiled and said, 'I was coming to that, Matron. We will need more nursing volunteers.'

'I am sure you will not find my nurses wanting,' said Olive Riley.

'I am sure we won't,' agreed Saithe.

'What about equipment?' asked Jenkins.

'Frankly we don't need much. Without antiserum there is little or nothing we can do for these people, save let them die with a little more dignity and in a little less discomfort than might otherwise have been so.'

'I see,' said Jenkins.

'Can we agree on the schools?' asked Saithe. There was universal approval, and Saithe called Beasdale to make his report. When he had finished speaking Beasdale asked, 'Is Dr MacQuillan there?'

MacQuillan cleared his throat and said, 'Yes, I'm here.'

'The antiserum, Doctor. Where is it?'

'I'm just about to contact Porton Down.'

313

'Call me back when you have.' The line went dead and people exchanged surprised glances at Beasdale's abruptness.

Saithe said, 'I think we are all interested in the outcome of that call. Shall we wait?'

MacQuillan left the room to telephone Porton Down and was back after less than a minute. 'They will call me back this afternoon,' he said.

'Is that all?' asked Saithe.

'Yes.'

Saracen was as disappointed as everyone else but more than that, he was afraid. He had just recognized that look of terror in MacQuillan's eyes, the one that he had first seen at the Palmer's Green flats.

THIRTEEN

Saracen found Tremaine in the locker room. He did not look up when Saracen came in, but instead continued to stare at the floor. His general demeanour made Saracen wait for the younger man to say something first.

'God knows what we are going to do with them all,' murmured Tremaine, still hanging his head. 'It was just an endless stream of people passing through on their way to the grave. There was *nothing* I could do...' Tremaine looked up and Saracen saw the despair in his eyes.

'Absolutely nothing. I might just as well have been a plumber or a postman...'

'There's nothing any of us can do until we get the antiserum,' said Saracen, resting his hand on the other man's shoulder. He told Tremaine about the opening up of the schools to cope with the increasing numbers of patients. He had intended to ask Tremaine to work on for a bit, but changed his mind after seeing how hard he was taking it. He would cover plague reception on his own and ask Jamieson to work a double shift with Prahesh Singh in Accident and Emergency.

Saracen found that the list of known plague contacts were two days out of date. He telephoned the public health department to find out why. When he got no reply he called Saithe's office and asked about it. He was told that there would be no more lists. 'Dr Braithwaite has suffered a complete nervous breakdown,' he was told by Saithe's secretary. No fewer than four of his staff had gone down with the plague and to all intents and purposes the public health department had ceased to function.

'Bloody marvellous,' said Saracen under his breath.

There was a telephone message, mid-morning, for Saracen. It was relayed to him from the unit and said simply that Staff Nurse Rawlings wanted him to contact her. Saracen knew that it had to be something important and called her back at the first opportunity.

'James? Thank God, it's Lindeman! She collapsed this morning. I think she's got it. I think we are all going to get it!'

'Calm down, Jill,' said Saracen, although his stomach was turning over. 'If Lindeman has got it she must have been careless, and that's not surprising the way she's been overworking; she was bound to slip up sooner or later.'

'But she was the one we all looked up to,' said Jill, with a sob in her voice.

'I know,' soothed Saracen. 'I'll come up and see her as soon as I can. I'm also going to see about some proper relief for you and the other nurses. It's about time you had a break.'

Two hours had passed before Saracen managed to find time enough to go up and see Moira Lindeman. By that time the first of the schools had been made ready and cases destined for it were to be cleared through the County Hospital. This took the pressure off the General until such time as the second school became operational.

Jill came forward to meet Saracen as he entered the plague ward. Like him she was dressed in full protective gear. She gave a wan smile and Saracen smiled back. Inside his head he was suffused with guilt over what had happened with Claire Tremaine. Telling himself that there was nothing to be ashamed of and that there was no commitment between himself and Jill had not helped. He still felt ashamed. Maybe the feeling was telling him something, he reasoned. Maybe he did have a commitment to Jill after all?

It did not take long to see that conditions in the ward were atrocious, and apart from the obvious overcrowding the air was filled with the stench of vomit and the moans of the dying.

'We can't get enough clean linen,' said Jill. 'People in the laundry are afraid to touch our stuff despite the fact that it goes through a sterilizer first.' Jill opened a door and led Saracen inside. The blinds were drawn but cold, grey shafts of light sought out the cracks and provided enough light for Saracen to make out the forms of eighteen sheet-covered corpses. They were lined up on the floor and were lying two deep. 'Our makeshift mortuary,' said Jill. 'It was emptied three hours ago.'

Saracen shook his head but could not find words. Jill led him out and along the corridor to another room. 'Sister is in here,' she said. 'This was her office; we thought she should keep it.'

A nurse was sitting by the bed; she stopped sponging Moira Lindeman's face and got up when Jill and Saracen entered. 'Give me a few moments alone with her, will you?' asked

Saracen, and Jill and the other nurse went outside. Saracen looked at the drawn face of Moira Lindeman and saw the sweat glisten on her forehead and the quiver in her lip. He sat down where the nurse had been sitting and gently wiped away the perspiration from Lindeman's eyes. She opened them and Saracen saw a flicker of recognition. It pleased him. He smiled and Lindeman tried to speak. 'Shouldn't...have...come...'

'I had to,' said Saracen, but then he saw that his protective gear had prevented Lindeman from hearing what he had said. He removed his mask and visor and repeated it, overriding her look of protest with a slight gesture of his hand. 'Don't try to speak,' he said gently. 'There have been so many times in my life when I've wanted to say something and ended up letting the moment pass, that this time I thought it had to be different. This time I am going to say it. For what it's worth, my lady, you are one of the finest nurses I ever met and one of the most noble human beings.'

The suggestion of a smile appeared at the corner of Lindeman's mouth but remained stillborn. 'It's worth...a lot,' she whispered, closing her eyes again with the effort.

'Get some rest, now,' said Saracen, and got up quietly to retreat to the door. 'Sleep.'

Saracen left the ward, suspecting that he would not see Moira Lindeman alive again. The thought added a bitterness to the depression that was growing inside him like a cancer. He telephoned Saithe about the need to relieve the nurses in ward twenty, but with little success. Saithe maintained that he and Olive Riley were well aware of the situation, but all the latest nursing volunteers had been used up in staffing the schools. There was nothing that they could do.

'Does Colonel Beasdale know about the shortage of nurses?' asked Saracen.

'The colonel has all the facts.'

'Then nursing volunteers could be brought in from outside Skelmore.'

'They don't want to do that,' replied Saithe haltingly.

'Why the hell not?'

'It's government policy to play down the situation in Skelmore as much as possible, keep the affair local at all costs. They are using the typhoid outbreak in Aberdeen in the sixties as a working model to handle things. If we start making nationwide appeals for help the cat will be well and truly out of the bag.'

'It's going to come to that sooner or later,' said Saracen angrily.

'They would rather it was later,' said Saithe.

'How much later?'

'They want to give the antiserum a chance. In theory there should be a dramatic improvement in the situation within a few days and we will have control again.'

'But we will need even more nurses when people start recovering,' said Saracen.

'True, but it will be easier and more acceptable to the powers that be if we have an effective vaccine and antiserum at the time of the appeal. If we can synchronize our appeal for help with the announcement that we can now cure the disease, then there will be no risk of panic. You do see the logic?'

'I see it,' said Saracen flatly. 'Let's hope the nurses in ward twenty appreciate it.'

'I'll have another word with Olive,' said Saithe in an effort to placate Saracen.

'They do have the option of walking out,' Saracen reminded Saithe.

'I can't see them doing that,' said Saithe. 'Can you?'

'No, damn it, but it's immoral to count on it; besides, some of them are so near to breaking point that they may not be able to carry on.'

'I'll make sure everyone concerned is aware of the situation,' said Saithe.

The second school was officially declared open at two thirty and for the next three hours it was agreed that the General would screen all plague cases to give the County Hospital a break. All confirmed cases would be sent on to the new school. Saracen screened twenty-two patients in the first hour. All were clear cut; men, women and children from all over the town.

The wild cards had sown the seeds of disaster.

Saracen knew that Jamieson in Accident and Emergency had been trying to get hold of him for the last thirty minutes, but he had been far too busy to get in touch. He had had to put a hold on all calls until his area was clear. It was clear at the moment, although he knew that this would not last for long; it was just a lull in the storm. He washed thoroughly and slumped down into a chair beside the telephone to ring Accident and Emergency. His limbs felt leaden and he rubbed his eyes as he waited for Jamieson to answer.

'I've got a patient here I would like you to take a look at,' said Jamieson.

'You've what?' said Saracen angrily.

'Before you say anything else, I know how busy you are and I wouldn't have called you unless there was a very good reason...'

Saracen calmed down and said, 'Tell me.'

'I really think you should come over,' said Jamieson calmly.

Saracen considered for a moment and then said, 'All right, give me five minutes.' He struggled out of his protective gear and washed again before hurrying over to the unit.

'He's in here,' said Jamieson, pointing to the end cubicle. He handed Saracen his notes and followed behind him as he read them on the move: Francis Updale, aged thirty-seven, heating engineer, 22, Bread Street, Skelmore; being treated for glandular fever, suddenly became so ill that his wife had put in a treble nine call after failure to contact their GP.

'But why wasn't he taken to the County?' asked Saracen. 'All fever cases go there.'

'The County has a problem,' replied Jamieson. 'They stopped admitting an hour ago and requested that we take their emergencies.'

Saracen could hardly believe his ears. 'What kind of a problem?' he demanded.

'I understand that Dr Moss and several others have been taken ill,' said Jamieson.

Saracen froze in his tracks. Never had any words sounded so ominous. 'Taken ill,' he repeated softly. 'Oh God!'

'Mr Updale is in here,' said Jamieson, to break Saracen's trance.

Saracen found the man conscious but in severe distress as he pulled back the covers to begin his examination. He made reassuring sounds to the patient, but in truth he was conducting the examination on autopilot. This went on until alarm bells started to ring inside his head. He was not finding what he expected to find.

'This isn't glandular fever,' he whispered to Jamieson.

'That's what I thought. That's why I called you over. I remembered what you said about taking nothing at face value.'

Saracen's pulse quickened. 'But he's not like the others, there's no pulmonary malfunction, he's...' Saracen examined the man's groin and found what he had been dreading. He showed what he had found to Jamieson and said, 'Do you know what that is?'

Jamieson looked and said, 'I saw it earlier but I haven't come across anything like it before. What is it?'

'It's the primary bubo,' said Saracen. 'This man doesn't have pneumonic plague, he has the *bubonic* form.' Jamieson's questions were lost on Saracen as his mind flirted with a new nightmare.

'You've got a patient with *what?*' exclaimed MacQuillan when Saracen called him. 'Are you absolutely sure?'

Saracen said that he was.

'And he was admitted to the clean area at the General?'

'No one realized what the symptoms were. He is different from the other cases.'

'What a mess,' muttered MacQuillan. 'How the hell did he get *bubonic* plague?'

'Doesn't that mean rats,' said Saracen.

There was a long silence before MacQuillan said, 'The disease can be transmitted by human fleas as well as rat fleas. If this chap has been living rough...'

'He's a clean-living, heating engineer, who lives with his wife and daughter in a nice area and has never been in contact with anyone who has since contracted the disease.'

'Then I don't understand.'

Frustration was beginning to gnaw at the edges of Saracen's temper but he refrained from pointing out that there seemed to be an awful lot that the experts failed to understand about the Skelmore outbreak. Instead he asked, 'How are things at the County?'

'You've heard, then?'

'That's why we got the patient.'

'Five of the staff have gone down.'

'Moss?'

'I'm afraid so.'

Saracen put down the phone and repeated the same expletive over and over again in a whisper. He pulled himself together and returned to the treatment room to arrange with Jamieson that Updale be admitted to ward twenty.

'Will you have a word with his wife?' asked Jamieson. Saracen said that he would.

'Could your husband have worked beside anyone who has since gone down with the disease, Mrs Updale?'

'Frank works for himself. He has his own business.'

'Did he do any work on the Maxton estate?'

'No, he has the contract for an installation in a hotel in Beverley Road; he's been working there since before all this business started.'

'Nowhere else?'

'No.'

Saracen shrugged his shoulders in failure and sighed.

'Wait, there was one day when Frank took on another job. A man called him at home, said he'd got Frank's name from the *Yellow Pages*, wanted him to have a look at his heating. Frank said that he was sorry, he couldn't manage it, but the man insisted that he would make it worth his while, so in the end Frank took the day off to do the job.'

'Whereabouts was this job?'

Mary Updale shook her head. 'I didn't think to ask and I don't think Frank ever said. Is it important?'

'Probably not,' said Saracen. 'But if you should happen to remember, please let me know.'

Tremaine came on duty at four and was apologetic about his earlier behaviour. Saracen assured him that there was no need and said that he was going to stay on at the hospital until MacQuillan had heard from Porton Down. In the event, Saracen joined Tremaine in plague reception a few minutes later on hearing that two military ambulances were on their way with two entire families on board.

'I'm not sure about this boy,' said Tremaine, as he and Saracen examined the latest admissions. 'Would you have a look at him?'

Saracen finished with the patient he was dealing with and went over to join Tremaine at his table. 'I don't understand it,' whispered Tremaine. 'His mother, his father and his eight-year-old sister are all textbook cases, but he is completely atypical.'

Saracen examined the twelve-year-old boy, who was only semi-conscious and in great distress. He knew within seconds what the problem was. 'He's the second,' he said, almost inaudibly as his throat tightened.

'The second what?' asked Tremaine.

'He's the second case of bubonic plague I've seen today.'

Saracen telephone MacQuillan as soon as the diagnoses were confirmed and the patients awaiting transfer to the school for hospitalization. The twelve-year-old boy, who was too ill to be moved, would remain at the General.

MacQuillan sounded as if he would rather not have been told when Saracen broke the news. 'No ideas at all?' asked Saracen.

'I suppose you could argue that the boy contracted the bubonic form and then gave his family pneumonic plague, but as to how he himself became infected I simply don't know.'

'But if we don't find out we could lose the whole town!' hissed Saracen, afraid of being overheard.

'Yes,' said MacQuillan.

Saracen was taken aback at MacQuillan's

apparent complacency. He also thought that MacQuillan sounded a bit strange. 'Are you all right?' he asked.

MacQuillan answered the question with a snort.

'Have you heard from Porton?'

'You had better come over.' The phone went dead.

'James!' came Tremaine's cry from the reception area, and Saracen hurried back to see what the matter was. He found that one of the women patients had gone into a coughing spasm. Bloody sputum frothed up from her lungs like lava from a volcano and her back arched in agony, making it difficult for Tremaine to keep her steady on the trolley. Saracen did what he could to help but the spasm continued until the woman's body suddenly went rigid, her eyes opened wide as if in disbelief, and her head finally fell back in death. The soldiers took her away.

Saracen and Tremaine cleaned the mess off the front of their suits before returning to the boy patient to find him delirious and clutching at something around his neck. Saracen thought at first that it was a doorkey, but it turned out to be some kind of medallion. He removed it and looked at it briefly before handing it to Tremaine while he dealt with the boy. It was rectangular, about five centimetres in length and had a simple design on it woven round the letter S.

Tremaine was surprised at how heavy it was. 'This is very old,' he said.

'Is it?' said Saracen, without much interest.

'In fact I've seen this motif somewhere recently. Now where was it...'

Saracen ensured that the boy was more comfortable before calling ward twenty with a request that he be admitted there rather than be taken on to the school. He took the opportunity to ask about Lindeman.

'She's very low, it can't be long.'

'It was on Claire's desk!' said Tremaine.

Saracen, who was washing his hands, could not think for a moment what Tremaine was talking about. 'What was?' he asked.

Tremaine continued to look at the medallion in his hand and said, 'There was a picture of this motif in one of her books on Skelmoris.'

'I think you must be mistaken,' said Saracen.

'No, I'm sure of it.'

'Right now we have two cases of bubonic plague to concern us. I've got a feeling they hold the key to this nightmare.'

'But this might be important,' Tremaine insisted. 'One of the cases had this round his neck. It might be some kind of a lead. Why don't you drop it off with Claire on your way home and see what she says?'

'All right,' conceded Saracen. He had no wish to see Claire but was too tired to argue. 'But first I'm going to see MacQuillan.'

Tremaine dropped the medallion into disinfectant and swirled it around for a while before rinsing it under the tap and handing it to Saracen, who slipped it into his pocket.

MacQuillan had his back to Saracen when he came into the room. Saracen coughed and he turned slowly to reveal the fact that he had a glass in his hand and, by the look in his eyes, had had quite a bit to drink already. Saracen looked at him quizzically.

'Drink?' said MacQuillan, with a humourless smile. Saracen shook his head. 'What did Porton Down say?' he asked.

MacQuillan looked at him for a long moment before saying, 'The antiserum we've all been waiting for...it's not coming.' He drank deeply from his glass.

'What the hell do you mean, it's not coming?' demanded Saracen in a hoarse whisper.

MacQuillan smiled bitterly and said, 'There is no antiserum; there will be no antiserum. They say that the Skelmore strain is so poorly antigenic that it's no use at all in antibody production. They can't make an antiserum; they can't make a vaccine. Finito!'

Saracen sank slowly into a chair. 'Jesus Christ,' he whispered.

'In my experience he's usually busy when you need him,' said MacQuillan.

Saracen ignored the comment. Drunken cynicism he could do without. 'We'll just have to ride the storm until it burns out, then,' he said.

'It's not going to "burn out",' said Mac-Quillan quietly. 'That bastard bug has won, just as it always did.'

'If we get help from outside and keep our nerve, we can still beat it,' said Saracen. 'We can't just give up hope.'

MacQuillan shook his head as though he were listening to a child telling him that the earth was flat. 'There is no hope,' he said. 'It's over.'

Saracen sensed that there was more than cynicism behind MacQuillan's last comment. 'What do you mean?' he whispered.

MacQuillan drained his glass and refilled it. He said, 'There will be no help from outside because none will be requested. The bug is immune to everything that medicine can offer. It's epidemiology is all wrong and we are helpless. Beasdale knows this, so there will be a reversion to traditional methods.'

'What "traditional" methods?' asked Saracen aggressively, but the aggression was born of fear.

'Fire,' replied MacQuillan.

Saracen's head reeled as he realized what MacQuillan was inferring. 'You must be mad!' he accused. 'Do you know what you are suggesting?'

'Beasdale will have his orders to carry out if things get out of control, and that is now the case.'

'But you cannot seriously believe that he will

destroy the town. Christ! This is England in 1990!'

MacQuillan's silence told Saracen that he did not retract anything. He started to pace up and down the room, occasionally shaking his head in unwillingness to believe what he had heard. 'It's obscene!' he protested. 'It's immoral! It's...'

'Practical,' said MacQuillan.

'But how can they just wipe out a whole town?'

'I told you. Fire.'

'Fire?'

'Oh, I don't mean soldiers running around putting torches to houses. I mean modern fire, scientific fire, liquid fire, all-consuming, chemical fire.'

'How do you know this?' demanded Saracen.

MacQuillan's Scots accent had become more pronounced with alcohol. 'Might I remind you, laddie, that I don't work at Woolworths.'

'So you work at Porton Down, the defence establishment.'

'Defence! That's a laugh. Have you noticed? Everyone is *defending*. No one ever offends, so if no one is offending, what the hell is all this defence for?' MacQuillan found his own philosophy hilarious.

'How do you know?' insisted Saracen.

'Contingency plans. There are contingency plans for this sort of situation. The strategy is to contain and destroy.'

'Contain and destroy,' repeated Saracen softly. 'A whole town?'

'The principle stands.'

'Just how does a government explain the destruction of a whole town to the general public?'

'A tragic accident, some awful consequence of the emergency, a factory explosion, maybe even the gasworks going up through lack of proper maintenance.'

'They'd never believe it.'

'They'll believe it if they want to,' said MacQuillan.

'What does that mean?'

'Any day now, mark my words, the authorities will start leaking the truth about the situation here in Skelmore. Stories of an incurable plague on his doorstep should put Joe Public in the right frame of mind to accept whatever happens next.'

'You're a cynical bastard, MacQuillan,' said Saracen.

'I'm a realist,' countered MacQuillan. 'A blessing in disguise, they'll say. The ways of the Lord are strange. Some kind of timely miracle. Thanksgiving services and now a look at the weather...'

'You're drunk,' Saracen accused.

'I am,' agreed MacQuillan, 'but that doesn't alter the fact that Beasdale, this afternoon, reduced the administration staff to a minimum and sealed off the waterworks. No one now leaves or enters. Don't bother trying to phone anyone either. STD has been suspended, it's local calls only.'

Saracen had had enough. He got to his car and headed for Claire Tremaine's flat.

'You look ghastly,' she said.

'I'm just tired,' said Saracen. 'Alan thought you should see this.' He handed Claire the medallion.

Claire took the object and held it closer to the table lamp beside her. 'Where on earth did you get this?' she exclaimed, and Saracen told her. A sudden look of concern filled her eyes and prompted Saracen to reassure her that the medallion had been disinfected. Claire got up and came back with a book. She showed him an illustration and said, 'Same emblem.'

'But it's what the emblem stands for!' continued Claire, her voice full of excitement. 'It's the crest of Skelmoris Abbey, the monastry we have been looking for!'

'Oh,' said Saracen, with as much enthusiasm as he could muster. This wasn't good enough for Claire who insisted, 'Don't you see? Don't you understand how important this is?'

Saracen reminded himself that Claire had no way of knowing what MacQuillan had predicted for Skelmore, no way of knowing the awful secret that made everything else unimportant to him. 'Of course, I'm sorry,' he said. 'I'm not thinking clearly.'

'Can you find out where the boy got this?'

asked Claire, her eyes bright with enthusiasm.

'He has plague, Claire,' said Saracen. 'He's close to death.'

Claire pursed her lips in frustration. 'Damnation! To be so near and yet so far,' she murmured. She became aware of the disapproving look on Saracen's face and had the grace to be embarrassed. 'I'm sorry, that was unforgivable,' she said. 'I know you must think this silly and unimportant and you're probably right, but seeing that emblem...' She held up the medallion. 'This is the most exciting moment of my career. It proves the existence of the Skelmoris Abbey beyond doubt.'

Saracen nodded. He respected professional enthusiasm but sometimes it was hard to take.

'Can you stay?' asked Claire softly.

Saracen shook his head. 'I've got to get some sleep.'

'Then sleep here.'

Saracen started to protest but Claire was already undoing his shoelaces. He sat down on the couch and put his head back on the cushion. He felt his eyelids come together.

'Don't worry, James Saracen,' whispered Claire, 'I won't take advantage of you, even if you don't realize how much you love her.'

Saracen awoke with a start, feeling disoriented, for he had no idea at all where he was until Claire said, 'Sorry, I woke you. I dropped my book.'

Saracen blinked against the light. He saw that Claire had put a blanket over him. 'How long?'

'Four hours.'

'I'd better get back to the hospital.'

'Don't,' begged Claire. 'You need more rest, go back to sleep.'

Saracen declined and sat up with a yawn.

'You're still dead on your feet.'

'I've just had four hours sleep, thanks to you,' said Saracen. 'I'm grateful.' He got to his feet stiffly and put on his jacket, shrugging the shoulders to make it fit better before moving to the door.

'Any idea what's wrong with the telephone lines?' asked Claire.

Saracen felt a chill run down his spine. 'What do you mean?' he replied.

'I tried to phone London, couldn't get through.'

'Happens all the time.'

'No, I tried several different numbers,' said Claire.

'Lack of maintenance due to the emergency?' lied Saracen.

'Probably,' agreed Claire.

FOURTEEN

Saracen drove back to the hospital through streets that were wet and deserted. As he turned into the hospital gates two military ambulances were coming out, and he had to give way. He watched them go, their deep-treaded tyres sending up orange-tinted spray in the neon lights, the hooded crews anonymous in their white plastic protection suits.

Saracen went to Accident and Emergency first and found the staff there subdued.

'Sister Lindeman died this evening,' said one of the nurses, and Saracen nodded in resignation.

'She was a fine woman,' he said quietly.

The nurse agreed and asked, 'When can we expect the antiserum? They seem to be taking their time.'

'Soon,' said Saracen, uncomfortable about having to lie. 'What's going on here?' he asked. He was looking at a group of men being attended to in the treatment room.

'They were injured while breaking into an off-licence,' replied the nurse.

Saracen nodded and did not have to ask why. The pubs in Skelmore had been closed under the quarantine order and, due to an administrative oversight, the off licences had been included in the non-essential shops register. On top of everything else, sudden alcohol prohibition had been a recipe for trouble. To Beasdale's credit the order had been rescinded to allow off licences to open for two hours a day, but the order would not take effect until the following day.

'There's a message for you on your desk,' said the nurse, and Saracen went to look. The paper said, 'Mrs Updale rang. Call her back', and gave the number which Saracen dialled. He did not bother to check the time. For him and, he suspected, Mary Updale, such considerations were a thing of the past.

'Dr Saracen, you asked me to let you know if I remembered anything about Frank's other job?'

'Yes.'

'Frank entered it in his diary. The customer's name was a Mr Archer and he lived on Palmer's Green. Does that help?'

'I think it does,' replied Saracen, as calmly as he could under the circumstances.

Once again the Archers had come up as the obvious link in the spread of the plague but the revelation raised almost as many questions as it answered. How could Timothy Archer possibly have given Updale the bubonic form of the disease? Then there was the time factor. Saracen hastily scribbled down some dates on the pad in front of him and discovered that for

Archer to have given any kind of plague to Updale within the limit imposed by the in-cubation time, Archer himself must have been in the advanced stages of the disease when Updale had seen him. Was Updale well enough to confirm this?

Jill was nowhere to be seen when Saracen got to ward twenty and for a moment he felt a chill of apprehension. One of the other nurses put his mind at ease; Jill was on her rest period.

Updale's breathing was shallow and rapid and his eyes had the look of a man running in a race that he knew he could not win.

'Hardgoing?' said Saracen.

Updale agreed with a single breathless syllable.

'I have to ask you some questions. The answers could be very important.'

Updale continued to stare at the ceiling and gave no sign of having understood.

'You did a job for a man called Archer down on Palmer's Green,' said Saracen.

Updale licked his lips and moved his head to the side. '...heating,' he said with great difficulty.

'Yes, on the heating system. Was Mr Archer ill when you saw him?'

Updale rolled his head from side to side on the pillow. 'No, not ill,' he breathed.

'Think carefully, it's very important.'

'Not ill, perfectly well.'

Saracen sighed wearily as he saw two and two add up to five. If Archer was well when Updale had seen him, how could he have passed on the disease? The answer was not difficult, it was just hard to face, but Saracen forced himself to come to terms with it. However unlikely it seemed, he had to consider the possibility that Updale had not contracted the disease from Archer at all, he had caught it somewhere else. The involvement of Archer had been a coincidence. Saracen baulked at the notion and remembered MacQuillan's same reluctance to consider anything other than the Archers as the cause of the death of all the residents in the block where they had lived. 'It's just too much of a coincidence,' he had maintained, and Saracen had agreed. He still felt that way, but there was something desperately wrong with the explanation somewhere.

'You just spent the one day down at Palmer's Green?' Saracen asked Updale.

'Thought it was going to be easy—found the air grille blocked—cleared it but flow still poor—fault was in the trunking—too big a job for me—removed the filters to improve the flow until he could call in a bigger firm...'

'You didn't go back to Palmer's Green again?'

'No.'

'Did you speak to anyone else when you were there?'

'The caretaker.'

'Was he ill?'

'No.'

'No one else?'

'No one.'

Saracen told Updale to rest and left quietly. He looked back once through the glass door to see him staring at the ceiling again, his chest rising and falling rapidly, as he continued an unequal struggle.

Saracen noticed that Philip Edwards, the boy with the medallion and the other case of bubonic plague, was in the next cubicle. He went in and approached the bed to see if he was awake or sleeping. He found him to be neither: Philip Edwards was dead.

The staff nurse was upset when Saracen told her. 'Oh no,' she moaned. 'He was stable when I looked in a few minutes ago. I had to go and help Nurses Rivers at the top of the ward. There's just so much...' She mopped her brow nervously.

'I know,' said Saracen.

Saracen thought about the name Edwards as he came back down the stairs. He felt that it should mean something to him, but for the moment could not think what it was.

MacQuillan telephoned to say that Dave Moss had died in County Hospital and Saracen took the news stoically, for he had been preparing himself for it. It still did not prevent an empty, hollowing feeling from settling in his stomach. 'Any more thoughts on the bubonic cases?' he asked.

'None,' replied MacQuillan. 'The game's over. We've lost.'

MacQuillan's attitude annoyed Saracen and he said so before slamming down the telephone. 'Damn the man,' he muttered. It was obvious that MacQuillan had stopped working on the epidemiology of the outbreak, and that was their last hope gone. Without establishing the true reason for the apparent random spread of the disease, there would be no chance of creating the right conditions for it to burn itself out. Plague would claim the whole town unless Beasdale pre-empted it.

Saracen began to write. He wrote down every single fact he knew about the epidemic in the hope that some new fact would emerge. Thirty minutes later he was no further forward. The best fit for all the pieces of the puzzle was still the one that MacQuillan had been using, but once more the bubonic cases stood out like a sore thumb. Could that mean that all the rest was wrong? Saracen tried to free himself from the blinkers of the obvious and started to question everything, right back to the very first assumption. Supposing, just supposing, that Myra Archer had not started the outbreak at all...

Saracen loosened his tie and tugged at his top shirt button. If the first assumption was wrong, how about the second? Could he test it? He got out the files on Archer and Cohen and felt excitement grow within him. Myra Archer had died on the sixth so that meant that she must have been very ill on the fifth and probably on the fourth as well. That being the case, she must have infected Cohen on the second or third, when she was relatively well, otherwise Cohen would have raised the alarm and called in a doctor for her. Cohen himself was brought in dead on the fourteenth. A man of his age, living on his own, would have succumbed to the disease after three days at the most. That meant that Cohen must have developed plague on the eleventh—an incubation time of nine days—it was too long! It was more than six days and that's what Chenhui Tang had been saying when she had had her 'breakdown'. More than six days! She had realized that Myra Archer could not have infected Leonard Cohen. That's why she had been so upset.

Saracen fumbled in his desk drawer for a marker pen and then highlighted the cases on his list that had been assumed to have evolved from contact with the Archers. What else did they have in common if it wasn't the Archers? The answer was plain for Saracen to see: it was Palmer's Green! Myra Archer had not brought plague to Palmer's Green. Palmer's Green had given it to her.

Saracen found that it was one thing to create

a new theory, but quite another when it came to finding evidence to support it. How could Palmer's Green have given all these people plague? He threw his pen across the room in anger and frustration as he failed to come up with anything. Somewhere in the distance he heard the wail of sirens and was reminded that time was running out. Suddenly he saw his best line of approach. It was Francis Updale.

Updale had spent only one day at Palmer's Green and yet he had contracted bubonic plague. Something he had done on that day had given him the disease. One day in Updale's life had to be re-created. Saracen needed help, and the public health department was *hors de combat*. It would have to be MacQuillan.

MacQuillan had been sleeping in his clothes and smelt strongly of whisky. 'We have to talk,' said Saracen.

'The time for talking's over,' growled MacQuillan.

'It's just beginning. Sober up,' said Saracen, pushing his way past.

'What are you talking about?' grumbled MacQuillan, scratching his head.

'You and the others, you got it all wrong. Myra Archer wasn't the source of the epidemic at all. It was a place, not a person. The source of the outbreak is the flats on Palmer's Green.'

MacQuillan looked at Saracen as if he were mad. 'What the hell are you talking about?' he demanded.

'Get cleaned up and then we'll talk,' said Saracen forcibly.

'Who do you think you are talking to!' exclaimed MacQuillan, trying to recover some semblance of dignity.

'Are you going to wash or am I going to stick your head under the tap?'

MacQuillan saw that Saracen was serious and capitulated. He went to the bathroom to emerge some five minutes later, subdued and more sensible. Saracen told him what he had discovered.

'I should have picked up on that,' said MacQuillan, when Saracen pointed out the discrepancy in the incubation period for Leonard Cohen. 'I saw it, but I couldn't let myself believe it.'

'The Wittgenstein problem,' said Saracen. 'It didn't *seem* right.'

'But this is all going to be too late,' said MacQuillan.

'No it isn't,' insisted Saracen. 'If we can establish beyond doubt where the outbreak is coming from, we can tell Beasdale that it's spread will soon be under control.'

'If,' said MacQuillan doubtfully.

'There's no time to lose.' Saracen told MacQuillan of his thoughts about Francis Updale. 'He only worked for one day on the heating system in the flats.'

'I'll talk to Beasdale,' said MacQuillan.

'Tell him we need the architect of these

flats, the builder, the site agent or anyone connected with the construction of the block.'

Fifty minutes later the site agent arrived with the plans.

'The heating system,' said Saracen, when asked if there was anything in particular he was interested in. He helped the site agent spread out the blueprint on the table.

'Show me the supply to flat fourteen, Myra Archer's flat.'

The site agent's finger traced out a line along the plan. 'This is the main duct for the first floor. It has four branch lines, each supplying two flats.'

'Two?' asked Saracen, looking closer. 'Which is the other flat on Myra Archer's line?'

'Flat G3.'

'Who lived there?'

The agent checked his list. 'A Mr Cohen.'

'That's got to be it, then,' said Saracen quietly. 'The bug is in the heating duct. That's how Updale got it too. He was working on the duct.'

'But how?' exclaimed MacQuillan. 'The bug can't survive on its own. It's not like legionnaire's disease, living in old water tanks for years, or anthrax lying dormant in the soil.'

'I don't know how but that's got to be it,' said Saracen, the bit now firmly between his teeth.

'But what about the other deaths in the building?'

Saracen thought back to what Updale had told him and said to the site agent. 'What effect would removing the filters in the system have?'

'There would be an increased air flow and everyone in the building would effectively be on the same line.'

This time even MacQuillan was convinced. 'That would explain why everyone in the building got infected at the same time,' he conceded.

'And the enormity of the dose,' added Saracen. 'They would be breathing it in constantly.'

'We'll have to examine the trunking,' said Saracen to the site agent.

'Now?' exclaimed the man in dismay. 'It's two o'clock in the morning!'

'Right now,' replied Saracen. 'What do we need?'

MacQuillan relayed the site agent's requirements to Beasdale, who agreed to have them delivered directly to the site. In less than forty minutes Saracen was down on Palmer's Green donning protective clothing by the light of arc lamps supplied by the military. Two more hours had passed by the time the trunking had been disassembled as far as the branch that served the Cohen and Archer flats.

'All ready,' said the site agent to Saracen, handing him an open-ended spanner. 'You'll have to squeeze through there,' he said, indicating a narrow gap between the trunking and the wall. 'You'll find an inspection cover on the left hand side secured by four hex bolts, that's what the wrench is for. You'll need this, too.' He handed Saracen a long thin probe. 'To check for obstructions.'

Saracen adjusted his respirator and eased himself through the gap. At first he found difficulty in seeing after the glare of the arc lights, but as his eyes became accustomed to the gloom he could make out the inspection cover in the wall of the duct. Three of the bolts gave in without protest, but the fourth refused to budge.

In the confines of the plastic suit and face mask Saracen felt the sweat begin to pour off him with the effort he was expending on the jammed bolt. He had to blink frequently to clear his eyes of the stinging perspiration that threatened his temper as much as his vision. He heard the site agent calling out to ask how he was getting on but did not reply; it was too much trouble. Instead he gathered himself for one last assault on the bolt.

Holding the spanner as near to the end as possible so as to exert maximum leverage, he strained until the veins stood out on his temples. He saw the paint around the bolt begin to crack, so slightly at first that he thought it might be his imagination, but then a piece flaked off and the bolt's resistance was over. Saracen let the cover clatter to the

347

ground and took a breather. He heard the site agent inquire again. 'I'm fine,' he replied.

Saracen inserted the probe to the right and found that it moved freely at all levels along the duct. He removed it and tried to the left. The probe stopped after half a metre; it had touched something soft. Saracen left the probe in position and reached inside with his gloved hand. His outstretched fingers could feel the obstruction. It was a pile of rags—no it was furry—soft, not rags, a body, an animal's body. He found what he thought was a leg and pulled the corpse back along the duct to the inspection hatch. In the gloom he thought he saw the partly decomposed body of a cat.

Moving backwards, for there was no room to turn around, Saracen emerged through the gap to look down at MacQuillan and the site agent. He held up the corpse and said, 'Here's the obstruction, a dead c...,' Saracen stopped himself for in the light he could now see that what he held was not a cat at all. It was the black carcass of a wild rat.

'Jesus God Almighty!' whispered MacQuillan.

'Is that what you were looking for?' asked the site agent, alarmed at the look on MacQuillan's face.

MacQuillan ignored the question. 'We'll have to seal all this up,' he said.

Back at the General, MacQuillan poured out two glasses of whisky for himself and Saracen.

348

He countered Saracen's look by saying, 'We both need it.' Saracen nodded and accepted the glass. 'Do you know what I don't understand?' he said. 'If we have plague rats in Skelmore, why don't we have bubonic plague all over the place instead of just two cases with the rest all pneumonic?'

'The answer must be that we do not have plague rats in Skelmore. They must be confined in some way to one area, the Palmer's Green site.'

'But the Edwards boy didn't live on Palmer's Green. He came from the Maxton estate,' said Saracen.

'Doesn't mean that he couldn't have been down at Palmer's Green for some reason, a delivery boy, perhaps?'

Saracen remembered something. 'Edwards!' he said out loud. 'Edwards' treasure!'

'What?'

Saracen told MacQuillan about the episode with the glue sniffers and the story of a boy named Edwards who had supposedly found treasure on the Palmer's Green site. Half way through the explanation Saracen saw the connection with the medallion that Edwards had been wearing when the ambulance brought him in. He gave MacQuillan a quick resumé of the legend of Skelmoris Abbey.

'Then the boy must have discovered the site of the abbey!' exclaimed MacQuillan.

Saracen agreed and said, 'It could have been

plague that wiped out the abbey all these years ago and anyone who went near it afterwards. That would account for the legend of the wrath of God. But how could the bug have survived this long?'

'In the rats,' said MacQuillan. 'The bug could live indefinitely in a rat colony and be passed on down through the centuries.'

'And if the rat colony had remained isolated from the town until developers moved in on the Palmer's Green site...'

'We would have a sudden outbreak of plague,' agreed MacQuillan.

'But can that really happen?' asked Saracen.

MacQuillan nodded. 'It's called sylvatic plague,' he said. 'There have been several recorded instances in the United States and in China, where plague has established itself in a colony of small animals in the wild. It's not a problem until man moves into their area, but when he does you then have the potential for disaster.'

'So we have to destroy the rat colony,' said Saracen.

'Not only the rats, but their fleas as well. Poisoning the rats isn't good enough, the fleas will just look for new hosts. Gas is the only answer.'

'We have to find them first,' said Saracen coming down to earth.

'Can we talk to the Edwards boy?'

'He's dead,' said Saracen.

'How about the glue sniffers?'

'At the time they hadn't managed to find out Edwards' secret, but they might have in the interim. It's our only hope.'

'I'll get the army to trace them.'

'Let's do it ourselves,' said Saracen. 'The addresses will be in the day book.' Saracen checked the book while MacQuillan brought round the car. They set off for the Maxton estate to be stopped twice en route by the army. They showed their identification and received an apology. It seemed that a growing proportion of Skelmore's population had taken to doing their shopping by night, using bricks instead of Barclaycards. Looting was rife in the town.

Frith Street was like many other streets on the Maxton estate. Walls were daubed with spray-paint slogans, ground floor windows were boarded up and gardens grew wild. The whole area breathed resentment and aggression.

'Number seventeen, this is it,' said Saracen. They drew up behind an abandoned Ford Cortina; they assumed it had been abandoned for it had no wheels.

'I was brought up in an area like this,' said MacQuillan quietly, 'in Glasgow.'

'A long time ago,' said Saracen.

'A long time ago,' agreed MacQuillan. They got out of the car.

'Third floor,' said Saracen, as they entered

the building. The passage stank of urine, so badly that they were forced to hold their breath as long as possible. Saracen managed it to the second floor landing. They found the door they were looking for and knocked. There was no reply. Saracen rapped again and this time was rewarded with shuffling sounds from within. 'What do you want?' rasped an angry female voice.

Saracen said who they were and asked to speak to her son.

'What's he done?' demanded the woman. 'What did he steal? The little bugger. I'll have his bloody hide before he's much older!'

Saracen assured her that her son had done nothing wrong and at this point the woman behind the door was joined by a man wanting to know what was going on. 'Two doctors from the General,' said the woman's voice. 'They want to speak to the boy.'

'We don't want anyone from that place coming in here,' growled the man. 'Don't you know what bloody time it is?'

'It's very important,' said Saracen, stretching his self-control to its limit. 'It's vital that we speak to your son.'

MacQuillan and Saracen exchanged glances while they listened to a whispered argument rage on the other side of the door. The woman won and the door was opened. They were ushered into the living room and the woman went to waken her son while the man went back to bed. MacQuillan sat down on a brown plastic arm chair that listed to one side under his weight. Saracen shooed a cat off the sofa where it had been wrestling with a greasy paper that had earlier held fish and chips.

The woman returned with the boy and picked up the paper. 'You do your best to keep the place nice,' she said, baring her teeth in what she felt was a smile. 'I sometimes wonder why I bother.'

'Remember me?' Saracen asked the boy, who rubbed his eyes and nodded in recognition. 'Your pal Edwards died tonight, I'm afraid.' The boy remained impassive while his mother made appropriate noises.

'You told me that Edwards had found treasure on Palmer's Green and I didn't believe you,' said Saracen.

'It was true,' said the boy.

'I know that now,' said Saracen quietly.

'Treasure? What treasure?' squawked the mother.

Saracen ignored her and addressed the boy again. 'Did you ever find out where Edwards found it?'

The boy shook his head but Saracen sensed that he was lying. 'A lot of people's lives depend on it,' he said. 'I'm not kidding.'

Saracen could see the boy hesitate. He swallowed hard and prayed that he would make the right decision.

'Yeah, I know where he got it.'

Saracen closed his eyes and gave thanks. Almost immediately he had to consider that the boy might be infected like Edwards. 'So you have been there too?' he asked.

'No, the watchman caught us. We went back last night but there was a bulldozer parked over it'

'Over what?'

'The entrance to Edwards' cave.'

'A cave?'

'The treasure cave where Edwards got his stuff.'

'Where exactly is this cave?'

The boy told Saracen while he took notes. 'That's exactly what we wanted to know,' he said, getting to his feet. He smiled at the boy and said, 'You might just have saved this whole town.'

The boy's mother shuffled along behind them to the door. 'Excuse me for asking,' she said with her bare-toothed smile, 'I just wondered, will there be any reward attached to this treasure?'

Saracen and MacQuillan returned to find chaos at the General. Military ambulances were blocking the access roads, engines were running and lights were blazing while their drivers gathered in small groups near the gates. Saracen found Tremaine, who told him, 'Ward twenty is full, the County Isolation Unit is full and both the schools are now full. We have nowhere

354

left to put the patients.'

'Then we stop admitting,' said Saracen.

'That's what Saithe said, but this is awful,' protested Tremaine. 'It's an admission of defeat and you know what will happen if there is no response from the emergency services when they are called out. The minute people find out that they are on their own, it will be every man for himself.'

Saracen nodded grimly.

'Surely Beasdale must know that,' said Tremaine.

'Oh, I think he does,' said Saracen quietly.

'Then why doesn't he get new premises for the sick and bring in volunteer help?'

Saracen deflected the question with one of his own. 'How many do we have out there in the ambulances?'

'Eighteen. We can't just send them back,' pleaded Tremaine.

'We'll bring them in and keep them in reception for the moment,' said Saracen.

'But...'

'It won't be for long. There will be that many deaths in the next hour, but we cannot admit any more.'

'Then you are admitting defeat, too?' asked Tremaine.

'I am facing facts,' said Saracen. He took Tremaine to one side and told him that there would be no antiserum and the reason why. Tremaine's will to argue all but evaporated

355

and he sat down, obviously feeling weak at the news. 'But the whole town will be wiped out,' he said distantly.

'There's still a chance that it will burn itself out if we can remove the source of the outbreak,' said Saracen.

'But the Archer woman was the source of the outbreak,' said Tremaine.

'No she wasn't,' said Saracen. 'They got it all wrong.' He told Tremaine about the real source of the disease.

'But why has it never happened before?'

'Because the rat colony was never disturbed before,' said Saracen. 'It was only when they started to build the flats on Palmer's Green that they unwittingly opened up access to the rats.'

'Skelmoris Abbey,' muttered Tremaine. 'All these years.'

'The Curse of Skelmoris,' said Saracen. 'It was plague.'

'Didn't they burn the place to the ground in the story?' asked Tremaine.

'I suppose the rats survived in the underground cellars and passages,' said Saracen.

'What are you going to do?' asked Tremaine.

'Find the colony and wipe them out.'

'Claire might be able to help there,' said Tremaine. 'She has plans of what the abbey was supposed to have looked like.'

Saracen agreed that the plans could prove invaluable when the time was right.

MacQuillan returned from contacting Beasdale and he and Saracen drove back down to Palmer's Green. 'What did he say when you told him?' asked Saracen.

'He kept asking about the "practical implications" of the discovery,' replied MacQuillan.

'I hope you stressed the importance of having uncovered the true source of the epidemic,' said Saracen.

'Of course,' replied MacQuillan. 'But I got the impression that he thinks things might just have gone too far already.'

Saracen felt a chill at what MacQuillan had said. 'But he did agree to help?' he asked.

'He said he would,' said MacQuillan.

Saracen looked at the site with his notes in his hands. 'That must be the bulldozer over there,' he said to MacQuillan, and pointed to a yellow machine near the western edge of an apartment block. They donned their protective clothing and approached the bulldozer, which was parked beside a small concrete bunker. Saracen asked what it was.

'It covers the air intake for the heating system in the flats,' said MacQuillan with a bitter smile.

Saracen squatted down and peered between the tracks of the vehicle but could see nothing unusual. 'Then we'll have to move it,' said MacQuillan. MacQuillan climbed up on to one of the tracks and looked into the cabin. 'The keys are in it,' he reported, and climbed inside. The whir of the starter motor gave way to a roar and a cloud of diesel smoke rose into the air as the engine sprang to life. There followed a series of hydraulic jerks as MacQuillan tried a row of levers in turn before finding the gear stick. When he did the machine lurched forward ten or twelve metres before MacQuillan killed the engine and silence returned to the site.

'I don't see anything, do you?' asked Mac-Quillan as they both examined the ground where the bulldozer had stood.

Saracen was about to agree when he did notice something different. 'These bricks,' he said, 'They've been placed there.'

MacQuillan could see what Saracen meant. Bricks were hardly out of place on a building site, but the six lying within a one metre area were the only ones on this side of it. Someone had placed them there, but for what purpose? Saracen moved them to one side and brushed at the dirt with his hands. Almost immediately he knew that he was on the right track because his fingers touched wood. MacQuillan helped him clear away the top layer to reveal a square block of chip-board. Saracen prised it up and found a hole.

'Well, well,' he said, 'Edwards' cave.'
'We'll need torches.'
'Beasdale's men should be here soon.'
A car drew up but it was not the army; it

was Claire Tremaine. 'Alan rang. I've brought the plans.'

'Thanks, but it's early days,' said Saracen. 'All we've found is a hole in the ground.'

'I could help,' said Claire. 'After all, holes in the ground are my speciality.'

'I don't think that's a good idea,' said Saracen.

Claire put her hand on Saracen's arm and said, 'Please, James, you know how much this means to me.'

'Did you inform your boss about this?' asked Saracen.

'No, there wasn't time,' said Claire, taken by surprise at Saracen's question.

'And being the first person in your team to find Skelmoris Abbey will do your career no harm at all,' said Saracen accusingly.

'All right, I admit there's something in what you say,' she conceded.

An army Land Rover arrived in a cloud of dust and interrupted them. Beasdale was in it. 'I thought I had better come down and see for myself what was going on,' said Beasdale. He was speaking to Saracen but his eyes were questioning the presence of Claire Tremaine. Saracen realized this and introduced Claire. 'Miss Tremaine is an archaeologist; she's an expert on Skelmoris Abbey and has agreed to help us with the excavations,' he said. Saracen saw the look of gratitude in Claire's eyes and the questioning look in MacQuillan's.

'Perhaps we can talk in the site office,' said Beasdale. 'Just Dr Saracen,' he added, when MacQuillan and Claire showed signs of following. Saracen felt uncomfortable but there was no time to dwell on it. Beasdale closed the door behind them and said, 'I've had Dr MacQuillan's views on this new discovery, now give me yours.'

'I'm sure they coincide,' said Saracen.

'Tell me anyway. I want a second opinion.' Beasdale smiled at his intended medical allusion.

'When we wipe out the source of the epidemic it will start to burn itself out.'

'But everyone will be dead by then,' said Beasdale.

'Not everyone,' said Saracen firmly. 'A lot, but not everyone.'

Beasdale adopted a pained expression as if what he had to say was difficult. 'I don't think you understand, Doctor,' he said quietly.

'Understand what?'

'My position.'

'Tell me,' said Saracen, though he feared that he would not like the answer.

'I believe that the situation in Skelmore will be out of control within seventy-two hours if I let it continue.'

'How so?'

'Any policing operation, civil or military, depends on the co-operation of the majority. When it becomes generally known in Skelmore that the emergency services have broken down and that people are being left to die in their houses, we will no longer have that co-operation. There will be an uprising and people will attempt to leave the town in large numbers. Under these conditions some would undoubtedly succeed and spread an incurable plague. I cannot allow that to happen.'

Saracen swallowed and said, 'The disease has survived for centuries in these rats. If we don't find the colony and wipe it out the chances are that it will survive any "misfortune" that should befall Skelmore. Afterwards, of course, the colony might have to look for a new home.'

Beasdale's face took on the hint of a smile. He said quietly, 'All right, Doctor, you've made your point. Find your colony, destroy it. I'll give you every assistance I can. The only thing I cannot give you is time.'

Saracen nodded and said, 'I understand.'

Beasdale got up and put on his cap. 'I'll leave a small detachment to help with the excavation,' he said. 'Keep me informed.'

FIFTEEN

Claire spread out the plans on the table in the site office and said, 'After the fire little was reported to have been left of the abbey itself, but it's likely that the cellars and vaults survived. As you can see, they were quite extensive.'

'And we know that there must be at least two outlets,' said MacQuillan.

'We do?' said Claire.

'There must be one that the rats used before the excavations gave them a new one here on Palmer's Green.'

'Of course.'

'Our immediate aim is to estimate the size of the labyrinth. Once we know that, we can work out how much gas we are going to need to destroy the inhabitants, fleas and all.'

The talking was over and it was time to examine the entrance hole on Palmer's Green. The three of them put on protective clothing, Claire's having been provided from one of the two army Land Rovers standing by. MacQuillan issued a warning. 'If we should come across any rats, back off, give them room. On no account come between them and their

362

escape route.' He looked at Claire and Saracen in turn to verify that his point had been taken.

'Let's get started,' said Saracen. He removed the wooden cover that the Edwards boy had fabricated to safeguard his find and shone his torch inside the hole, before dropping down and examining the walls. Once more his hands touched wood. This time a piece of chipboard had been wedged into the side wall. He levered it out and handed it to MacQuillan, who put it to one side.

'Can you see anything?' asked Claire as Saracen bent down to peer through the opening with the aid of the torch.

Saracen grunted. He could see that he was standing on the roof of an arch that spanned a stone passage below. There was a two metre drop to the floor. He told the others.

'Can you get down?'

'I think so,' replied Saracen. 'It must have been easier for the boy, but here goes.' He manoeuvred backwards through the opening and lowered himself into the darkness, taking most of the strain on his arms as he searched for footholds. He found two on the way down and let out a sigh of relief as his feet touched the floor of the passage. He could feel the cold and damp of the atmosphere permeate his protective suiting as he looked up to see the circle of light blotted out by Claire as she put her head into the opening.

'To your left,' Saracen advised her, as he saw

Claire's foot seek out a grip.

'Got it.' Claire lowered herself gingerly and stood beside Saracen. She reached out her arms and could touch both walls. 'Not much room,' she said.

MacQuillan joined them and they set off along the passage in single file with Saracen leading. 'I don't remember anything like this in the plans,' he said, as the passage stretched beyond thirty metres. No one replied, 'Any suggestions?' he asked, as they passed fifty metres.

'It's beginning to make sense,' said Claire behind him.

'Glad to hear it,' said Saracen drily.

'I think this is an escape tunnel.'

'For whom?'

'For the brothers of the abbey.'

'Why?'

'These were troubled times when violence was a way of life. Many castles, palaces and monastries were built with secret escape tunnels that would not be marked on any plan.'

'That would explain why it's so long,' said Saracen.

'And why it's so narrow,' added MacQuillan, 'If its only function was as a means of escape.'

Saracen reckoned that they had covered the best part of a hundred metres when the passage suddenly widened out into a circular chamber, closed off on the far side by an iron grilled gate. Tugging at the bars failed to budge it. Saracen shone the torch all round the edge but found no lock. Subsidence of the ground above them had driven the bars into the floor. He froze as a dark shape flitted quickly in and out of the torch beam. He heard Claire's sharp intake of breath. 'Was that what I thought it was?' she asked.

''Fraid so,' said Saracen.

'Over here,' said MacQuillan. Claire and Saracen joined him and saw that he was holding a crucifix in his hand. 'I found it on the shelf here,' he said, running his torch beam along a stone lintel set into the wall.

'Can I hold it?' said Claire quietly, and MacQuillan handed it to her. She took it gently in her palms and whispered, 'To think that this belonged to the monks of Skelmoris.'

Saracen swept his torch beam around the floor of the chamber and paused as it picked out a red Coca Cola can. He picked it up and said, 'Well, the monks never held this. I think we can be fairly certain that this was young Master Edwards' treasure cave.'

MacQuillan looked at the way the gate was jammed and said, 'He couldn't have got past here.'

'Any idea what this chamber was for, Claire?' Saracen asked.

'Hiding,' replied Claire. 'They would wait here for a while before deciding whether to go back or use the tunnel.'

'And the gate would be the last line of

defence in case the searchers found the entrance to the tunnel?'

'I think so,' agreed Claire.

'We are going to need help with the gate,' said MacQuillan, and the others agreed. Saracen led the way back along the passage to seek the assistance of the military.

While they were waiting for the soldiers to deal with the jammed gate, Claire took the crucifix to the site office to record its details. Saracen and MacQuillan took a breather and sat with their backs against one of the Land Rovers. Saracen said, 'I've been thinking. If plague has survived in the rat colony for more than six centuries, the rats must obviously have some kind of immunity from it.'

'That's usually the case in sylvatic plague. Some animals are immune and others aren't.'

'Is it known why?'

'No, but a healthy carrier state has been described in human beings, too. A study carried out in Vietnam showed that a number of people were carrying it in their naso-pharynx. What's on your mind?'

'If the immunity factor could be identified it might be possible to use it.'

'But that kind of study could take years,' said MacQuillan.

'It might take years to do it scientifically and describe the immune mechanism in detail, but I was thinking in more practical terms.'

'Go on.'

366

'If we could get blood from an immune rat and have Porton Down compare it with the blood of a rat that had succumbed to the disease, they might be able to spot the immunity factor without having to know what it was. If they could get enough of it we could use it to treat people.'

MacQuillan thought for a moment before saying, 'That, my friend, is a bloody good idea.' He asked one of the soldiers to call up Beasdale on the radio. The soldier did so and handed him the handset.

Saracen listened while MacQuillan told Beasdale of the new plan. He could not hear what Beasdale was saying but it was obvious that some kind of argument was developing.

'Of course there can be no guarantee,' MacQuillan stormed. 'But there is a real chance— no, I'm not stalling—damn it man, listen to reason!' MacQuillan put down the handset and looked at the ground for a moment, trying to compose himself before saying anything.

'Well?' asked Saracen.

'No extension to the time limit. We have forty-six hours left.'

'We'd best get started, then,' said Saracen. He asked the soldier for pen and paper and made out a list. 'We need these things as quickly as possible,' he said to the man, and the soldier snapped to it.

'What did you ask for,' asked MacQuillan.

'Sterile glassware, anticoagulants, scalpels,

specimen containers and rat traps.'

The other three soldiers who had been down in the tunnel emerged and relayed their tools and equipment to the surface. 'The gate's open,' said the sergeant. 'And we've left you better lighting.'

Saracen thanked him and dropped down into the hole again.

'One more thing, sir,' said the sergeant. He handed Saracen a revolver and a box of shells. 'Colonel Beasdale thought you'd better have this.'

'I've never used one of these things in my life,' said Saracen. MacQuillan said the same. The soldier took back the gun and ran through the rudiments like a schoolboy reciting a poem, the words of which he hadn't considered. 'This is a Smith and Wesson 0.38 calibre, double action weapon. It requires a trigger pressure of...'

Saracen listened politely and deduced what to squeeze and which end to point.

As they prepared to re-enter the tunnel the soldier said, 'Colonel Beasdale is arranging for a truck with the required chemicals to be on site within the hour, sir.'

Saracen gave a last thoughtful look across the site and said, 'Don't let any heavy vehicles cross the line of the tunnel, will you? The roof might not take it.'

'Very good, sir.'

'These are a vast improvement,' said Claire, switching on one of the lamps that the soldiers had left for them.

Saracen saw where the bars had been cut away from the bottom of the gate and pushed it gently back on its hinges to stand on the threshold.

'Shall we continue?' he asked. The passage went on for some twenty metres before taking a turning to the left. Saracen was about to round the turn when he stopped in his tracks and said, 'Can you hear something?'

'What?'

'A scuffling noise. There, it's getting louder.'

'Someone is coming up behind us,' said Mac-Quillan.

Saracen led out the breath he had been holding and felt embarrassed at having let his imagination run away with him.

'Dr Saracen?' said a voice from the blackness. 'It's Corporal Jackson, sir. I've got the things you asked for.'

'Only two?' exclaimed Saracen when he saw the rat traps.

'All we could lay our hands on, sir.'

'We'll need more.'

'How many, sir?'

'As many as possible. The more traps we set, the more chance we have of catching one in time.'

'I'll tell the sergeant, sir.'

MacQuillan said, 'I'll set one back by the

gate where we saw one of the damned things.'

'Mind your hands,' said Saracen, as he gingerly handed him one of the primed and baited traps.

'Surely you don't plan to catch them individually?' said Claire, while they waited for MacQuillan to come back.

'I need some rat blood,' said Saracen. 'I'll explain later.' MacQuillan re-joined them and they continued in single file.

The passage grew ever-narrower until they felt that the cold, damp walls were closing in on them. Saracen stopped and said, 'Now what?'

'What's the matter?' asked Claire.

'We've come to a blank wall.'

'This must be where the tunnel meets the abbey. Try pushing, pulling, sliding things.'

Saracen's hands moved over the stone without success. He was about to say so when he felt one of the stones move and his heart leapt as he pushed it and the wall opened up in front of them, causing him to marvel momentarily at the hidden counterweight mechanism. They stepped through into a long, low cellar with an arched roof.

'Oh my God!' exclaimed Claire.

Saracen wheeled round and saw the skeleton of a man caught in Claire's torchbeam. 'And another,' said MacQuillan from further along.

'And another and another,' said Saracen, as he slowly walked the length of the cellar past fifteen skeletons lying parallel to each other and about a metre apart.

'It's a dormitory,' said Claire.

'Not a dormitory,' said Saracen quietly. 'An infirmary.'

'God, yes,' murmured MacQuillan. 'We are looking at a medieval ward twenty.'

Claire screamed as the black shadows of two rats scampered across the floor and disappeared again. She apologized.

'Don't,' said MacQuillan. 'I feel the same way.'

Saracen asked Claire if she could work out where they were in the abbey from her plans, and she unfolded them and looked for a place to spread them out. She considered the floor briefly before remembering the rats and opted instead to lay them gently across two of the skeletons.

'I think we are here,' she said, pointing to a rectangle near the foot of the paper. 'That would mean that there should be a doorway over there.' She swung round her torch and saw what she wanted to see. 'Yes, there it is. If we go through there we should come to a round chamber that we think was used as a wine cellar, and after that there is a room off to the right where the treasures were kept.'

'But that's not what we are here for,' Saracen reminded her, on detecting the excitement in her voice. He turned to MacQuillan and said, 'Do you think it is going to be possible to gas

371

a place of this size from the outside?'

'Doubtful,' said MacQuillan. 'We can ask the army for advice but first we have to find the other exit and block it up and, of course, catch you a rat.'

Saracen looked at his watch and saw that they had been in the tunnel for an hour. They moved into the next chamber and found, as Claire had predicted, that it was round. Claire moved to the right and Saracen and MacQuillan followed. They heard her gasp and then saw that she was holding a golden crucifix in her hand.

'It's the altar piece!' she exclaimed. 'The altar piece of Skelmoris Abbey!'

'And the candlesticks,' said MacQuillan, delving into the chest from which Claire had taken the cross, 'and communion goblets and...'

'We don't have time,' said Saracen.

'But the Skelmoris Chalice must be here!' protested Claire. 'We must look!'

'There is no time,' insisted Saracen.

Claire became angry. 'What difference will a few minutes make?' she demanded.

'There are some things you don't understand,' said Saracen. 'We have to hurry.'

'No!' Claire exclaimed. 'You go on if you must, catch your damned rat, seal up your exits, but I'm staying here and I'm going to find the chalice!'

Saracen could see that to argue was pointless

and he had no wish to tell her what Beasdale had planned for the town. 'Very well,' he said softly. 'Perhaps you can tell us what to expect in the other cellars.'

Claire opened up the plan again and ran through the presumed location and uses of the remaining chambers. Her voice was subdued with guilt but an overriding ambition maintained her resolve.

When she had finished Saracen asked, 'Have you any idea at all where the other exit might be?'

Claire pointed to the plan and said, 'The steps leading down from the abbey came out in this room. Perhaps they still give access to the world above.'

'Could there be a second escape tunnel?'

'It wasn't unknown for there to be two. One was often built as a decoy and accordingly was quite easy to find. It took the heat off the real one.'

'Any thoughts?'

'If there is a second one I would guess at somewhere along the north wall.'

Saracen and MacQuillan moved off and left Claire on her own. They came to the room where Claire had said that the steps would be and shone their torches up at the ceiling. There was no longer any way up to the outside world. Instead worn treads rose into the ceiling to disappear into solid, unbroken earth. There was no way through, even for a rat.

Saracen was examining a crumbling section of a wall on the north side when he heard a sound. He stood up and listened, urging MacQuillan to do the same.

'It's someone calling,' said MacQuillan.

'Someone screaming!' said Saracen. 'It's Claire!'

They raced back through the cellars towards the chamber where they had left Claire looking for the chalice. As they approached the screams became louder but still seemed strangely muffled, and by the time they had reached the room they had stopped altogether.

'There!' said MacQuillan, swinging his torch round. They could see the lower half of Claire's body protruding from a small opening in the back wall. 'She's stuck in the gap,' said Mac-Quillan.

'She must have panicked and fainted,' said Saracen, trying to free Claire's limp body but finding it stuck fast. There was a frantic scratching sound from the other side of the gap and both men started to make soothing sounds assuming that it was Claire clawing at the dirt in fear. Then Saracen looked down at Claire's motionless legs; he saw the visor that she had taken off, and a nightmare was born. If Claire was still unconscious, what was making the scraping sound?

'Oh Jesus Christ Almighty!' said Saracen, in a faltering whisper. His lungs went into a spasm of revulsion as he realized the awful truth. MacQuillan too had realized the significance of Claire's lifeless legs and the scraping noise.

'Rats!' he said, as though he were afraid of the word.

Saracen nodded. 'She must have been trying to crawl through the gap and got herself stuck between the rats and their route to freedom.'

'Is she dead?' asked MacQuillan.

'She's dead,' replied Saracen, who had been searching for a pulse.

'Oh my God,' said MacQuillan, mesmerized by horror.

'The rats are still trapped inside,' said Saracen. 'We'll have to be careful when we pull her body out.'

MacQuillan did not need the warning for his imagination had gone into overdrive. They pulled Claire's body back through the gap slowly, pausing before the final tug.

'Ready?' asked MacQuillan.

Saracen nodded and they moved Claire's body so that a space between her shoulder and the roof of the gap appeared. As soon as it did a rat *flew* through the space and spreadeagled itself across Saracen's face visor, before scrambling down over his shoulder and off into the blackness. Saracen looked down and saw that a rat was still fastened to Claire's face. He overcame a tide of nausea and swung his torch at the thing, sending it flying across the room. Several other rats joined in the exodus from the chamber and then there was silence.

Saracen looked at Claire and had to swallow hard to contain the urge to vomit. He heard MacQuillan do the same. 'God, and she was so beautiful,' he whispered, looking down at the featureless tissue. MacQuillan turned away.

When they had both sufficiently recovered MacQuillan said, 'You've got your rat.'

Saracen followed MacQuillan's torch beam and saw that it was resting on the rat that he had hit with his torch. It was lying in a heap in the corner. MacQuillan fetched it while Saracen prepared his equipment. He opened the lids of several containers in readiness, then removed the guard from a scalpel blade as Mac-Quillan held up the rat to expose its throat. Saracen cut straight across it and collected the blood, filling one container after another until the animal was completely exsanguinated. Then MacQuillan tossed the carcass away.

Saracen was packing the bottles into his bag when he heard MacQuillan say, 'Good God, look at that!'

Saracen saw MacQuillan reach through the gap where Claire had been trapped and remove something. He held it up and shone his torch on it. It was a gold chalice encrusted with rubies as big as birds' eggs. 'So that's why she was trying to get in there,' said MacQuillan. 'Have you ever seen anything so beautiful? It must be worth millions!'

'Leave the damned thing,' said Saracen. 'God knows how many people have died for it.'

'Let's not over-react,' whispered MacQuillan, examining the chalice from every angle. 'Surely you don't believe that old curse nonsense.'

'Let's get this blood back. We'll take Claire's body with us.' said Saracen, arranging the body so that he could grip her arms. 'You take her feet.'

MacQuillan stuffed the chalice inside his protective suit and gripped Claire's ankles. 'Ready.'

They had almost reached the iron gate when they heard footsteps coming towards them. It was the soldiers and they had brought more rat traps. Saracen thanked them but explained that they had managed to catch a healthy rat. He handed the blood samples to the sergeant, telling him to get them to Beasdale as fast as possible. 'He knows where they have to go.'

'And the traps, sir?'

'Just leave them.'

As the soldiers took charge of Claire's body and turned to head back along the passage, the air was filled with a rumbling sound from above. It grew louder and they could make out the characteristic throb of a diesel engine. Saracen looked at the sergeant in alarm and said, 'You did warn them about not crossing the line of the tunnel?' He could see by the look on the man's face that he had not. The man turned on his heel and started running back to the entrance while the soldiers bearing Claire's body followed as quickly as they could.

As the truck passed overhead the roof of the tunnel collapsed. It was quite sudden; there was no warning trickle of dirt, no creaking sounds. The roof just imploded some thirty metres from where Saracen and MacQuillan were standing.

Saracen stared at the wall of rock in stunned silence. The sergeant, the soldiers, Claire's body, the blood samples were all gone, buried under tons of black stone. Two more stone sets fell from the roof and broke the spell.

'The rest is going to go!' Saracen yelled. They turned to run but MacQuillan tripped and fell. The chalice he had been clutching flew from his grasp and sailed between the bars of the gate. 'Leave it!' urged Saracen, but Mac-Quillan was determined. He crawled over to the bars and stretched his arm through to grope blindly for the lost chalice in spite of Saracen's warning.

Instead of the chalice, MacQuillan's hand found the rat trap that he had set earlier by the gate. The hammer released and smashed down on his fingers, making it impossible for him to pull his hand back through the bars. He cried out in pain as he tried to free himself and overhead the roof began to move. One stone fell, then another. Saracen threw himself backwards as the whole lot collapsed. As he did so he caught a glimpse of the terror on MacQuillan's face just before a huge stone fell and crushed him.

Saracen was alone in the infirmary of Skelmoris Abbey, save for fifteen skeletons and the rats. He was exhausted physically and mentally and could not be certain how long he had been sitting there in the darkness. He had switched off his lamp to conserve the batteries after a fruitless search for another way out. Was there any point in going on, he wondered. The odds were hopelessly against him and time was running out. He brought out the revolver that the soldier had given him and weighed it in his hand while he considered his position. God, he was tired. Revulsion, fear and anguish had conspired to drain him of every last vestige of hope. He brought the cold muzzle of the gun to rest against his temple and curled his index finger lightly round the trigger. He caressed the curved steel and flirted with an increase in pressure. The thought of Jill stopped him.

Ye gods! How clear it all seemed now. The hurt and pain that Marion had caused him had been much greater than he had ever cared to admit. His reluctance to acknowledge that he had fallen in love with Jill had been just fear that it might happen all over again. Claire had been right about that. He did love Jill; of that he was now very sure. The guilt he felt after his fling with Claire should have told him, but he had fought against it and now it was too late. He would never be able to look into Jill's beautiful eyes and tell her how much he loved her, how much he adored her and wanted her. The thought of her hair on the pillow and her face smiling up at him filled him with an almost unbearable sadness.

The spectre of death was returning to court Saracen when the sound of scurrying paws startled him out of his trance. He whipped the gun round and blazed away at where he thought the sound had come from. The chamber was transformed from being a silent tomb into an echo chamber filled with endlessly reverberating thunder and the blackness was punctuated with flashes of orange lighting. 'Bastards!' Saracen yelled. 'Stinking, verminous bastards!'

He started to tremble all over and hysteria made his breathing erratic. Curses were interspersed with sobs as he dropped the gun and placed both hands over his face, taking what comfort he could from the feel of his fingertips massaging his skin. The moment passed and he came back from the brink. 'For God's sake, get a grip,' he muttered, as he got to his feet. If only he could find a way out there might still be time to destroy the rat colony before Beasdale acted. If only. He reloaded the gun, picked up his lamp and returned to the north wall of the cellars.

At the end of another fruitless search, in which he had felt his way along each stone from ground to shoulder level along the entire north face of the abbey cellars, Saracen sat down to rest. The silence was broken periodically by the sound of running feet in the blackness but he had now come to terms with this. As he sat there listening it occurred to him that the movement of the rats was not entirely random. There seemed to be a constant east to west movement along the corridor outside the chamber where he sat. He tested his theory by waiting for the next sound. There it was again! Two animals running from east to west along the passage. Where were they going?

Saracen got up and followed the passage along to the last chamber. It was at the north-west corner of the cellars and seemed to have been some kind of wash or bath house for there were five large stone troughs standing in line, each with its own spur to a main water channel. A rat scurried across the floor and over Saracen's feet, making goose flesh spring up on his neck. He swore viciously to maintain his fragile courage and break a silence that threatened to smother him. Another rat shot across the floor going in the opposite direction from the one that had hurdled his feet. He squatted down cautiously to see if he could see where it had come from.

Saracen's pulse raced as his torch beam picked out an opening in the wall under the end trough. It was not difficult to work out what the opening had been for; it was the drainage channel for the troughs but it was much bigger than it had to be for the volume of water it had been liable to encounter. It was about two-thirds of a metre high in the centre and slightly narrower in width. At a pinch a man could crawl inside and escape to the outside world. This was the decoy tunnel!

As yet another rat flew from the mouth of the drain Saracen knew that he had found the primary entrance and exit that the rats used, and the thought filled him with dread. He had found his way out but it was going to be full of rats. Once committed there would be no room for manoeuvre inside the channel, because it was too narrow and his body would practically fill it. Rats would be coming towards him and up behind him. The image of Claire's face after the rats had finished with her haunted his subconscious like a vision of hell. Did he have the nerve?

Saracen sat down with his back against one of the stone troughs and took deep breaths. He moved his head restlessly from side to side as variations on a nightmare invaded his mind. But it was the only way. There was no alternative.

He crawled back to the entrance to the drain and rested his hand on the stone above it. Was it his imagination or was the air sweeter here? Fresher? The thought of sky and fresh air strengthened Saracen's resolve. He would do it. He had to. But first he would do something about improving the odds. If he could somehow block up the entrance to the wash house, he could eliminate the possibility of rats coming up behind him in the tunnel when he could not turn round. That would leave the ones coming towards him, but for them he would have the gun. He would hold the lamp in one hand and the gun in the other as he wriggled along on his belly. There might even be a chance that oncoming rats would turn and flee when they saw him coming and that would be much better than having to use the gun.

He set about blocking up the entrance to the chamber with whatever came to hand and discovered that it was difficult because anything that remained in the cellars after all these years tended to be hard: wood, stone or iron. There was nothing soft that he could use to plug up small gaps with. He did what he could with his shirt and sweater and consoled himself with the thought that the barrier did not have to last long, just until he had crawled along the length of the drainage channel. He tried not to dwell on the fact that he had no idea of how long that was going to be.

Saracen's throat was tight as he checked the pistol for the last time and dispensed with the remaining cartridges because, once inside the drain, there would be no room to draw his arms back to re-load again. He could feel the blood start to pound in his temples as he knelt down in front of the channel entrance and, frightened to delay too long in case his nerve snapped, he slid his arms into the mouth and wriggled inside. Almost immediately he hit trouble; his face visor prevented him from raising his head to see where he was going. He withdrew and tore it off to throw it across the chamber in anger, venting his pent-up frustration with every obscenity he could think of and several that didn't make sense.

As he calmed down and steadied himself on his emotional tightrope he could hear scratching at the barrier he had erected. The rats were trying to get through it already. He went over and shouted and banged it to scare them off, then all went quiet and he entered the drain again.

He had moved forward about twenty metres when he had to stop because his elbows and knees demanded a break from the pain of continual bruising against the unforgiving stone. He comforted himself with the thought that, as yet, he had seen no rats. On the other hand there was nothing but blackness ahead of him in the tunnel. How long was it going to be, and what if the exit should be barred with an iron gate? It was the first time he had considered this possibility and it ate at his stomach like acid. He had rested enough. He gripped the lamp and the gun and started crawling again.

The lamp picked out two eyes in the darkness; there was a rat five metres ahead! Saracen's sense of fear was already on overload so he could find no extra emotional response. He stared at it, then yelled at it, and the creature turned and fled. He crawled on for another ten metres. Another two eyes, no this time there were four. He shouted again and two disappeared, but two remained.

Saracen yelled again but this time the rat did not move. This was a braver rat. He inched forward but the animal held its ground so Saracen's fingers left the lamp and moved across in front of him until he held the gun in both hands. He looked along the barrel and held the front sight between the glowing embers. The index finger of his right hand squeezed harder and harder until the deafening report filled his ear drums and the rat's head exploded on impact.

Saracen coughed and spluttered in the acrid gun smoke. The paroxysms had the side-effect of relieving some of the tension that had built up inside him and made him feel marginally better, although his ears were ringing painfully. He edged forward again until he encountered the carcass of the rat and found a new problem. There was no room to push the corpse behind him. He would have to push it along in front of him with the heels of his hands. The smells of its innards, together with the gunsmoke and the ever-encroaching claustrophobia of the drain as he edged in ever-deeper, conspired to push Saracen once more to the verge of hysteria. No vision of hell could have outdone the situation in which he now found himself.

The merest suggestion of a movement in the air caressed Saracen's cheek. There was still no light ahead, but there was definitely a faint breeze, he was sure of it, and it rescued his sanity. But elation was to turn to despair when the tunnel ahead of him filled with eyes.

Terror became blind fury as Saracen fired three times in rapid succession and ignored the agony in his ears. He was waiting for the smoke to clear when a rat loomed up in the torch beam and he fired again, but only to miss it in his state of panic. The rat launched itself at him and he dipped his head to protect his face. He felt the rat's claws scratch on the back of his head as it struggled for balance, and he waited for its teeth to gnaw into the back of his neck, but it didn't happen. The animal had found enough space between the top of his body and the roof of the tunnel to be able to pass along. He felt it run down the centre of his back and leave him. Another rat followed using the same route, and Saracen felt this one pause for one dreadful moment on the back of his upper thigh, but then it too continued on its journey and scampered down over his ankles and away.

The path ahead was now clear.

Desperately calling on what little energy he had left, Saracen wriggled forward, ignoring all pain as he pushed a pile of rat corpses ahead of him, using his forearms as angled blades. The drain channel curved to the right and he could see daylight. Five metres, four, three, two, one and he was free of his stone prison! He raised himself painfully to his knees and took great gulps of fresh air for a full half minute before he even thought to look around. With a final, superhuman effort he pulled himself up a two-metre bank, and found himself on a hillside. He was on the hill behind Skelmore Municipal Rubbish Dump and rubbish had never smelt sweeter.

Saracen lay on his back for a moment and looked up at the drifting clouds, taking pleasure from the feel of the watery sun on his face. He gripped handfuls of coarse grass and rejoiced in its feel before throwing it to the breeze as pale rays of sunshine broke through the clouds like a poster on a Sunday school wall. He wanted to sleep; he desperately wanted to sleep, but there was no time. He had to tell Beasdale how to get at the rat colony.

In the distance Saracen heard an engine. He got up and saw that a military vehicle was coming down the road towards the dump. He yelled out but the trucks showed no signs of stopping until he pulled out his pistol and emptied it into the air. The truck stopped and a soldier jumped down. Saracen waved his arms and saw the soldier put his weapon to his shoulder and point it at him. 'No!' he cried. 'For God's sake, no!'

It was Saracen's protective suit that saved him, for the soldier registered it at the last moment and realized that any person wearing it must have an official role to play. The man lowered the weapon and Saracen stumbled down the hill to say who he was.

'Christ, you were lucky, sir. I nearly...'

'I know what you nearly did,' said Saracen wearily. 'Call Colonel Beasdale, will you?'

'Dr Saracen. You're alive!' said Beasdale's voice.

'All the others died and the blood samples were destroyed when the tunnel caved in, but I do know where the rat colony is and where the old exit is. You must destroy it.'

'No, they weren't,' said Beasdale.

'Pardon?'

'The blood samples, they weren't destroyed. Sergeant Morris got out. The rock fall just missed him. Your samples were flown to Porton Down and analyzed.'

'And?'

'They've identified the relevant factor as an—adjuvant—is that how you say it?'

'Yes.'

'Apparently this adjuvant stimulates antibody production against the Skelmore strain.

In short, they say they can make an antiserum and a vaccine. Are you still there, Doctor?'

Saracen had gone weak at the knees. He rubbed his forehead and said, 'I'm still here. You won't be destroying the town, then?'

'I don't know what you mean, Doctor.'

'Thank God,' whispered Saracen.

'You say you can show us how to gain access to the rats?'

'Yes, but gassing them is probably a non-starter. The cellars are too big.'

'The sergeant was of the same opinion,' said Beasdale. 'We are going to use Parapalm.'

'What?'

'Parapalm, liquid fire. It will generate enough heat to incinerate anything in the cellars.'

'And you just happen to have it handy,' said Saracen.

'Is there anything I can do for you, Doctor?' asked Beasdale, choosing to ignore the comment. 'Anyone I can get in touch with? We all thought you were dead.'

'Yes, there is,' said Saracen weakly. 'I'd like you to contact Staff Nurse Rawlings at the General.'

'What shall I say?'

'Tell her—tell her I love her very much, will you?'

Consciousness was slipping away from Saracen. So the plague from the abbey was going to be treated with fire just as it had been

389

six hundred years before. The Skelmoris Chalice was safe again. Those who had dared touch it had been destroyed. Just a coincidence, just a legend. Saracen smiled and passed out.

'Poor bugger,' said a soldier. 'He looks all in.'

The publishers hope that this book has given you enjoyable reading. Large Print Books are especially designed to be as easy to see and hold as possible. If you wish a complete list of our books, please ask at your local library or write directly to: Magna Print Books, Long Preston, North Yorkshire, BD23 4ND England.